A stubborn cowboy has sworn never to forgive or forget—but one special woman may find a way to change his mind . . .

Hospice nurse Laken Garlington helps people face the end with peace and dignity, surrounded by their loved ones. But the son of her new patient didn't come home to reunite with his dad. So why *is* Cyler Myer back in horse country? It's clear the sexy, six-three hunk with the steely eyes has a score to settle, and Laken doesn't plan on being collateral damage . . . no matter how irresistible she finds the prodigal cowboy.

Dying is too good for the father Cyler will never forgive—not in this lifetime. Showing up at his family's Washington State ranch is the first step in his plan. But revenge takes a back seat to desire when Cyler meets a bossy beauty who arouses feelings he isn't ready to face. As they work together to save an ailing mare, Cyler realizes he must decide where his true destiny lies. With darkness . . . or with the woman who offers the promise of redemption with every kiss.

"Obsessed. That's how I felt while reading this book, like every page was better than the previous. Just try to put this down, I dare you." --#1 *New York Times* **Bestselling Author Rachel Van Dyken on** *The Heart of a Cowboy*

The Heart of a Cowboy

Elk Heights Ranch

Kristin Vayden

LYRICAL PRESS
Kensington Publishing Corp.
www.kensingtonbooks.com

Lyrical Press books are published by
Kensington Publishing Corp. 119 West 40th Street New York, NY 10018

First Electronic Edition:
eISBN-13: 978-1-5161-0562-5
eISBN-10: 1-5161-0562-1

First Print Edition:
ISBN-13: 978-1-5161-0563-2
ISBN-10: 1-5161-0563-X

Printed in the United States of America

This is for my husband, Harry. Who answered a million questions about ranch life, who put all five kids to bed so I could stay up and write, and who educated me on how to actually do a proper wine tasting. You're the best of everything, baby. I love you more than I could ever say.

And also for my sister, Rachel Van Dyken, who encouraged me, reminded me that the middle is always where you feel stuck, and who is all around amazing. Love you so much!

Chapter 1

Warm air breezed through the open window whipping Laken's hair across her face. In her rearview mirror, she could see a cloud of dust billowing behind her Honda, but thankfully the way ahead was clear, offering her an intimidating view of the huge log house growing bigger by the moment. Iron and cord fences lined the dusty gravel driveway, longhorn cattle dotted the landscape as they lazily grazed, but none of it calmed her nerves.

If anything, it made her more anxious.

"You're quiet. Are you still nervous?" Kessed asked across the Bluetooth connection, and Laken twisted her lips.

"Maybe?" She sighed.

"You're fine! Seriously. Chill. It's going to be great. Turn on that country girl charm, be yourself, and you're good to go." Kessed's tone was almost bored, since she'd basically given Laken the same speech the night before.

Normally, when her company sent her a new assignment, it was just that, an assignment. As a hospice nurse, she treated those who usually weren't in the position to be selecting their care. That choice was left up to the family. But when she received the call last week, it was to an interview. The patient wanted to hand-select the care nurse, and judging by the size of the property and house, the patient didn't have to worry about what insurance would, or wouldn't, cover.

"I'm here. I need to go. I'll call you later, 'kay? And if you have any leftover Pike Place after closing, it better have my name all over it. Just saying." Laken grinned as Kessed sighed over the phone.

"Is that the only reason we're friends?"

Laken nodded. "Yes."

"You suck."

"You love me! I entertain you."

"True. Now go and be awesome, and let me marinate in the amazing scent that is my workplace."

Laken sighed dramatically. "Starbucks is my lover."

"You're going to get cut off if you keep talking like that." Kessed giggled. "Gah, just get off the phone, stop stalling, and win over whomever needs the best nurse ever. Okay? Okay. Bye!"

The connection ended, and Laken grinned and shook her head as she navigated the car.

The road split into a circular drive, and she kept to the right, pulling up just before the hewn log entrance. *Ugh, why did I say yes?* Heart pounding, she tried to keep her nerves in check, but deep down she knew the reason. Because someone inside that huge house needed someone like her.

Someone who cared.

Someone who would be a guide in that terrifying transition, when everything seemed completely uncertain and hopeless. Someone who wouldn't care about the will or who got the house, someone who had no investment in their death. More often than not, families pulled together in the end, but it was usually after they had fought for most of the time before the final passing.

So with a deep breath, Laken strode to the front door and rang the bell. The slight breeze stirred, and a chime echoed in the stillness. When she turned, she saw an antique triangle, just like the ones she'd always imagined on the ranches in books. A smile broke through her lips, and her heartbeat slowed.

"Hello there, love."

Laken turned, blinking as she took in the low and gravely tone of the man before her. He couldn't be older than seventy-five, with deeply tanned skin and a full head of more salt than pepper hair complete with a handlebar mustache.

"Hello." She reached out a hand, and when he took it, she was sure to squeeze tight.

His brows rose, then he grinned, showing off straight white teeth. "Nice handshake, girl. I like you already. C'mon in." He gestured with his head to the long hall, and Laken entered, noticing the heady aroma of old wood, pipe tobacco, and some sort of cleaner.

"What's your name, love?"

She spun, immediately berating herself for forgetting something so basic. *So much for first impressions.* "I'm sorry. I'm Laken Garlington. I'm here for the hospice nurse interview."

"I figured as much. You're the nicest looking one of the lot. I think I'll hire you." He nodded once then turned and continued down the hall.

"Uh, thanks." She tilted her head, curious. "Just where is the patient, if you don't mind my asking?"

"You're looking at him, sweetheart." He turned. "Jackson Myer. Doc says I have less than three months. Cancer. I don't want any drugs till the pain gets too bad." He shrugged as if talking about the weather or something just as benign.

Not cancer.

Not three months left of life.

Her trained eye started to notice the few telltale signs that could be easily overlooked. His tanned skin had a yellowish hue, now recognizable as jaundice, meaning his liver function was compromised. His rolled-up sleeves showed bruises dotting his arm, along with several Band-Aids, meaning his blood wasn't clotting either.

Then he coughed.

And with a weathered hand, he pulled out a once-white handkerchief, stained a brownish red, and wiped the fresh trickle of blood from his lips.

"I see." She nodded once, taking a step toward him. "And you've refused treatment? Is that what you mean about not taking any meds?"

"Drugs, sweetheart. Yeah." He cleared his throat, and as he continued, his voice grew raspy. "It's a losing battle. I waited too long and, well, I'm not going to fight fate."

"Why?" It was a simple question, but in her experience, the answer was anything but.

"Don't beat around the bush, do you?" He gave her a sad smile. "If we're going to chat, I'm going to need to sit down. I'm a bit slower these days."

The foyer opened into a wide hall, a wall completely of windows in the A-frame-style room. Indian-red leather couches sprawled across the large expanse, and he took a seat in a large chair facing the view the windows offered. Light spilled in, accenting the wide space. He ambled to a large chair and slowly sat, easing himself into the cushions. As his weight settled, he sighed and closed his eyes briefly.

"Have a seat, honey." He opened his eyes and nodded toward the couch.

"Thanks." The leather squeaked beneath her as she sat and set her purse to the side. "So, Mr. Myer—"

"Jack, sweetheart. Mr. Myer was my daddy." He gave a dry chuckle.

"Got it. Jack, then. Why are you refusing treatment?" She leaned back, crossing her legs, and watched him as he absently toyed with a worn spot on the leather armrest.

"I've seen what chemotherapy can do. Radiation, all of the damn stuff. I asked Doc straight up what my chances were if I tried any of it, and even if it worked, it would only buy me some time. I figure I'm as ready to go now as I'll be in six months, so why make those three extra months I *might* get, only full of suffering from the side effects of the chemo? You know?" He shrugged and leaned forward, resting his elbows on his knees.

"I see." She chewed her bottom lip, pulling it between her teeth. It wasn't uncommon for people in advanced stages of cancer to feel that there wasn't any hope, but the problem came when they were facing the final few days of life, and they regretted giving up that hope earlier.

The dying had a sharper perception of the value of life because with each second, they felt it slipping through their fingers.

"You're quiet. I'm betting you disagree. Don't worry, you're not the first, nor will you be the last to think I'm just giving up." He sat back and shrugged.

"Jack, I can't tell you what's right or wrong. I'm not in your shoes, or boots, rather." She grinned slightly as she glanced to his feet. At his small laugh, she continued. "But life is precious. I've seen more people regret their refusal of treatment than you'd expect. I just don't want you to be one of them." She hitched a shoulder.

"That's kind of you, sweetheart. But I'm not going to be regretting anything. I've got plenty in my life I can regret. I'm not going to add another foolish thing to the list."

Tilting her head, she offered him a warm smile. "Okay. I just want to always be honest."

"And that right there is why you're hired." He smacked his knee.

"Ah, and here I was under the impression you just thought I was cute," she shot back in a teasing tone, arching her brow.

He shrugged slightly. "That, too. But it sounds better if I say I'm hiring you for your candor."

"Keeping it classy. I like it." She reached for her purse and took out a card. "HCEW sent over my resume, right?" Hospice and Care of Eastern Washington was usually on top of things, but it was always smart to double-check.

"Yup. You're experienced for someone so young." He nodded, acting impressed.

"The great thing about having a direction when you're young is that you can work hard to get there faster. After my grandma died, I knew what

I wanted to be. The hospice nurse who cared for her was incredible. She left an impression, and I've never looked back."

"Conviction is good, too."

"Everyone has to have a reason, Jack. If it's not conviction, it's something else driving you, but chances are it won't be as strong of a motivation."

He rubbed his whiskery chin. "How old are you?"

"Old enough. Now where are your doctor's notes?" With a quirk of her brow, she stood and walked over to his chair, offering a hand, dodging the question she knew she'd inevitably be asked. The question concerning her age always crept up one way or another. It wasn't common to be a twenty-six-year-old hospice nurse, but she wouldn't trade it for the world. People assumed her age meant a lack of experience, but that wasn't the case.

"I don't need your help," Jack grumbled.

"No, but sometimes it's nice to have help even when we don't need it."

He gave her a sarcastic glare, even as a grin broke through. "You're going to be bossy, aren't you?"

"Yup."

"Damn it."

"Lucky you."

"Ha, ha." He took her hand and stood. "Fine, but I'm not going to like it."

She bit back a giggle at his disgruntled look. "We're going to get along just fine. I can tell already."

As she followed him down the hall, she mentally made notes of what needed to be arranged. Empty walls held no pictures, and as she thought back to the living room. There weren't any there either. Odd. Was he alone? Did he no longer have living family? Or maybe they were estranged? Either way, she needed to find out.

"Here." He pointed to a large wooden desk, neatly organized with several white files with the St. Luke's logo on front. "You can sit if you want. I'm going to go and get some more coffee. You want some?"

"Nope, I'm good."

He started toward the door and paused. "You do drink coffee, don't you?"

She glanced up. "Every day."

"Good. I was worried for a minute. You can't trust a person who doesn't drink coffee. Unnatural." He walked away, the sound of his boots thumping the wooden floor.

Laken studied the charts and notes; it was textbook Adenocarcinoma in its advanced stages. The cancer had spread to his liver and lymph nodes, which confirmed her earlier suspicions. The specialist was Doctor Damien

Wills, an expert in the field and one she'd worked with before. If Dr. Wills said three months, then three months was a good assessment.

Three months also wasn't much time.

And time would only go quicker as the end grew closer.

As a general rule, she'd live in with Jack, providing care as it was needed. At first it would be less hands on, yet as time progressed she'd give round the clock care. She made a mental note to line up an on-call backup nurse so that Jack wouldn't ever be without care, even on her rare days off.

"Jack?" Laken called, setting aside the charts and listening to a soft click from down the hall.

"What, darlin'?"

She left the office and walked down the hall to find him pouring steaming black coffee into a Starbucks mug. "Jack, do you have time for a few more questions?"

"I can spare a minute or two." He gave a wily grin and rested against the counter.

Laken pulled out her phone and opened up her chart app to make notes. "Sweet. Okay. First things first. Family. Do you have living relatives, and are they aware of your condition?"

Jack took a long sip of coffee. "Yup and nope."

She glanced up. "Yes, relatives, and, no they don't know?"

"Yesss." He glanced away.

"Alright. Do you want any of them to be made aware?"

"I should probably tell Cyler, but I don't want to be around for the bonfire he'll throw to celebrate." He took another sip.

"Pardon?" She paused typing in the name.

"Cyler. My son. It's complicated."

"I see. So, he doesn't know." She studied his expression, trying to read between the lines.

"No, but I'll tell him myself." He lifted his mug and sighed, his shoulders rounding out as if insecure. "He deserves to hear it from me."

"Anyone else that needs to be informed?" She sidestepped the other questions about this Cyler guy. When it came to rifts in families, she stayed out. Period.

"Nope, he's all I've got. Wait. Damn it. I bet you Breelee will get wind of this." The kitchen echoed with the sound of his coffee mug hitting the stone countertop abruptly. "Damn woman. She'll be like a vulture, circling me till I drop dead. I gotta call my lawyer." He closed his eyes and pinched his nose. "Damn females. Okay, sweetheart, what other questions are you going to pelt me with? Let's rip it all off like a Band-Aid." He grabbed his mug, sloshing coffee onto the countertop, and stomped back into the living room. "What are you waiting for, girl? And grab my phone. I gotta make a few calls apparently. Damn, this day is just getting better and better," he muttered.

"And so it begins," Laken whispered under her breath, grabbing a sleek iPhone from the counter beside the coffeepot and walking to the living room. The questions were the easy part.

Especially if Jack's only living relatives were anything like he'd described.

Death really sucked.

Chapter 2

Cyler Myer tapped his pen on his pickup dashboard, watching as they lifted one of the frames into position. The house was coming along nicely, and even nicer would be the payout when this subdivision was fully established. It would sell quickly, just like his other three. It had taken years, sleepless nights, and scraping every last penny together, but he'd made it. *His* construction company. *His* design. *His* success.

And he hadn't needed one cent from Jack.

And he sure as hell didn't need his approval either.

Speak of the devil, as Cyler's phone buzzed, Jack's name lit up the screen.

It was a satisfying feeling, rejecting the call and tossing the phone aside to the passenger side. Let him leave a message.

One he wouldn't listen to.

He was just about to drive on to the next project when his phone buzzed again.

Jack.

Ignoring it, he threw the truck into drive and started down the gravel road, kicking up dust behind him. As the next project came into view, his phone buzzed again. He glanced over, expecting to see Jack's name. Odd that he'd call three times in a row when they hadn't spoken in years, but it wasn't his name that lit up the screen. It was a random number, and Cyler swiped to answer. "CC Homes."

He put the truck in park just before another house.

"Hello...son."

The voice haunted him, filling him with both anger and bitterness. "What the hell do you want?" He bit out each word.

"There's something I have to tell you." Jack sounded old, nothing like the pain in the ass that he'd always been. And as much as he wanted to throw the phone out the window, he paused, listening.

"Well?"

"Well…it's like this. I've got three months, and I'd like to say I'm sorry before I don't have that chance anymore."

His words echoed in Cyler's head, and he replayed them before answering.

"Three months, huh?" He glanced down at the brown leather seat.

"Yup, cancer. And I'd like for you to come home. If you can."

Cyler pinched the edge of his nose. "No, I don't think I'll be doing that, *Dad*." He spat the name. "And quite honestly, three months is still too long for me. You said you're sorry. I listened. Let's just be done." *At least this time it's final.*

"I see."

"Unlikely, but okay. You have a good three months." He ended the call and closed his eyes. He was justified in hating the old coot. But part of him whispered that even though Jack deserved it, he shouldn't have treated the old man that way.

Regardless, it was a moot point anyway. Three months wasn't long, and soon enough, it wouldn't matter.

As he got out of the car and walked toward the construction zone, he mentally started a countdown.

Ninety days left.

And soon Jackson Myer would answer for everything.

May he rot in hell.

As the day progressed, Cyler kept pushing thoughts of Jack to the back of his mind. Evening came and went, and as he lay down to sleep, he stared at the ceiling, till finally he couldn't take it any longer. Glancing to the clock, he groaned.

4:00 a.m.

Damn it.

Cyler rolled over, the rustling noise waking him up even further, if possible. He'd never had an issue falling asleep, but tonight…tonight he had simply watched one minute pass after the other.

He refused to believe it was because of Jack's confession.

Ha.

That was comical. As if the man would ever admit to being wrong. Cyler breathed a humorless laugh. Even as he was facing death, Jack had used it as emotional collateral to get what he wanted.

Well, it wouldn't work. Cyler laid his head deep into the pillow, closing his eyes and sighing deeply, pushing—shoving—every thought of Jack from his mind.

But just as he'd started to feel slightly peaceful, another question would tease his mind, and he'd be fully alert once more. *Damn, this sucks.*

"Why the hell would he want me back there anyway?" he mumbled, rubbing his hand down his face, his shadow of a beard rasping against his palm.

It was strange as hell, asking for him to come home. After all, Jack was the one who'd told him to never set foot on the property again, not that he'd ever intended to, not after—

He stopped the thoughts in their tracks. He couldn't go there. Wouldn't go there. It was a dark place he was still recovering from.

He rolled over once more, only this time, it was to reach for the remote. With a click, the screen lit the room with blue light before the news started. Frustrated, he rose from the bed and stalked to the bathroom. If he couldn't sleep, he might as well start working.

His job had been his salvation, his motivation; it had rescued him before, and he was betting it would save him again. As the business grew, he'd found himself doing more paperwork than manual labor. Some would appreciate the break, but he missed it.

Especially after nights like this past one. As he started the shower, he waited for the room to start filling with steam. After tossing his boxers in the laundry basket, he stepped into the water, his tight muscles slowly relaxing under the hot temperature. He braced the wall with his hands, leaning into the pressure, letting the water travel down his head and back, pouring off him. Forcing himself to not think, he focused on the heat.

Soap in hand, he made quick work of getting clean, never once trying to scrub the stained calluses on his palms. It was a losing battle, trying to make them look clean. Even with the increase in paperwork, his calluses were still deep, and he was proud of them.

Never forget where you came from.

Don't think of yourself as better than others.

He gave a humorless chuckle. He certainly didn't learn any of those ideals from Jack.

"Damn it." He growled as he turned off the shower. Shaking the excess water from his head, he angrily dried himself off. Why in the hell couldn't he just let this go?

It's not like the old man ever cared about me. I shouldn't care about him either.

Just as he finished the thought, he paused, and for the first time in the past twenty-four hours, something actually made sense.

Jack hadn't ever been successful in the one thing he wanted—for Cyler to be just like him.

And this was proof.

Suddenly, having half a heart didn't look so bad.

Rather, he was thankful for it, because it meant that in spite of Jack's best efforts, he'd failed.

Damn. He probably didn't even want him showing up, just wanted to sound good saying it.

That made a hell of a lot more sense than actually wanting him around. A smile tickled his lips as he wondered just what the old man would do if he actually did show up.

Probably die from shock.

Talk about temptation.

As Cyler dressed, he glanced to his old duffle bag, hiding in the bottom of the closet. He couldn't believe he was actually considering it.

Going back.

The memories would be like ghosts, and he wasn't sure he could deal with that. But on the other hand, it would be a sweet revenge, doing the unexpected and being a thorn in the man's side. He deserved far more, and showing up didn't mean he forgave Jack.

Hell no.

The wounds were far too deep, the blood far too bad. What kind of a man would sleep with his son's fiancée? What type of man would use it as leverage to hurt his wife enough that she'd finally sign the divorce papers?

What kind of a man would then run off with his son's now *ex*-fiancée to Mexico, only to arrive six months later and act as if nothing had happened?

As if Cyler's world hadn't completely burned to ashes.

As if Cyler's mom, Leslie, hadn't drunk herself to death shortly after the divorce finalized.

No. There would be no forgiving Jack, and he deserved far worse than three months of cancer condemning him.

Cyler ran his fingers through his damp hair, squeezing his eyes shut and thinking. Was it worth it? Seeing the devil himself again, just to get some sort of revenge?

Taking a deep breath, he filled the duffle bag, telling himself he would only be gone for only a day. Surely, he could do some damage in just twenty-four hours.

One night, maybe.

If Jack didn't die from shock first.

His chest constricted with both anticipation and cold fear at what the next day could hold. But one thing was utterly true.

Revenge could be sweet, especially when it was completely unexpected.

Chapter 3

The next morning, Laken blinked awake, the movement reminding her of when sand had once blown in her eyes. She glanced at an old Seahawks poster, focusing on the yellowed edges. It was a decidedly masculine room with football trophies, blue tones, and even old clothes in the closet, but no pictures. If she were betting, it was probably exactly as Cyler had left it, whenever that had been.

It wasn't the first time she'd moved into someone's old room, but this time felt different. Usually when a parent kept a room exactly as a child had left it, it was because they'd never really let go, or they'd had to let go too soon because the child had passed. As she replayed yesterday's phone conversation between Jack and Cyler, she was even more confused.

Ideally she'd have taken the guest room, but it was located at the back of the house. She'd never hear Jack if he needed her. But Cyler's room was directly across the living room from the master suite, so if Jack kept his door open, she could hear if he started a coughing fit or worse.

It was part of the job, being available when the patient needed help most. Night was usually that time, meaning Laken had become very fond of taking naps. At night, the body would wind down, and if the day had been particularly taxing, this could lead to complications. Cancer patients had a hard time falling asleep. Their bodies being so fatigued from the internal fight and the various drugs they were taking all took their toll. Add in an emotional event, and sleep usually didn't happen.

Which is exactly what had happened last night. Jack had been up coughing, requiring more breathing treatments to simply relax his lungs. Once he finally agreed to sleep meds, it was four in the morning. She rolled to her side and picked up her phone from the dark wood nightstand. Six-thirty.

Two-and-a-half hours of sleep. Today would be a nap day for sure. But first, coffee—copious amounts of coffee—preferably not made by Jack. The guy loved his coffee black and stronger than anything she'd ever tasted. She gave a quiet huff. It was probably exactly what she needed, but it didn't sound appetizing at all. She thought of how Starbucks was just a ten-minute drive. Her stomach rumbled in appreciation of the thought, and she sat up in bed, slid her feet out quietly and arched her back in a stretch. After yawning, she padded over to the suitcase she had packed and pulled out some fresh clothes. As she stepped into the hall, she heard Jack's snoring, and with a smile she went into the guest bathroom and clicked the door shut.

Dear Lord.

Laken looked rough. Her blond hair was in a tangled mess from when she'd put it up in a messy bun the night before. Tugging the band free, she tossed a few hairs into the trash and mercilessly brushed it out. After quickly braiding it, she put on a swipe of mascara, calling it good. She brushed her teeth and dressed, then tiptoed out of the bathroom, the sound of Jack's snoring still coming from his room. He'd easily sleep for at least another hour.

As she exited through the kitchen door, she jumped slightly when the coffee maker beeped and started to brew its scheduled morning pot. With a quick glare at the thick black sludge pouring into the clear carafe, she closed the door and walked to her car. She sent a quick text to Kessed, saying she was coming in for her fix.

The air was already warm, but the dry heat gave it a crisp feel that only the desert mornings could bring. Laken cast a glance to the faded red barn. Jack had a mare boarded there, and she almost made a detour to say good morning to the chestnut horse. Jack had mentioned the mare's soft spot for sugar cubes, and Laken had readily snuck her favorite treat outside more than once. But the siren call of coffee overpowered the impulse to pet the horse's velvet nose. Crickets chirped as she slid into the driver's seat and started up the Honda. Her phone beeped with Kessed's reply, saying she would have it ready.

Soon she was driving into the barely waking town of Ellensburg. She parked beside an oversized Chevy pickup and slid out of her door, using caution not to dent the overly close truck. The parking lot was notoriously small, and large rigs took up more than their share. Only slightly irritated, she walked into the coffee shop, the warm aroma of the brew wrapping around her like a quilt on a cold day. Immediately energized by the scent alone, she grinned as she saw her friend.

"Hey beautiful!"

Giving a small wave, Laken almost cried tears of joy when Kessed held out a coffee cup toward her, a knowing grin on her face.

"You're just saying that since I'm your dealer for your drug of choice." Kessed grinned, swiping her espresso colored hair over her shoulder. Green eyes curved up into half-moons from her wide smile.

"Bless you," Laken whispered, taking the offered cup and inhaling deeply. "You're so handsome." She whimpered at the beautiful black contents.

"Yeah, you're going too far with the coffee-lover thing. It's getting weird." Kessed rolled her eyes as she rang up Laken's order. With a furtive glance to the side, she leaned forward slightly. "And believe me, your coffee has nothing on that over there." She flicked her glance to the right then back, arching a dark eyebrow.

Laken resisted the urge to glance over; rather, she pulled out her phone and scanned the app. "I need a mobile Starbucks," Laken murmured, her gaze returning to Kessed.

"What? Am I not good enough for you? Seriously. You don't even have to order. Some people are so lazy." Kessed's eyes flicked back to the right for a moment before fixing on Laken.

"I guess that will have to do." Laken sighed, earning an eye roll from her friend. "Ok, I gotta go. But I'll text you later."

Kessed saluted, her grin anything but innocent. Laken ignored her and turned to leave. Taking a step toward the door, she scanned the room, curious as to what Kessed had referred to earlier. Coffee sloshed as she almost tripped. The guy looked like Scott Eastwood, only broader in the shoulders and with bluer eyes. Lips twisting into a smile, she couldn't help staring, but she tried to pass her gawking as a friendly hello, so she waved. *Ugh, lame.*

He nodded once, holding her stare for a moment then turned to his coffee, playing with the sleeve and rotating it around the cup as if anxious. He turned his attention to the window, and she noticed how his shoulders held their shape, as if overly tense. Not wanting to pry, she glanced away and walked toward the door. But before it swung closed, she cast one more glance behind her, meeting his blue gaze. She sucked in a startled breath, and walked to her car, pulling out her phone.

Laken: *Uh, whoa. You were right. He gives my coffee some serious competition.*

The little bubble popped up as she slipped into her car.

Kessed: *Dibs.*

Laughter shook her shoulders slightly as she rolled her eyes.

Laken: *Fine. But if he has a brother...*
Kessed: *You got it.*
Laken: *Enjoy the view.*
Kessed: *Believe me, I am.*

Laken started the car and slowly backed from the parking lot then drove back to Jack's ranch, grinning the whole way.

Jack wasn't in the same kind of cheerful mood when she arrived. He was sitting on the front porch with his coffee mug as she drove up. Feeling guilty about her Starbucks run and the fact that she hadn't brought him anything, she debated between leaving the cup in the car and taking it.

Screw guilt. She needed coffee.

"Good morning!" she called out cheerfully.

Jack glared.

"Aren't you sweetness and light today?" Laken teased as she took the seat beside him, taking a sip of her black Pike Place brew.

"Traitor." He nodded to her cup and arched a brow, a grin teasing his whiskery cheek.

"Just feeding my addiction. The heart wants what it wants."

"My coffee ain't good enough for you?" he asked, taking a long sip from his cup.

"Jack, I'm not woman enough for your coffee." She shook her head teasingly.

He gave a chuckle. "You tried. That's more than most men will do."

"What can I say? My heart belongs to Starbucks."

Jack rolled his eyes. "I don't see what all the fuss is about. Never could stand the stuff."

"Take it back!" Laken gasped, jokingly.

"Nope. The heart wants what it wants." He tossed the words back at her. "Mine likes my own coffee, thank you kindly."

Laken rolled her eyes. "To each his own."

After a few moments of silence, she asked, "How did you do after the different sleep medication?" It was important to know for future reference.

"It was fine. I still don't like it, but it did help me sleep a spell, so that's good, I guess. I kinda feel like a Mac truck hit me this mornin' though." He gave his head a quick shake.

"Gotta love sleep deprivation." Laken raised her white and green cup in a toast.

"We're not all young like you, honey." Jack chuckled, but also raised his mug.

"I'm young, and I hate missing sleep, so I can't even imagine how you feel. Did the coughing subside after that last treatment?" She knew it had but needed to know how it felt to Jack. Just because a treatment or medicine was good didn't mean it was necessarily effective for that patient. Odd side effects happened sometimes; it was never wise to just assume the drug did exactly what it was supposed to do.

"Yeah, that last one really nipped it in the bud. What was the change?"

"I increased the dosage but only slightly. Your doctor said it might need some adjustment and gave me the specifications."

"Nice."

Next came the subject that she wasn't excited about bringing up, but needed to regardless. She was pretty sure that last night's episodes had been brought on by the phone conversation with Cyler. It was important for Jack to process everything so that tonight was not a repeated cycle with ruined sleep.

"How are you feeling about yesterday?" She slid a glance up over her cup as she sipped.

"I did it. I called him. I'm at peace with the idea that I did what I needed to do." He gave a firm nod and took a determined sip of coffee.

"The ball's in his court now."

"Yup. At least he can't say I didn't try."

"Exactly. And that gives you a clear conscience. Jack." She placed a hand on the shoulder of his soft flannel button-up shirt. "You're only responsible for your own actions. You can't be held responsible for others."

Jack turned and looked at her, his blue eyes sharp and clear. "If only that were the truth, honey." He shook his head and placed his hands on his knees, standing, causing her hand to slide from his shoulder. "If only that were true. But, girl, it ain't. Because you're forgetting to factor in one thing."

She watched as he slowly took a few steps toward the house and turned, meeting her gaze.

"Sometimes the reaction we get…it's exactly what we deserve. And in this case, Cyler's right. All I can do is be happy that I tried, and you know what? In a week, I'll try again—till the end of the damn three months. I'll keep trying because his reactions are exactly that. Reactions. I made the first move a long time ago. And it was wrong. And I can't expect that one right move negates all that I screwed up. And darlin', you can't either."

Laken swallowed, watching the intense furrow of his brow as he took a deep breath, coughed, and walked toward the kitchen door.

As much as it sucked, he was right. And if he did something terrible to his son, then one phone call couldn't fix it.

Only time could somehow heal that wound.

And time was always the enemy.

Chapter 4

It's now or never. The unmistakable scent of sagebrush and Russian Olive trees hung in the air as Cyler's tires crunched the gravel road till he put the truck in park just before the semi-circular drive. An older model Honda Civic was parked to the side, but he dismissed it. *Probably a maid or a nurse.* He gave a small humorless laugh. That gave purgatory a whole new meaning. *Poor nurse!* Hopefully, whomever the insurance company sent over to deal with Jack's worthless hide was well-seasoned and unwilling to take his crap.

Or charm.

In that order.

With a bravery he certainly didn't feel, he stepped from the cab and shut the door, making sure the sound was loud enough to warn of his arrival. He debated on whether to bring in his duffel bag but decided leaving it in the truck was smarter, just in case he wanted to abandon this whole forsaken idea and hightail it out of there.

After a few steps, he remembered his half-full coffee left in the car. Normally he wouldn't care, but Jack's coffee was like tractor oil, thick and dark, and tasted just as bad. He swung open the door and reached across the seat and grabbed his Starbucks cup. He took a sip before starting toward the door once more.

He had stopped at the coffee shop in an attempt to clear his head. *That didn't happen*, he thought sarcastically as the memory of the blond he'd seen there passed through his mind. She was beautiful, but in a girl-next-door kind of way. Probably early twenties and finishing up her summer quarter at Eastern Washington University. He'd only made eye contact for a few seconds, but it had felt like she was reading him, seeing things that other people would have just ignored. The feeling had stuck with him ever since, distracting and irritating both at once.

A few lonely crickets chirped, but the ranch was otherwise quiet. Setting his resolve, he walked toward the house and stepped on the porch. The front windows were wide open, letting in the morning air.

"Damn it, woman! Are you trying to kill me before the cancer does?" Jack's unmistakable voice filtered through the screen, and in spite of himself, Cyler grinned.

Some things never change.

"No. But if you don't sit still when I take your blood, then you're going to have a needle permanently embedded in your arm, and the next nurse to take care of that issue won't be nearly as nice as me," a woman answered, her tone sounding almost bored, as if well accustomed to dealing with his outbursts. But something about the voice seemed vaguely familiar.

Odd.

"And here I thought you'd be sweet since you're so pretty."

"And here I thought you'd be a gentleman since you're so old," she shot back, and Cyler felt like giving a little cheer for the poor woman having to deal with Jack, but clearly, she could hold her own.

There was a pause in the conversation, and Cyler waited, curiosity making a small smile linger on his face.

"Are you done yet? Bloodsuckers, all those doctors. Vampires, the lot."

"Are you done complaining? Jack, really, I thought you were tougher than this."

Cyler choked on his laugh, not wanting to give away his presence but proud of whatever woman just hit his pain-in-the-ass of a father between the eyes with a well-placed setdown.

"Needles are unnatural," he answered after a moment, his argument pathetic sounding.

"You're unnatural," she replied. "Okay, done. Now put your feet up and close your eyes. We don't want a repeat from last time."

He heard some grumbling, and something close to a swear word.

"Jack. Really. You want to do that again? You're still black and blue on your shin, elbow, and eye. I'd rather your pride hurt than your body, okay?"

"Fine."

Jack's acquiescence was startling. Never had he heard him give up anything without a fight—whether he was right or wrong. Pride had a crazy way of making men more stubborn than mules, Jack being king of those types of *jack*asses.

It seemed like they were done with whatever they were doing, so now would be a good opportunity to strike when Jack was weak.

Even as he thought the words, he hated how they sounded, hated even more how necessary and true they were.

He knocked twice then stepped back from the door, taking a deep breath. His heart pounded hard as he waited, hearing the decidedly feminine footsteps draw closer to the door.

The handle turned, and as the door opened, everything he was thinking came to a skidding halt.

"Uh-uh," Cyler stuttered as the girl he had just seen at Starbucks blinked at him, and by the furrow in her brow, she recognized him, too, "hi." He lifted a hand in a pathetic wave, feeling completely off-centered. *How in the hell is she old enough to be taking care of Jack?* The old bastard *would* find the prettiest nurse in the county.

"Hi. Can I help you?" she asked, her head tilting slightly, her green eyes taking on a curious glint.

"Yeah—"

"Well, I'll be damned."

Jack's voice drew his attention, and his gaze shifted, the sight punching him in the gut.

The woman stepped to the side, turned and walked toward Jack. "Jack, you're going to pass out again, and I'll have to carry your sorry as—carcass to the couch. Like last time." She put her hands on her hips, looking like a pissed-off mother hen.

"Well, I don't think I lost that much blood, but I think I'm seeing things, honey." His gaze shifted to the girl then back to Cyler, narrowing.

Cyler nodded once. "Hi, Dad."

* * * *

For once, Laken was thankful for Jack's ornery streak. It was a needed distraction from the Scott Eastwood look-alike from Starbucks. His voice was deep, rich, and bitter, immediately setting her teeth on edge.

She spun around, her gaze narrowing on the guy as he took a step over the threshold and walked into the house like he'd been there a million times.

Because he probably had.

This was Jack's son?

He was taller than Jack by several inches, making him at least six feet and three inches of taut muscle and crystal-blue eyes. His dark walnut hair was cut short, but long enough to be tousled, giving him a younger appearance. Tan skin highlighted the strong cut of his jaw, drawing her attention down to a broad chest and—

"Laken?" Jack put an end to her study of his son. Her gaze jerked up, a burning blush heated her face as she made eye contact with the subject of her focus.

The look this newcomer gave her was annoyingly mocking, as one side of his mouth tipped up in a knowing smirk.

Arching a brow, she held his gaze, not backing down.

"Laken, this is my, uh, son, Cyler Myer." Jack made the introductions.

"A pleasure, ma'am...or is it miss?" Cyler asked. His voice was more alluring with the bitter tone absent.

"Ah, nice to meet you, Cyler. It's always great to finally put a face to the name." She gave a sweet smile, forcing it to be genuine when she wanted to be more cutting. She avoided answering his last question.

"You can't believe everything you hear, *miss*." Cyler reached out a hand, his steely gaze flickering from it to her. A dark brow arched in question.

Or is it a dare?

"Isn't that the truth?" she answered, taking his hand and squeezing tightly and continuing to hold his stare.

"Why don't we head to the living room? All this standing is making me dizzy," Jack mumbled.

As Laken released Cyler's hand, she turned to watch Jack. His steps shuffled as he made his way toward the living room, and she rushed to give him help. When she reached out and grasped his arm, she felt his body trembling. "Jack?" she whispered, just loud enough for him to hear.

"I'm fine, sweetheart. Just a little weak and even more shocked." He took a long breath, the rattling in his chest faint but present. "I guess I never thought he'd actually come." He gave her a quick glance and gripped her hand tightly.

When they made it to his favorite chair, she turned to watch Cyler stride in with hesitant familiarity. His gaze scanned the room, as if taking inventory of what was different. How long had it been since he'd been there?

"So, Cyler...I'm really glad to see you." Jack paused; an awkward silence filled the room.

"Yup." He took a seat on the adjacent couch and leaned forward, setting his elbows on his knees and watching Jack, a cruel smile on his face.

As if he was enjoying Jack's discomfort.

What an ass.

It wasn't as if Laken hadn't seen family animosity before, but this was cold, clinical, as if it was a pre-calculated move made to cause injury.

But it wasn't her place.

Biting her lip, she slowly stood. "I'm sure you both have a lot to discuss. I'll be in my room if you need me. Jack, is there anything else you'd like at the moment?" She turned, watching as the poor guy swallowed hard.

"No, honey. I'm…fine."

The usually aggravatingly confident man was hesitant and insecure. It ripped at her, and more than anything, she wanted to snap at Cyler for being a jerk but, honestly, what had he actually done wrong? Nothing! He'd shown up, just like he'd been asked to, and he was actually in the living room with his dad when only yesterday he had refused his calls. As much as she wanted to find fault with him, there was nothing.

"Alright. Cyler, do you need anything? Water, coffee?" She gave a small smile, hoping to lighten the heavy atmosphere of the room.

It worked. He grinned, the action softening the grim lines on his face and making him even more handsome. "I think I'm good." He raised his Starbucks cup and gave a wink.

"Let me know if you need anything, Jack." And with a small smile in his direction, she left.

Odd how silence could be louder than shouting.

And cold.

She wasn't sure if hell had frozen over for Cyler to actually be there, but she was sure it wasn't going to be an easy road.

For any of them.

* * * *

Well, I'm here. Now what the hell do I do? He expected for it to be simple. See Jack, shock him into an early grave, and leave. Boom, done.

He should have known that life was never that simple. He was there but had no clue as to what to do next.

So he waited, and watched, and tried to take some sadistic joy in the way Jack fumbled with his jeans, rubbing his hands over his knees and glancing around, focusing on anything but him.

He should wait. Let the awkward silence be part of the punishment, but damn it all, it was punishment to him too. So, against his better judgment, he spoke. "I should have guessed you'd pick a nurse like that."

So maybe it wasn't the high road, but at least he'd broken the silence.

Jack's gaze snapped up, zeroing in with that same precision that immediately sent Cyler back to his childhood. "Don't go there."

Cyler swallowed the compulsion to stand down. "Just calling it like I see it...Dad." He held up his hands in mock surrender.

"Don't *Dad* me. You haven't called me that since your mother—"

"I wouldn't go there either, *Jack*," Cyler interrupted, his body tensing with too many memories.

Jack's eyes narrowed, and Cyler braced himself, but rather than restart an old fight, Jack broke their stare-down and lowered his head. "I'm sorry, Cyler."

It wasn't enough. It wouldn't ever be enough. "Sorry isn't worth the dirt on your boots."

"No. No, it's not." Jack lifted his gaze, a light sheen of moisture shocking Cyler like a swift punch to the gut. But a moment later, he steeled himself against it. Probably another attempt at manipulating him. He'd tried every other trick in the book, so why not this?

"You're not here for me. Are you?" Jack asked after a moment, his body still and tense as if waiting for a blow.

Cyler sensed it. It would hurt; it would be a deep blow if he told him the real reason. It would be everything he'd dreamed of, everything he'd wanted it to be. He jumped at the opportunity. "Hell no. I'm here to make sure you're suffering," Cyler whispered low, his gaze piercing through the man who had tortured him for years, and, when he'd needed him the most, betrayed him deeper than any man should endure.

"I see."

"I don't think you do. I've heard that when people are passing...they need to feel at peace. Jack, there's no way in hell I'm giving you that. I want you to be so restless, so deeply tortured that you know what it was like"—Cyler swallowed—"to be me. That you feel everything you caused me to feel, and in the end, you know it's completely and utterly hopeless." Cyler stood and walked over to Jack, watching as the old man trembled and his gaze took on a narrow and furious glint, reminding Cyler of the man he recalled. "Because I will never, ever, *ever* forgive you, Dad." He waited, letting the words sink in, marinating in the air.

Jack slowly stood. Gave a small nod.

And swung.

Chapter 5

Cyler woke up with a pounding headache. The pain radiated from the back of his skull to the front then started over. "Aw, hell," he whispered, closing his eyes against the sunlight in his room.

His eyes blinked open again as he took in his surroundings. Was he dreaming? What the *hell* was he doing in his old room? He thought back over the past day, piecing together events and trying to make sense of it all.

"Hey there, Rocky. How are you feeling?"

He watched in fascination as a faintly familiar and startlingly beautiful blond leaned over him. Her ponytail slid from her shoulder and lightly thumped against his chest as she tenderly prodded his head with her fingers.

"Rocky?" he asked, unable to put anything else coherent together.

"Yeah, you know, the boxer?" she answered, her eyes still trained on his head as she slowly moved her hands from the front of his head and to the sides, her green eyes narrowing slightly.

He winced as her fingers grazed an especially tender spot on the right side of his head.

"Right there, huh? I think the coffee table did more damage than Jack." She straightened, giving him a wry grin.

Damn, that grin is sexy.

Wait. Coffee table?

"Say what?" He rose on his elbow, trying to ignore the way his head throbbed when he moved.

"You're lucky your head is harder than oak." She gave him a wink and stood. "When Jack swung and collided with your jaw, you lost your footing and smacked your head on that monster of a coffee table in the living room."

He leaned back on the pillow, closing his eyes as the throbbing slowly ebbed. "Damn thing. I used to stub my toe on it as a kid. Did I do any damage to it? Please say yes."

"Yes."

Cyler opened one eye. "Liar. Stupid piece of shit is probably still there," he mumbled.

Her soft laughter had him fighting his own smile, but he bit it back as his jaw ached with the slight movement. "Damn, that old man can still hit."

"You'll be a little tender, but I think Jack's the one that suffered the more serious injury," she added softly.

He turned his head and glared at her. "Oh really? Is his *tender* heart all bruised up?" he asked with thick sarcasm.

A loud laugh echoed in the small room before she covered her mouth with her hand and gave him an apologetic smile. "Sorry. Uh, I don't think I'd ever use *tender* as a way to describe Jack." She shook her head but sobered. "No, I'm talking about his hand." She arched a brow.

"Oh. Son of a bitch deserves it."

"Yeah, well, people with cancer don't exactly heal…"

He waited for her to finish, but she didn't. "Don't heal…" He let the sentence linger, waiting.

"Period." She blinked at him, her expression curious. She opened her mouth then closed it. "I think you need to have a conversation with Jack. One that uses words." She gave a quick roll of her eyes. "Think you can do that, Rocky?"

"No."

"*A* for effort."

"I'm not here to try."

She sat down on the bed, tilting her head slightly. "Then why are you here?"

He exhaled a deep breath, debating on what exactly to say.

"Never mind. Not my business." Laken held up her hands in surrender, stood, and walked to the door. She paused, placing her hand at the doorframe. As she glanced over her shoulder, she bit her lip, her body tense. "Just talk."

As she left, Cyler closed his eyes. He wasn't going to let her soft spot for Jack mess with him.

Rolling over, he slowly rose into a sitting position, the dull throb in his head going into a mad pounding. "Damn, I'd kill for some ibuprofen," he muttered.

"That won't be necessary."

"You again?" Cyler glared through his narrowed eyes, trying to see through the pain.

"Yup. Sorry." She shrugged, handing him two small brown pills and a glass of water.

"Laken, right?" he asked as he took the meds and water, giving her a quick glance.

"Yup. Laken Garlington." She extended a hand.

"Cyler Myer," he answered as soon as he swallowed. "But I guess you probably already knew that."

"The general animosity gave me a clue," Laken answered, a slight grin at her lips, pulling them wider and capturing his attention. Her lower lip was plumper than her top one, the off balance of it somehow perfect.

"Really? That's what gave it away?" He slowly stood, his body aching, but it was better than being worthless and in bed.

"Easy there. Pretty sure you got a small concussion."

"Damn it, old man will never let me live it down, even if the blasted coffee table did his dirty work."

Laken's laughter filtered through the room, lightening his mood.

"It's not my first concussion. Probably won't be my last." He narrowed his eyes as he watched her. "There's only one of you, so I'm good to go." He slowly grinned and started toward the door.

"Just take it easy. It might be a better idea if you laid—"

"I'm fine," he clipped, bracing his hand on the doorjamb, his head pounding like mad.

"Backing off." She held up her hands and took a step back, but before he turned away, he noticed she started forward again.

"Look, I'm fine. I'm sure you're used to having to care for whomever you're stuck with—" He paused. "That came out wrong."

"I'll blame it on the concussion," she answered, her tone serious.

He shifted back to her, concerned that he'd offended her by his careless remark. But as her full lower lip twitched at the corner, he relaxed.

"I've got thick skin." She shrugged and walked toward him, waiting as he walked through the door and into the hall. "Jack's in the living room, in case you were curious."

Cyler watched her walk toward the kitchen, the slow sway of her hips capturing all his attention. She filled out her jeans damn well, just the right amount of muscle and curve. His lips twitched as she paused, placing her hands on her hips and taking a deep breath as if facing a huge endeavor, rather than just standing in a kitchen.

As he turned, he heard stainless steel pots clanging together. It was both comforting and painful; memories of his mother in that very same kitchen came flooding back.

With a firm set to his jaw, he walked into the living room. Jack was sitting in his recliner, flipping through the satellite guide, and making annoyed grunts with each highlighted show. "A thousand channels and not a damn thing on."

"I've heard that before."

At the sound of his voice, Jack jumped, the remote launching out of his hand and landing on the coffee table, sending the plastic backing and batteries sailing across the surface.

"Well, that sucks." Cyler watched as a battery rolled off the table. He took a seat on the other side of the room. *This seems familiar.*

"I'm sorry I cuffed you," Jack grumbled, his expression wary and shockingly apologetic.

What the hell?

"As I understand it, the coffee table needs more credit than you," Cyler replied, leaning back into the sofa.

Jack huffed, casting a glare at the offending piece of furniture.

"Angry that it stole your glory, old man?" Cyler grinned, unable to resist poking the bear.

"You damn well know it," Jack retorted then gave him a sidelong glance. "For being so hardheaded and stubborn, you should have at least dented the damn thing."

"When you kick the bucket, that coffee table and I are going to have a bonfire," Cyler shot back. Like hell was he going to let him forget that his time was ticking, slowly sifting away. And when it was gone, there wasn't a damn thing the old man could do to stop Cyler from doing whatever he wanted.

"Don't sound so happy about it."

"I'll try to put a damper on my excitement."

"Damn it, Cyler. I know you're just trying to be the largest pain in the ass, but think for one moment." Jack turned in his seat, facing Cyler. His jaw was set in a firm line as he lifted his hand to gesture then winced.

White gauze wound around his fist, blood staining the white with a deep red. Cyler glanced away. The last thing he wanted was to feel sorry for him. It was the last thing he deserved anyway.

"Cyler, look at me," Jack commanded.

It was the same tone Jack had used when he was just a kid. The same edge to his voice that made Cyler remember the sting of the apple tree switch across his ass and the tears of his mom when she tried to protect him.

Defiantly, he glanced up, daring Jack to continue.

"Did it ever occur to your thick head that maybe, even though you're the biggest pain in the ass that ever did walk this earth, that I'm happy you're here?"

"No. A lot of things crossed my mind, Jack. But I can honestly say that not once have I ever deluded myself into thinking you actually wanted me around. You made that abundantly clear when I was about twenty-one. You remember?"

Cyler leaned forward, watching his reaction. It wasn't fair; it wasn't even right, but he was spoiling for a fight. Call it preying on the weak, but Lord only knew how many times Jack had done the same to him. It was payback.

"I remember." Jack's gaze slid away, his shoulders caving slightly as he turned his attention to the TV.

"Lucky me. I haven't forgotten either."

The silence stretched as Cyler trained his gaze on Jack, feeding off the tension that rolled off him as the old man tried to ignore him. *Try to pretend I'm not here. I'm not going anywhere.*

"Jack?" Laken broke through Cyler's concentration, shattering the tension with one word. She walked into the living room as if there hadn't just been a declaration of war. "Are you getting hungry?" She placed a gentle hand on his shoulder, tilting her head slightly as she cast a curious glance back to Cyler.

"Not now, sweetheart. I think I'm going to just take a rest." Jack glanced up, giving her one of his trademark grins, one that Cyler had watched him use on every single female at every rodeo they'd ever attended.

He barely resisted the urge to roll his eyes.

To hell with it. He took an annoyed breath and rolled them anyway. "Hey, Casanova. She's not going to keep you warm, so stop trying."

"Ass," Jack answered back.

"I learned from the best," Cyler retorted.

"Yeah, we're going to get you out of hostile territory, Jack." Laken scowled a warning to Cyler.

He flashed her a grin. He wasn't about to cave to her scolding just because she had a nice ass and a sexy smile. He'd learned that lesson long ago.

Laken frowned a moment then helped Jack rise from his recliner. His movements were stiff, but as he took a few steps, his swagger returned. Her arm braced his back as he walked, helping him along. And just before they made it to the hall, Jack looked over his shoulder, giving him a challenging glare. He hunched farther, requiring more of Laken's help, and Cyler ground his teeth. The old codger was taking shameless advantage of her!

Was he surprised? No.

But that didn't mean he had to like it.

With a snort, he stood and all but stormed out of the room. He needed to clear his head, and he knew just what would do the trick.

Chapter 6

Laken glared at Jack. "Don't think I don't see what you're doing," she hissed as they walked down the hall. "You're not helping. Trust me."

"Aw, let an old man have some fun in his last days."

"You're not having fun. You're planning your funeral, and your son—"

"Son. Ha!"

"Whatever, he's going to be the one who gets you there early."

"At least I'd take him down with me."

"Hey! What happened to calling him and wanting to make things right?" Laken asked as she released her support from his back and helped him ease into his bed.

"He's an ass."

"So that justifies you being an ass too? Logic at its finest," Laken replied with heavy sarcasm.

"Yes."

"Liar."

"Nope. I'm simply immature."

"Such an accomplishment at the ripe old age of seventy-five."

"It's taken hard work to get here."

"Alive," Laken added, pulling up his blankets.

"Eh." Jack shrugged, closing his eyes. "Just make sure he doesn't ride her too hard and fast."

Laken coughed. "Say what?" She blinked, replaying exactly what she'd heard. "Who?"

"Margaret. She'll be hell to deal with later. And you'll be the one taking care of her because I'm not feeling up to dealing with her drama in the barn." He yawned and rolled over.

"I'm missing something."

"Margaret." Jack rolled back enough to meet her gaze. "You know, that old mare you keep eyeing in the barn? She's a beauty but has a stubborn streak a mile wide. And I'd bet my last bottle of scotch that Cyler's out there saddling her up." He narrowed his eyes. "You ride?"

Laken bit her lip. "Yeah?"

"That's always what a horse responds well to. Uncertainty." He huffed.

"I'm sure it will be fine." She took a step back, watching as Jack rolled to his side.

"You're the one dealing with it if it's not *fine*," Jack mumbled.

As she walked into the hall, she glanced to the kitchen then turned to study the back door. She should finish prepping for dinner, but her curiosity beckoned her toward the barn. Jack was right. She had been slipping sugar to the chestnut mare. With her long black mane and four white socks, Margaret was a beauty with a sweet temperament as well. At least she was sweet when she had her nose stroked and was given a treat.

Would Cyler ride her too hard?

Her curiosity made the decision for her, and soon she was making her way to the barn. The thick scent of sagebrush and hot dusty earth swirled around her as she crossed the gravel between the house and yard. Yet as soon as she stepped through the large red-and-white doors of the barn, the sweet smell of hay and leather tack welcomed her. She glanced to the mare's stall, noticing that she was still there. As soon as Margaret saw her, she nickered and stomped, sending up a faint cloud of dust.

"Hey, baby," Laken crooned, walking toward her, and reaching to rub the warm velvet of her nose.

Warm breath huffed out as Margaret gently rubbed harder against Laken's hand; then she dropped her head and sniffed as if searching for her treat.

"I'm sorry I didn't stop in the kitchen before I came out. I'll sneak you some sugar later." Laken leaned in to whisper.

The mare tossed her neck slightly as if offended but calmed down as soon as Laken gently petted her nose once more.

"I take it this isn't the first time you and Margaret have had a chat." Cyler startled Laken, and she gasped.

Margaret's ears turned forward, but she didn't seem afraid; rather, she nickered welcomingly.

"You two have a history?" Laken asked, taking a step back so that she could see Cyler better.

"You could say that." His lips twisted to the side, showing off a dimple.

"I sense a story." Laken gently pushed the topic.

Cyler's brows rose as his grin broke through, showing off straight white teeth. "Well—" He reached up and scratched the star in the middle of Margaret's head. "Let's just say that some kids dream of driving their dad's sports car. And all I ever wanted was to ride Margaret." He shrugged. The gesture was self-deprecating. "So, I did. Whenever the old man turned his back or pissed me off enough, I'd take her out and ride her."

"Ah, that explains what Jack said." Laken shook her head.

The bolt squeaked as Cyler unlocked the stall and swung the door open. Laken stepped out of the way, letting the worn wood door pass her by.

"I know I'm going to regret asking." He clipped a lead rope to Margaret's halter. "But what did Jack say?"

The mare stomped but followed Cyler out of the stall and into the hall of the barn. He lined her up with the tack room and tied her lead to the post. The wood was worn smooth from age, giving it a dull shine.

Laken eyed the rear of the mare with caution and walked a wide circle around her. "Just that you rode her."

"Yeah, I'm betting he didn't say it like that. Don't protect him." Cyler gave her an irritated glance, all remnants of his earlier grin evaporating.

"More or less." Laken shrugged.

"Yeah, I'm betting on more. But that's fine. I don't need more ammunition against him. I've got plenty." He placed an old Navajo blanket on the mare's back and settled it so that it was even.

Laken stepped to the side, watching as he gently patted the horse's hindquarters, whispering gently. He lifted an intricately detailed western saddle then slowly rested it on the blanket. She imagined that the weight of the saddle caused the muscles in his shoulders to tense, molding around his back, tightening into a V toward his waist. He made a few adjustments, each one causing his shirt to shift under the tension of his muscular back moving. Laken watched in fascination at the strength, yet was impressed by the contrast of his gentle care of the mare.

Cyler patted Margaret's neck, smoothing it as he leaned down, grasping the cinch and securing it. When she nickered, he glanced up, watching carefully.

"She'll bite if I'm not careful. Gotta watch your backside," Cyler murmured as he cast a furtive glance from Margaret to the cinch and back.

"I'm guessing she's done that before?" Laken asked with a thick tone. She cleared her throat delicately, hoping he didn't notice.

If he had noticed, he didn't indicate it as he shrugged, patted Margaret's leg and quickly secured the cinch. The mare huffed, turning her head, and giving what looked like a glare at Cyler.

"I don't think she likes you right now." Laken leaned against an empty stall, resting her hip against the wooden door.

"She never does when I saddle her. I used to ride her bareback. That ended when she shied from a rattler out toward the ridge and threw me." He rose and turned to her. "My nose was laid over, and I got a nice gash on my head. My mom about had a fit. Blood was everywhere." He chuckled as if reliving a great memory, rather than a traumatic one.

"Head wounds bleed like none other," Laken replied, giving a delicate shudder. Just because she was a nurse didn't mean she enjoyed the triage side of her career.

"You're not kidding. This scare is my only lasting war wound from the ordeal." He traced a faint line across his right eyebrow. "It's also why my nose is oddly perfect." He winked.

Laken chuckled. "Perfect, huh? When you were thrown, it obviously didn't damage your ego," she shot back, grinning.

"Nope. Happy to say my ego was the only thing not bruised." He gave her a sidelong glance. "My nose is perfect because...well, when it was jacked up to hell, I had to have some fancy doctor in Seattle fix it up. Plastic surgery isn't just for cosmetic stuff. Sometimes it's really damn helpful." He flashed her a grin and turned back to the mare. Margaret stomped her foot impatiently.

"You're fine, girl. Don't get your dander up." He leaned in, whispering loudly. "You're prettier anyway, so don't get jealous."

Laken rolled her eyes.

Quickly, he made sure the cinch was tight enough then put on the bridle. Margaret chewed it, causing the metal pieces to click together.

"Ready, aren't you, baby?" he crooned.

Laken took a silent breath, simply amazed by the way he and Margaret worked together, as if this were an everyday occurrence.

And it probably had been.

A decade ago.

"How old is Margaret?" she asked, trying to add pieces of the story together.

"About seventeen. She's not a young filly anymore, but she's far from being an old nag."

As if to accent Cyler's words, Margaret whinnied.

"I think she agrees with you."

"She always was a smart one." Cyler swung his leg over the saddle and mounted effortlessly. The leather creaked then settled as he placed his boots in the stirrups.

"When did you get those?" she asked, remembering that he hadn't been wearing them earlier when he was laid out on his bed.

"In my closet. When I left, I didn't exactly take the time to pack up everything. I pretty much jetted out of here with the shirt on my back," Cyler responded, gathering the reins. "Can you unclip her halter?" he asked.

Laken took the lead rope off and wound it around the pole, setting Margaret free.

"Well, you have fun." She took a step back as Margaret tossed her head and stomped.

"What? You don't want to come with me?" Cyler asked, but his gaze held a challenging glint.

"Where?" She glanced around the barn. Margaret was the only horse.

"Just around. It's beautiful country, and I can only assume that being with Jack wears you a bit thin at times. He's a pain in the ass on a good day." He reached out a hand, watching her.

Waiting.

"Can she handle us both?" Laken asked, fighting between wanting to throw caution to the wind and ride and doing what was probably wiser and stay with Jack.

"Easy. She's half quarter and half thoroughbred. She's a big girl." He gave Laken a lopsided grin. "Unless you're afraid."

He started to pull back his hand, but Laken reached out and quickly grasped it. The warmth of his fingers tightened around her, and he tugged. He lifted her from the ground as she placed her foot in the stirrup he had vacated and swung onto the horse's back. Immediately, she wrapped her arms around his waist and realized she was in trouble.

Every part of her body came alive. She tried to ignore the warmth of his back against her breasts, the tight expanse of his shoulders, so solid and broad. His soft T-shirt brushed against her, the scent of fresh laundry, horse, and some spicy cologne swirled about, causing her to lose the internal battle of ignoring the millions of sensations.

"You ready?" Cyler's voice rumbled, teasing her senses further.

"Yeah." She tightened her grasp around him, feeling the tight structure of his abs.

"Hold on." He eased Margaret into a slow walk out of the barn, but it may as well have been a gallop as her heart pounded with both anticipation and tension.

They never taught her how to handle this kind of attraction in nursing school.

And it terrified her.

Because the last thing she could risk was her heart.

And something told her it was a losing battle.

Chapter 7

This was a bad idea.

With every shift of the horse, he could feel Laken's front pressed against his back. It was difficult to concentrate on the horse's soothing rhythm when each step caused Laken's body to rub against his. The normally calming scent of old leather and horse was accentuated by a light floral fragrance that made his heart pound faster—harder. It had been a long while since he'd been that close to a woman, and his body was painfully aware of the fact. He needed a distraction or else was going to do something stupid.

"So, tell me about yourself, Laken. All I know is that you're a nurse with the patience of Job, and that you aren't afraid of horses." He focused on the passing sagebrush, on the height of the sun in the cloudless sky. Anything but the way she tightened her grip around his waist, holding him closer. *Damn.*

"The patience thing might be a stretch"—she gave a small laugh, the sound warm and inviting—"but I've been a nurse for almost four years, a hospice nurse for about three. I do love horses, and no, I'm not afraid of them. It's been a while since I've ridden on one this tall though…." Her voice trailed off, and he felt her shift as if looking down to evaluate the height once more.

"Yeah, she's about sixteen to seventeen hands. Not draft-horse height, but close. It's the thoroughbred in her," he answered, watching as a coyote ducked behind a crop of rocks, hiding. "Do you have any brothers or sisters?" he asked, wanting to keep the conversation moving.

"Yeah. I have one brother, Sterling. He's older by five years. I haven't seen him in about a year." Her tone softened.

He turned his head slightly, not enough to see her fully but enough to notice the way her shoulders caved slightly. "Why so long?"

"He's stationed in Afghanistan. Marine recon," she answered, and he saw her shoulders straighten as if saying it gave her strength and pride.

"Wow. You miss him?" He asked the obvious.

"Yeah, a lot. He's a pretty great guy. I usually get to talk with him more, but this last assignment has him out of range for long periods of time."

"So, you guys are close?"

"Yeah. Real close. It's hard with him over there. My mom is in a constant state of anxiety." He felt her shrug behind him.

"I bet." He shook his head, his own memories flooding back. "My mom, she always said I could be anything I wanted to be, except go into the military."

He felt her stiffen behind him. "Why's that?"

"Don't be offended. It's nothing against it. You see, my mom's two brothers were killed in action in Vietnam. She never really got over the loss, and the thought of her only son in some sort of foreign war was enough to give her chest pains."

"Oh, that's hard. I can't even imagine. I know that I freak about Sterling whenever I think of it." She tightened her grip around his waist as if trying to pull some security, some strength, from it.

"Reconnaissance?" he asked, clenching his teeth, attempting to ignore the way her arms around him woke up a million senses he'd rather remained dormant.

"Yeah. He likes to be in front. It was a pain when he was younger, and I'd get shoved back behind him. It's more of a pain when I can't yell at him for it because he's so far away. But he's happiest there, doing only heaven-knows-what, but there's always this edge of excitement to his voice, even when he's exhausted."

His gaze strayed to the horizon as he led Margaret down a deer path that led toward one of the canyons. "When was the last time you got to talk with him?"

"About a month ago. It was a short phone call. He just wanted to wish me happy birthday." There was a smile to her tone, and Cyler found himself returning the gesture, even if she couldn't see him.

"Well, happy belated birthday." He turned his head again, glancing back toward her then again to the trail.

"Thanks." She chuckled. "It was actually about six months ago."

"Oh. Well happy *really* belated birthday. I guess it's better late than never, right?"

"That's what Sterling said." She laughed louder, scaring a pheasant from its hiding place. Its wings beat furiously as it crowed and fled the scene.

"Damn thing." Cyler flinched and glared at the bird as it flew. "About scared me out of my skin."

"Margaret didn't even glance up." Laken shifted so that she was looking over his shoulder.

"Yeah, she's what you call bomb-proof. Nothing fazes her, well, except for that one rattler."

There was a lull in the conversation, but he didn't want to break the peaceful silence.

"If only we could be like that, huh?" Laken spoke up.

"Be like what?" he asked, intentionally choosing to misunderstand her question.

"Bomb-proof. If we could just live as if nothing really phased us, regardless of how startling or horrible it was."

"Would save us a lot of pain." He took a breath and released it in a sigh. "But that's not how it works."

"No. It's not."

He waited for her to bleed platitudes, to say something about how there was beauty in the pain, or how it all worked out, something equally as asinine. But she didn't; she just moved in quiet grace with Margaret's strides. He could feel her intake of breath, but not once did she hold it as if trying to break the silence.

Oddly enough, it created a tension inside of him, one that needed to be broken, but he wasn't sure how. Finally, when another minute passed, he caved and spoke. "I keep waiting for you to say something profound about life, and you're taking too long."

He felt her body shift as if regarding him. "Oh? And what do you think I should be saying?"

He shrugged. "Something about life being beautiful in both the pain and the high points."

"Alright. Why would I say that?" she asked, her tone soft.

"Because, isn't that your job? I mean, you deal with people dying all the time."

"Are you dying?"

"No, but—"

"But you think that since I've faced death so often, I have the answers." She finished for him.

He paused, thinking over what she'd said. "No…" He gave a humorless chuckle. "No, I don't. In fact, I'd bet you were more confused than the rest us."

"I knew you were smarter than you looked," she teased lightly, no doubt trying to lighten the mood.

"It's how I catch people unaware. They see my pretty face and think I'm all beauty, no brains."

"I can't say I had that impression."

"Yeah, well, being taken out by a seventy-year-old and his coffee table sidekick didn't exactly help that."

"Ha! No. No, it did not."

He felt her shake her head.

Cyler noticed the canyon growing closer and nodded in its direction. "See that shadow over there?"

"Yeah?"

"It's actually part of the Manastash Ridge, but it's a pretty incredible canyon. There's a few of them around here, but they aren't as big as the Yakima Canyon."

"The one with the bridge?"

"Yeah."

"My whole body tingles when I cross that bridge. I'm just thankful that whoever engineered it made it so that you can't see over the edge very well. You can see the depth in the distance, but not right beside you."

"Don't like heights?"

"Don't like driving seventy miles an hour over cement then air," she replied with an exasperated tone.

"I took you for a braver soul."

"We all have a chink in our armor. Yours is just a coffee table. Mine is several thousand feet of a sheer drop. Mine is way more badass than yours," she teased.

"Hey, I see why you get along so well with Jack. You're a pain in the ass too."

"Yup, and don't you forget it."

"I don't think you'll let me."

"Probably not."

"At least we understand each other." He pulled up on Margaret's reins and commanded her to whoa. As she came to a stop, he shifted slightly to face Laken over his shoulder. "I'm going to slide off, so watch my boot." He waited for her nod then slowly slid from the saddle.

"Here, let me help." He held his arms up to help her dismount the horse, but she shook her head.

"I've got this." She placed her foot in the stirrup and arched her leg over, giving him a prime view of her butt as she stepped onto the ground.

Damn it, all that hard-fought self-control went back out the window. He turned around and adjusted himself, trying to think about anything that would distract him from the sweet view he'd just enjoyed.

Enjoyed far too much.

"Wow, that is amazing!"

Laken's voice didn't help his state of arousal, and he concentrated hard on thinking about freezing lakes and clowns, anything that he hated.

"Yeah, it's pretty epic." He forced his body into a calmer state and walked over to her, thankful her attention was on the canyon to the north and not on the issues happening in his southern region.

"How far down is it?" She took a tentative step forward, even though the canyon cliff was at least fifty feet ahead.

"It drops about six hundred feet. Not too far, but enough to make it a sight."

"Yeah." She breathed. "I bet you came out here a lot as a kid."

He snorted. "Yep, I sure did." He slid his hands in his jean pockets, noticing that his previous issue was no longer present. He'd have to remember that thinking about his childhood was more effective than a cold shower.

The sun was arching over the Rattlesnake Hills, making its final descent into sunset and creating shadows across the canyon. "It's a good place to think," he added.

"I'm betting you needed that."

"I still do." He turned back to Margaret. "She could walk out here blindfolded."

"I don't doubt that," Laken replied, heading back toward the mare as well. With a small grin, she rubbed her hand over the horse's velvet muzzle, crooning to it softly.

Warmth spread throughout his chest at the sight. He glanced away, trying to fight the unwelcome emotion.

"Cyler?"

He looked back to her, steeling himself internally. "Yeah?"

"I know you don't know me well, but if you ever want to talk...I'm here." She shrugged. "Sometimes it's easier to talk to someone you don't know very well, rather than someone you do. I'm a good listener." She held up a hand as if warning him that she wasn't done yet. "That's all I'm going to say. I'm not going to push you. And I do not expect you to talk now. Just know I'm here."

It rubbed him wrong, but rather than explore just why, he snorted and did what came easily, retreat behind the hard shell he'd erected so long ago. "While I appreciate the sentiment, I'd like you to just mind your own business. I knew that you'd have some sort of plan or ulterior motive to try and have me mend things with Jack, but hell will freeze over first. Do you get that?" He ran his fingers through his hair and walked away, back toward the canyon.

He kicked the dirt with his boot, sending the particles in the air and watching as the wind took them.

"You ready to go?" Laken called, and he turned, narrowing his eyes at the fact that there wasn't any firm set to her mouth, no flashing of anger in her expression, just...acceptance. As if they were talking about the weather.

"Uh, yeah," he answered, eyeing her cautiously. He'd learned long ago that a woman's emotions were not to be trusted.

"Thanks. I need to finish up everything for dinner. Are you staying?" she asked.

He should say no.

He should ride like hell to get back to the ranch and take off as soon as his boots hit the gravel.

Yet he found himself mounting the mare, helping Laken saddle, and swearing a blue streak in his head as he answered, "Yeah. I'll stay."

A month ago, he would have said that hell would have needed to freeze over.

Apparently, hell was starting to get a lot colder.

Chapter 8

The ride back to the ranch was a test in her self-control. With each step of the horse, Laken's hips would sway slightly, her breasts pressing into his back—his solid, warm, and very sexy back. She needed to refocus. But damn, it was hard! Professional, she had to be professional. And she didn't even like him a few hours ago! Was that all it took? A sexy back and warm laugh? Ha! No. This was her job, her *calling*. She wasn't about to let some jerk who hated his father come waltzing in and distract her from what was important: celebrating life and making each day count for those starting the countdown. Jack deserved better than her dreamy musings.

Laken leaned back slightly, keeping a few inches between Cyler's back and her all-too-aware breasts, and focused on what needed to happen next.

Dinner.

Gah. Of all the details her job entailed, cooking was her least favorite.

Of course, that was probably because she sucked at it. No matter how many episodes of *The Pioneer Woman, Cutthroat Kitchen,* or *Food Network* in general, she couldn't quite get the hang of it.

Just another reason she should let the whole Cyler thing go. If she'd been trying to win his heart by way of his stomach, that would mean a fail of epic proportions.

"You're quiet back there." Cyler's voice was a low murmur above the singing crickets.

"Thinking. I feel I should warn you. I'm great at a lot of things, but cooking isn't one of them." She sighed, glad she had been honest.

"Ha!" Cyler shifted in the saddle, tossing a quick smile over his shoulder before navigating through a few rocks on the trail. "So, are we talking just burnt food or are we talking food poisoning? Because if it's food poisoning, that might change my mind about staying." He chuckled then added darkly, "Though it might make Jack's trip to the afterlife a bit quicker."

Laken smacked his shoulder. "Burnt food. No one's gotten sick from my cooking."

"Yet."

"Hey!"

"There's always a first time," he said. "So, you're saying I should maybe cook. Is that what you're getting at? Just what did Jack tell you?"

Laken blinked, tilting her head in curiosity. "You cook? Jack never said anything. He's remarkably tightlipped concerning you. Which is interesting since Jack likes to talk."

"Likes to hear the sound of his own voice, you mean," Cyler shot back.

"Both," Laken replied, grinning.

"Huh, well, Mom really sucked in the kitchen. Only she was the kind who gave food positioning." He groaned slightly.

"So, you taught yourself to cook out of self-preservation," Laken suggested.

"Call it a dogged will to live."

Giggling, Laken watched as the barn grew closer and closer. It was bittersweet. Needing to get away from the temptation warred against wanting to stay, talk…learn. It was dangerous ground.

"So, what's your specialty? Most guys have this one thing they are epic at making. Or is it grilling? My brother is King of the Grill. Granted, he named himself that, but we go with it as long as he grills the steaks."

"There's nothing better than grilled steak." He sighed appreciatively. "But I'm actually pretty good at most things I set my hand to." He shrugged. "I watched a lot of cooking shows going up and experimented a lot. It was a good way to keep off Jack's warpath."

"It was your escape." Laken spoke quietly as they entered the barn. Margaret stopped by her stall and nickered as if telling them to please get off her and get her some oats.

"One of the many." He slid from the mare's back and dusted off his jeans. He lifted a hand to Laken, offering help.

She shouldn't take it. To slide off would be simple, yet the desire to simply touch him overpowered her common sense, and she grasped the warm, callused hand. Rather than guide her, as soon as she started to set her foot in the stirrup, he reached up around her waist and eased her down effortlessly.

Dear Lord.

Laken could feel her heart pound as his hands spanned her hips, slowly setting her on the barn floor. Frozen, she took a shallow breath then forced a step away.

Turning, she offered a small smile. "Thanks."

Cyler nodded once, his gaze cool yet anything but indifferent.

Taking a step backward, she cleared her throat. "I'll, uh, just be inside."

"I'll be there to help in a moment." He turned away, breaking the intense gaze, and freeing her.

Spinning on her heel, she forced herself to walk slowly to the house. As she swung open the door, she heard the TV. The sound wasn't overly loud, but she could hear Jack flip through the channels restlessly.

"Nothing good on. Ever." Jack sighed. "How did it go? Is Margaret doing well?" he asked, crossing one foot over the other and regarding her from his favorite recliner.

"She's fine. Cyler's taking care of her now. She had a nice ride, and he was super gentle." She glanced away, feeling like she was a teacher giving a good report on a student.

"Good, good." He sniffed. "Uh, so—" Jack wiped his fingers along his mustache, smoothing it. "Do you know if he's planning on staying at all?"

Laken hesitated. It really wasn't any of her business nor was it her place to tell Jack about Cyler's plans, or was it? "I think you better talk with him about it."

"Throwing me under the bus, eh?"

"Let's just say I have more faith in you than you have in yourself. You guys can talk, can't you? Not fight, not argue, not throw punches"—she arched a brow—"but talk."

"I tried!" Jack threw his hands in the air.

"Try again."

"It's hard."

"So?"

"So…" He trailed off. "Can't a man have his last days in peace?"

"You're not on your last days yet. So, no." She grinned, earning a scowl from Jack. "I'm going to go get us something to eat, okay?" She patted his shoulder and walked toward the hall.

"Damn woman, trying to kill me one way or the other," Jack mumbled.

"I heard that."

"I'm not sorry!" he shouted back, and Laken grinned in spite of herself.

Once in the kitchen, she pulled out a container of frozen, pre-cooked pulled pork and a bag of rolls. "Honestly, I can't mess this up."

Quickly she warmed up the meat in the microwave and set the rolls in the oven. It really did suck that she wasn't great at cooking. Each patient she'd worked with had required different meal plans, and it was the most tedious part of her job. Most of the time, she just ordered the assembled food from a center that worked with cancer patients or even the hospital cafeteria. Patients who were taking chemo usually wanted spicy or very strong-tasting food. Chemo could wreak havoc on taste buds. Others were diabetic and required special menus. But Jack? He didn't fit into any of those categories, so here she was, totally out of her element.

The microwave dinged, and she opened the door and groaned. The lid to the barbeque pork had melted slightly. Pulling the container out, she shook her hand from the slight burn of the plastic on her fingertips, and tossed the lid aside. A quick fork prick showed her the middle of the dish was still cool. "Shit."

"I'm sure it's better than that." Cyler's voice came from the doorway of the kitchen. He leaned against the wall, his blue eyes reflecting the grin he wore.

"It's close. Okay, you. Fix this." She waved her hand over the stupid container and stepped away.

"Did you defrost it or just cook it?" he asked as he walked over to the counter, his brows furrowed slightly.

"I'm not sure." Laken blushed and called herself a million types of idiot. Seriously, did she just do something that stupid? Who in the world doesn't know how to operate a microwave?

Me.

Only. Me.

"So, uh, get me a pan, would you?" he asked as he unbuttoned his sleeves then rolled them up. A partial tribal tattoo wrapped around his forearm, the rest of it hidden under his sleeve on his bicep. Shaking her head, Laken grabbed a pot from the overhead rack and set it down.

"Close enough." He tossed the contents into the pot and set it over the gas stove, the lighter clicking as he turned it on. "What else have you got going?"

"Rolls." She pointed to the oven.

Biting her lip, she waited for smoke to billow out as he opened the oven door. Thankfully, no smoke emerged.

"Looking good. What else?" He faced her.

"What do you mean, what else? Oh! I can slice up an apple! And—"

Cyler held up his hand. "Jack hates apples. Wait, yeah, go chop some up." He headed toward the fridge.

"Who hates apples? Seriously?" Laken marched over to the fridge and put a hand on the door, halting Cyler's intentions. "Mature. What? We slice them up and watch while he doesn't eat them? Really?"

His eyes narrowed, his full lips twisting in a wry grin. "Damn it, you're right."

"I hear you talking about apples! You better not be hiding them in my food, you son of a bitch!" Jack shouted from the living room.

"As if one little apple could kill the devil himself," Cyler shot back, but some of the heat was missing, giving Laken a small sliver of hope.

"Wait. Is he allergic?" she asked, skeptical.

"Possibly." Cyler turned away, walking back toward the simmering pot on the stove.

Goodbye hope. "So, you were thinking of giving him an allergic reaction? Lovely. Between him throwing punches and you trying to poison him, I'm way out of my league." Laken braced herself on the counter with her hands, taking deep breaths. She'd experienced family drama, just not any this insane!

"I promise I won't try to poison him." Cyler's tone was bored. "At least not tonight."

"Ever. You mean ever." Laken lifted her head and glared at his broad back.

"Whatever makes you happy. Hey, can you see if there's any garlic powder in the cabinet? I need cumin and cinnamon as well." Cyler started to whistle quietly as he stirred the pork.

After casting a suspicious glance at his back, she went to the spice cabinet, pulled down a few bottles, and set them beside the stovetop.

"Perfect. Thanks." He started to add in small amounts of each spice, and soon the room began to fill with a delicious aroma.

"Cyler's cooking, eh? Should have known. Girl, you're going to have to make sure I'm not poisoned. Though, by the smell of it, poison might be a better way to go than cancer. Just sayin'." Jack sauntered to the small kitchen table and pulled out a chair, the legs scraping against the wooden floor.

"As if I'd give you an easy way out," Cyler shot back then pulled open the oven and took out the rolls. With effortless grace, he pulled the rolls apart, releasing puffs of steam. "Plates?" he asked, turning to Laken.

"There." She pointed to a cabinet to the left and went to fill water glasses while Cyler finished putting the food on plates.

Soon they were all sitting at the table, and that sliver of hope started again as Laken watched Cyler sit beside his father, no punches thrown, no insults—at least not yet.

"Damn, I miss your cooking, boy. Is that cinnamon? Perfect." Jack spoke with appreciation.

"I didn't do it for you."

"Never said you did."

"As long as we're clear."

"I think we've established our mutual aversion to one another."

"Aversion is a pretty tame word."

Jack glared at his son. "There is a lady present."

"And that stopped you before? Fine. *Aversion.*" Then Cyler mumbled under his breath, "Aversion my ass."

"Okay! We're done." Laken eyed both men, giving her best glare, only to have both men grin back unrepentantly. "It's going to be a long night," she remarked, feeling the previous night's sleeplessness weigh on her, combined with trying to keep the fighting at bay.

She was torn; half of her wanted Cyler to stay, to be that redemption for both him and his father. Heaven only knew that as the end approached, they would both need that closure. Yet the other half wished he'd leave, and quickly. He was already wreaking havoc on her heart and self-control, let alone his established animosity toward Jack. Yeah, it was messy all around.

She bit into the pulled pork sandwich, her mind momentarily forgetting about all the issues at hand. Damn, the guy could cook. *Add one more sexy trait to that list.* Maybe if he stayed, it wouldn't be so bad. *At least then I wouldn't have to cook, right?*

Just then, Cyler glanced up, meeting her gaze. He winked seductively, and Laken almost choked on her bite.

Leave. He definitely had to leave.

And damn it all, he needed to leave soon. Or else what self-control she had was going to melt away like that stupid lid.

She needed to find her balance; she needed level ground.

She needed to call Kessed.

But something told her that Kessed wasn't exactly going to be on her side.

Chapter 9

The sound of footsteps pulled Cyler from sleep. Pausing, he listened intently, piecing together why there would be footsteps in his house. Had he gotten drunk last night? Was there a burglar? His hand clenched as he slowly reached under his pillow only to feel the vacancy where his 9 mm usually rested. *What the hell?*

Soft humming distracted him, and he opened his eyes and stared into a vaguely familiar wall. Red wallpaper dotted with flowers brought back a menagerie of random childhood memories, and everything finally clicked.

Jack, Laken, the ranch—hell. He'd woken up in hell. And oddly enough, it was utterly voluntary. The humming sounded again, and he rolled over and saw shadows flicker from under the door. He picked up his phone and groaned.

Why the hell is she up at six a.m. on a Saturday?

Rising from the bed, Cyler glanced around the guestroom at the ranch. As a kid, he hadn't ever been allowed in this room; it had been kept nice for company, not that they ever had much. His mother had been many things, but especially an optimist. Stretching, he glanced around for his jeans then slid them on. His belt clinked as he cinched it, and he shrugged on a new shirt from his duffle bag. He visited the adjoining bathroom and then slipped into the hall.

A flash of blond hair disappeared out the front door and he strode toward the window. Laken got into her Honda, pulled on to the driveway, and disappeared behind the hill.

"Wonder where she's off to," he muttered. The coffeepot in the kitchen beeped, and he glared in the general direction. *Hell no* was he going to drink that tractor oil Jack called coffee. After heading back to his room for his wallet, key, and phone, he darted out the door as well. *Starbucks.*

He thought about parking in the small lot, but instead chose to park at the gas station across the street. It had been hell getting out of that parking spot last time, and he didn't want to have to navigate that again if it wasn't necessary.

The roads were silent as he crossed the street over to the blessed green sign. A familiar Honda caught his eye as he passed the parked cars, and a grin tipped his lips.

He should have known.

Was this her everyday routine? He couldn't blame her. With a smile, he opened the glass door and paused as Laken's voice carried across the aromatic air.

"I'm dying, seriously. This job might kill me." Laken groaned as she lifted her cup in a salute. "To my sanity. I think I need stronger," she muttered to the barista. She was the same coffee-girl as yesterday, a brunette with almond shaped eyes hinting at Asian ancestry.

Those eyes slid by Laken and widened slightly as they focused on him.

"Well, it looks like your day is getting better and better." Her lips tipped into a suppressed grin as she glanced back to Laken.

"Because of coffee," Laken replied, lifting her cup and inhaling deeply.

Cyler shook his head, amused. He sauntered across the tiled floor and stood beside Laken. "Aw, and here I thought she was talking about me."

Laken's head whipped around, her eyes widening as a pretty pink blush stained her cheeks.

"Don't worry. I didn't over hear much. Your secrets are safe." He chuckled. "Pike Place, venti, no room," he ordered and pulled out his phone.

"Sounds familiar," the barista murmured, almost too low to hear, but she cut a sharp gaze to Laken, smiling widely.

"I take it you two are friends." Cyler glanced between the two, waiting for someone to fill in the blanks.

"She's my dealer." Laken shrugged.

"I rock her world." The barista winked. "It doesn't take much."

Laken rolled her eyes. "Yeah, friendship timeout." She pointed between the two of them.

"Well, then I'll just have to talk with blue eyes over here." She turned to him. "You must be Cyler?"

Laken groaned. "Thank you, Kessed."

His lips widened into a knowing grin. "So, you know me, huh?" He turned to Laken, clicking his tongue in a scold. "Whatever happened to client confidentiality?"

"You're not my client."

"Thank the Lord." He shook his head, still grinning. "So, Kessed, is it?" He leaned against the counter, softening his gaze, and turning up the charm. "Well, what did she say about me? You can't believe everything you hear, you know."

"This is so not happening. And you, *you* are not talking. Because there's nothing to say!" Laken pointed to Kessed then stalked off to a table.

Kessed shrugged and made a locking gesture with her hand across her mouth then tossed the pretend key to Laken, who acted like she caught it.

"Please?" he asked, lowering his chin so that his gaze sharpened.

Kessed visibly swallowed, her gaze flickering to Laken then back to him. "Uh, you know. I seem to remember something about you cooking?"

"You know what? I need to get back to the ranch. Cyler? You coming too?" Laken was glaring daggers at her friend, all while stepping toward the door.

"Hmm, I'm really enjoying my time here. And I haven't exactly gotten my coffee yet." He let the words linger, watching as the barista jumped as if shocked she had forgotten his order.

She then quickly poured him a cup. "We can't have that now, can we?" The barista recovered, handing him the steaming venti.

"Nope, it would ruin a very promising start to the day." He bit back a grin, loving the way Laken had responded to his teasing. It was endearing, and sexy as hell with that pink blush staining her cheeks. It had been a long time since he'd seen a woman blush, let alone find pleasure in some innocent flirting.

"Okay, you have your coffee. Now let's go." Laken pointed to the door once more.

"Bossy, isn't she?" Cyler turned to the barista.

"You have no idea." Kessed rolled her eyes. "But entertaining."

"I'm starting to see that." He took a tentative sip of his coffee, hissing as the hot brew singed his tongue.

"I'm leaving. I'll see you back at the ranch." Laken started to open the door.

"Actually, you won't," he called to her, taking a more cautious sip of his coffee as she paused.

"Oh, well then, uh…I guess…goodbye?" She took a hesitant step back inside the shop, her expression unreadable.

It was frustrating not being able to determine her reaction. Was she happy he was going? Disappointed? And why the hell did it matter?

"I need to check on a few things at home, but I left my bag at the ranch. I expect I'll be back in a few days, just to check on things. Jack hasn't sprayed the back roads that wind around the property, and I saw the Kochia weeds making themselves a nuisance. I don't expect stuff like that is included in your duties."

Her brow furrowed. "Wow, that's really kind of you. I didn't notice. And even if I had, I wouldn't know the first thing to do about it."

He scoffed. "It's not kind. It's necessary. When the old man says *sayonara*, that ranch is mine, and I don't want it to go to hell in a handbasket."

Laken's gaze dropped and she sighed. "Should have guessed. Okay. Good enough then." She gave a forced grin, one that didn't reach her eyes.

Part of him wanted to give her what she wanted, a sort of hope that he and Jack would reach some kind of truce, but that was impossible. Better to be honest; let her know exactly what he was thinking. No one would get hurt; no one would expect more.

Cyler took a breath, hesitating. "Uh, in the meantime, just do me a favor and make sure Margaret is combed? Last night I spent more time than usual currying her. It hadn't been done in a while. And call Vince, the farrier. She's more than due for a good shodding." He gave a decisive nod and lifted his cup to his lips, needing something to do to distract from the way her lips parted as if hesitating about saying something or the way intuition flashed across her green gaze. Yup, he needed to run fast from this one.

"Got it. Comb and clip. I can do that. Well, it was nice…to see you." She slowed the words at the end.

"Ha, yeah. We'll just pretend that's true. At least life was more interesting, huh?" he teased, chuckling.

"Interesting. For sure, it was interesting. We'll see you then." She lifted her cup in a quick salute and then shifted her glance to her friend. "Zip it, lock it, put it in your pocket." Laken tossed an imaginary key back to the barista.

"Yes, Mother," Kessed remarked, smirking.

With a narrowed gaze, Laken slowly opened the door once more then left.

"Gah, I thought she'd never leave. Okay, cowboy. What gives?" The barista wagged her eyebrows and leaned her elbows across the counter, still wearing that smirk.

Cyler glanced to her nametag. "What do you mean, Kessed?"

"You, her, the tension." She waved her hand in the air and stood straight. "Nothing? Am I totally off-base?"

Cyler felt a tick in his jaw, his spine stiffening at her intrusion into his personal life. "And why the hell do you think I'm going to say anything to you?"

"You don't have to." She shrugged. "Guess I misread something. Or you're just scared. Yeah, I'm betting on scared. Okay, that's all I needed. Have a good day." She turned and walked toward the room in the back.

Cyler blinked then narrowed his eyes. "What the hell? Who do you think you are?"

Kessed paused before turning slowly. All traces of teasing gone. "I'm her best friend. And with Sterling away in Afghanistan, I'm the next best thing to looking out for her." She sighed. "Laken is used to rescuing people, helping them, giving everything she has with her whole heart. I just want to make sure you're not playing games with that same heart. We clear?"

He glanced away from her intense gaze, sliding his empty hand in his pocket. "Damn it all, I've been here one day. You're crazy!"

She gave a harsh laugh. "You have no idea. So, don't mess with me. Mmm-kay? After all, sometimes it only takes one look. One day is more than enough to start something." She took a deep breath then flipped her long black braid behind her shoulder. "Enjoy your coffee." And with a tight smile, she disappeared into the back room.

He watched as the swinging door moved back and forth then rubbed the back of his neck, glaring at his coffee cup. "So much for my morning." He sighed deeply and strode to the door. The dry summer air was a welcome distraction from the way his mind was spinning. It was crazy, insane, utterly loco for him to even consider half of what that crazy female ranted on about, yet what she said about Laken rang so true it was startling.

And it made so much sense.

That was why she was good at her job.

It was also why he needed to stay away.

Because what Kessed said was true. One look could start something; one look had. And he'd been denying it, distracting himself from it, lying to himself ever since he'd first seen her at the ranch. He wasn't what Laken needed, and he could see that she was a good person and deserved better than what he had to offer, even on his best day.

And she most certainly hadn't seen him on that best day, rather on one of the worst.

As he crossed the street then climbed into his pickup, he was thankful for the distraction of work. There was always something that needed doing, always something to distract him, something he could build with his own two hands and have it stand the test of time.

Relationships were never as reliable.

Chapter 10

The ranch felt different. Cyler had only been gone for a few days, yet it felt as if he'd created a hole in the fabric of the house, even though he'd only been there for a short time.

Laken shifted the load of laundry to her hip and walked out into the living room, giving Jack a quick smile before setting the basket on the sofa. The on-call nurse would be stopping by later to meet Jack, and Laken wanted to get a few things done before she arrived.

"Sit down for a spell, honey. You're workin' too hard."

Laken rolled her eyes. "I'm running out of things to keep me busy, more like it."

Jack chuckled then glanced to his phone. Did he realize that he'd been watching it closely? Was it all subconscious? His weathered hands slid up and down his denim-covered thighs. The movement gave away how tense he'd become. That Cyler hadn't tried to contact Jack was obviously wearing on him.

The doorbell rung, and Jack grumbled. "I don't want to meet her."

"She's going to be taking care of you if I'm out for a few hours."

"I can take care of myself."

"I know you can, but think of it this way, you're getting your money's worth, alright?" Laken gave him a wink and strode to the door.

Paige was waiting with a small smile. Her salt and pepper hair was cut in a short bob and her gray eyes danced with warmth. "Hey, Laken."

"Hi Paige, come in." Laken moved to the side, and Paige strode in, her iPad tucked under her arm.

"Do you have any questions concerning Jack's information that I sent?" Laken asked as they walked down the hall.

"Seems pretty straight forward." Paige nodded.

"I hear you talking about me." Jack called out as they approached the living room.

"Hello Mr. Myer, I'm Paige Langston." She held out her hand, offering Jack a warm grin.

"Nice to meet you." Jack shook her hand.

"I'm going to familiarize Paige with the house and where I'm keeping the medical supplies should she need to access them. We'll be right back."

In short work, Laken had showed Paige everything she needed and was soon waving goodbye as she drove away. Laken closed the front door and strode to the living room. The TV echoed down the hall, the announcer narrating about a strike out.

Jack was in his chair, his shoulders tense as he stared at his phone again.

"Who's playing?" Laken asked, trying to distract him.

"Who? Oh, uh, it's the Mariners. Losing." He clicked off the TV. "You know what, honey? I'm going to take a short nap. Why don't you go and love on Margaret when you're finished with that? Maybe take her out for a walk. She was nickering this morning. She's bored." He gave a stunted smile then slowly rose from his chair.

Laken watched, observing the hesitant movements. His skin had taken on a slightly yellower hue, and she'd noticed this morning that the whites of his eyes were a bit discolored. His breathing treatments were still effective, but she knew they were simply a Band-Aid, and soon they'd need to be increased. Thankfully, he'd started to sleep better at night, but that was the nature of the beast. At first, sleep was hard, then as the cancer progressed, the demand for sleep would increase, till finally the patient was bedridden. Tears pricked at her eyes, thinking about Jack in that final state. A man who was so strong, had done everything for himself with his own two hands, bedridden and relying on her help for each basic need. It tore at her.

But that was life and death, at least with cancer. But that's also why she was so devoted to her job, to the people she served. Jack deserved to pass knowing he was in good hands, and she was blessed to have those hands be hers. She glanced from the pile of laundry to the door then back. It could wait.

She stopped in the kitchen to pull out a few sugar cubes she'd purchased at the grocery store a day before and slid them into her back pocket. The sunshine was welcome on her face as she opened the door and started toward the barn. The warm breeze teased a few wisps of hair that were free of her messy bun and tickled her face. Smiling to herself, she kicked a bit of the dust and watched it as the wind carried it away. The wide barn door squeaked a bit as she slid it open and strode inside.

"Hey girl."

Laken glanced to Margaret's stall, but the mare didn't welcome her. Rather, she heard a low nicker. Frowning, Laken jogged to the stall. Margaret was lying down, her head arching as she thrashed at her stomach. When she caught sight of Laken, she tried to get up only to roll back to her side and groan, huffing out a sigh that blew away some of the chaff from her hay beside her head.

"Margaret, what's wrong?" Laken opened the gate and walked inside, kneeling beside the mare and stroking her neck. "You're sick, aren't you?" She studied the mare from head to tail, looking for an injury. Her stomach looked slightly bloated, but there weren't any other signs of trauma. Rubbing the horse's nose, she pulled out a sugar cube with her other hand and offered it.

Margaret sniffed at the treat but didn't take it. Whinnying, she laid her head down. A moment later, she thrashed again, kicking her legs, and Laken stumbled back, getting out of the way of the hooves.

"Whoa, girl. Easy." Laken slowly stood and left the stall. Her brow creased as she started to walk back toward the house then picked up her pace to a run. She opened the door quickly and jogged down the hall. "Jack? Jack!" She knocked on his door.

"Huh? What? Come in."

She heard his groggy voice and opened the door. He was blinking at her from his bed, his brow furrowing immediately as he gave her a look.

"It's Margaret. I think she's sick." Laken's heart pinched as she watched Jack's color grow ashen. But a moment later, he sat up, his eyes sharp. "What's she doing?"

"Thrashing, lying down, not eating sugar." She gave the rundown of her symptoms.

"Damn it. Sounds like colic. You gotta call Vince. He's the vet and farrier who's supposed to be coming tomorrow. Tell him it's an emergency and that Margaret's down. He'll know what to do. In the meantime, try to get her up. Pull on that halter and don't let her give you any excuses. She stays down, she dies. Do you hear me, girl?" Jack's eyes bored into her.

Laken nodded.

"Call Vince first. I'll head out there and help you get that bitch to stand. She's going to be stubborn. I'll tell you that much."

"Jack, you can't." Laken took a step forward. "She was thrashing hard. If I hadn't moved, she would've kicked me. If she kicks you..." Laken let the implication linger. Jack wouldn't just get hurt; it could kill him. He wouldn't heal; he wouldn't survive a broken rib or leg. Cancer had a way of making bones far more brittle than people expected.

"I let you boss me around plenty, girl. This is one area I'm going to be as stubborn as Margaret. That horse is the best thing in my damn life, and I'm going to help her." He growled, rising from bed with determination rather than strength.

"Let's just call Vince first, okay? Maybe he's nearby." Without waiting for a reply, she rushed to the kitchen and grabbed her phone, thankful that the man's number would be in her phone's history from calling to set up the appointment yesterday.

She quickly pressed send and held her breath as it rang. "Jack, you better be staying there."

"To hell with it all!" he replied, and she heard the door slam.

"Hello?" A man answered, and Laken sighed in relief.

"Hello, Vince? This is Laken Garlington. I'm Mr. Jack Myer's nurse. We spoke yesterday about a shodding appointment for Margaret. She's sick, and we need you to come immediately. Jack say's its colic," she gushed out, not giving the man a chance to reply.

"I see, uh. I'm actually here at the Wilson's farm down the street. I'm in the middle of a calving that's going sideways. My nephew is putting chains on the calf as we speak, and I'm prepping to assist with this delivery, and then I have one more that's just as bad. It will be about an hour tops though. Just—" He shouted something to someone. "Just keep her upright. Don't let her lie down, 'kay? That's what's most important. And tell Jack to keep his sorry ass out of that barn. He's going to get himself killed. I'll be there as soon as I can."

The line went dead, and Laken closed her eyes. She didn't know much about colic for horses, but she did know that an hour was more than enough time for Jack to get himself in trouble.

She looked at her phone then to the barn. She opened her history once more and scrolled through the past week. Her finger hovered above the phone number she shouldn't call. Biting her lip, she pressed the number and closed her eyes, waiting as the phone rang.

"CC Homes."

"Cyler? It's Margaret." She didn't say anything else, just waited.

"Wait, say what? Who is this?"

Laken slowly released her lip. "It's me, Laken. Margaret has colic, and, uh, I need help. I don't know what to do, and the vet can't be here for at least an hour, probably more and—"

"Give me twenty minutes." The line went dead.

Laken sighed in relief, thankful that help was on the way. She placed her phone on the counter and ran to the door. She wrenched it open and ran across the gravel drive till she reached the barn. Jack's yelling filled her ears before she made it to the door.

"C'mon, you lazy son of a bitch, get up!" Jack was tugging on her halter, pulling Margret's head, and the horse wasn't moving an inch. "Get in here, girl. She needs some help." His breathing was labored, and Laken rushed forward to the stall.

"Let me try." She reached for the halter, and Jack gave it up willingly, stepping back and leaning against the barn wall, his breathing still irregular.

"Rest." She speared him with a gaze and leaned down to stroke the mare's face. "C'mon, Margaret, let's get up, shall we? It's not too hard. You're so strong. You've got this," Laken crooned, rubbing Margaret's soft muzzle. Grasping the lead rope, she placed a hand under the mare's chin at her halter and gave a tug.

Margaret lifted her head and moved so that her feet were tucked beneath her, her head up.

"So far so good."

"I got her that far, then she just wouldn't budge and collapsed back down. The thing with colic is that her insides are all twisted, and if we can get her to stand and walk around, it helps things move through a bit better. But if she just lies down, the twist will kill her." Jack spoke softly, his breathing growing more consistent.

"Well, we can't have that," Laken replied, patting Margaret's head once more and grasping beneath her halter again. "Let's go!" She tugged, lifting as she stood, and Margaret huffed, rising up on her front legs. "C'mon, baby, you can do it." Laken groaned, pulling up on the halter.

"C'mon, girl!" Jack called.

Margaret started to tuck her back legs and rise, then with a mighty huff, she collapsed; her head rested on the straw, her big brown eyes blinking slowly as if giving up.

"No, Margaret, don't do that." Laken sat beside the mare, stroking her nose once more.

"We'll, that's farther than I got. When did Vince say he'd be here?" The sound of straw rustling alerted her of his movement from the barn wall.

"An hour. Maybe more? I'm not sure. He's helping with a couple of calving's, one gone sideways, whatever that means."

"Damn." He sighed, crouching beside her. "Would be nice to have Cyler here." He rubbed a hand down his face. "Words I never thought I'd utter. And if you ever tell him, I'll deny it." He gave her a mock glare.

"Well, uh, that's good because I-I called him." Laken glanced away to the mare, waiting.

"Meddlesome female." Jack swore under his breath. "I'll never live this down." He stood.

"I figured he was attached to the horse and—"

"But that didn't give you the right to call him, Laken!" Jack's voice rose, and Laken turned her head to watch him kick the stall door open and storm out, swearing a blue streak with each step.

The sound of gravel crunching made Laken wince. Unless she was lucky, that wasn't the vet. It was Cyler.

"Aw hell, speak of the devil, and he shall appear." Jack groaned and marched right back into the barn.

Definitely not the vet.

A few moments later, Laken watched as Cyler strode into view; her gaze greedily took in the sight of him, knowing it was a foolish thing to do, but helpless to stop it. His jeans were faded and dusty, the blue more brown over the front of his thighs down to his shins; his boots were covered with a powdery dust that settled off him with each step. Blue eyes met hers, sending a shiver down her spine and pooling in her belly as she watched him quickly pace toward them. He gave a curt nod then slid his gaze to Jack.

Laken tensed, wondering just what fireworks were about to be set off. Jack was like a spring bear. Between the stress about Margaret and the arrival of Cyler, it could be interesting. Of course, that Cyler all but hated Jack only added gasoline to the already-smoldering fire.

"How long?" Cyler asked, turning to Jack, and tucking his hands in his pockets, and he waited.

Jack narrowed his eyes, his shoulders tense as if spoiling for a fight.

At that moment, Margaret whinnied. It was a shrill noise, and both men's stares cut to the mare.

Laken quickly knelt beside her, patting her neck, then looked back to the men.

Jack sighed, his body sagging with defeat. "Not sure, Cyler. Laken, she was fine last night?" he asked.

"She wasn't overly hungry, but she ate her hay. It was this afternoon that I noticed her lying down." Laken regarded both men.

Cyler nodded, his lips set in a grim line. "Well then, we best get started." He strode toward Margaret's stall while unbuttoning his sleeves, then rolling them up, displaying his chiseled forearms and tattoo.

Laken moved aside and watched as Cyler knelt beside the mare.

"Okay, Margaret. Don't make this more difficult than it needs to be, alright? I'm going to get you up, and you're going to walk. That's it. Not hard, but I'm not taking no for an answer. Got me?" He whispered softly, but there was intensity in his voice that was unmistakable.

Margaret must have heard it as well, because she sighed heavily, as if already tired of trying.

Cyler took the lead rope and grasped under her halter, much like Laken had done, but as he tugged on the halter to get her up, he placed his shoulder under her head, helping her rise. The mare groaned, faltered, but managed to get her feet beneath her, even as her head was almost resting on Cyler's shoulder.

"Good girl, that's a girl…" Jack murmured, striding toward the stall.

Margaret sighed, moved one back hoof, and started to lie back down.

"Aw hell no, you don't." Cyler growled, pulling her head back up and shoving her shoulder so that she stumbled to correct herself, standing once more. "Let's go. No rest for you." He crooned softly as he continued his firm grasp on her halter then led her from the stall out into the open area of the barn. "You've been lying about all day from what I hear, and we need to get that twist out of you, okay, girl? Let's walk a bit."

Never once releasing her halter, he led her around a wide circle within the barn. The usually surefooted horse tripped often, leaning some of her weight against Cyler as he walked beside her. "C'mon, lazy ass, don't knock me over," he'd reply, but there wasn't any heat to his words, just a dogged determination lacing the tone.

Jack took a few steps to stand beside Laken. "She's up. That's good," he muttered, then Laken watched as he heaved a big breath. "I'm sorry I yelled at'cha. You did the right thing calling him. As much as I hate to admit it, I'm not in any shape to be shoving around big mares, and sorry, sweetie, but you're not big enough to push around a fly, let alone this stubborn thing. So yeah." He shrugged then turned back to watching Cyler and Margaret make circles.

"I'm sorry I didn't ask you first."

Jack gave her a sideways glance. "Well, I probably wouldn't have asked me either, so we'll just call it good, 'kay?"

"Okay." Laken bit back a grin then turned to Margaret. The mare kicked a leg up as if trying to thrash at her stomach again.

"None of that now," Cyler scolded as he reached up with his free hand and patted her leg encouragingly.

"Have you checked her gums yet?" Jack asked, his white eyebrows drawing together.

Cyler shot a glance to Jack and shook his head. "We need to get her moving first, then I'll check that once she's up for a bit. There's no way I can tell if it's a twist or something else." He gave Jack a small shake of his head and turned his attention back to the mare.

"Is there anything we can do?" Laken asked.

Cyler regarded her as he and Margaret continued the circle in the middle of the barn. "Yeah, actually, check her stall. Is there much manure there, or is it pretty clean?" He jerked his chin toward the stall.

Laken strode to the open gate and glanced in, kicking around some straw to check fully. "Looks like there's some." She regarded the floor. "But not a lot."

"That's good," Jack replied, his words giving Laken some hope.

"That means she's probably backed up. Check her water." Cyler spoke next, continuing the circle.

Laken glanced to the basin; it was nearly full. "She hasn't drunk much."

"Vince will need to pump her stomach then. He'll bring the tube, but Laken, can you take that bucket over there, wash it out, and fill it with warm water? We need to get her to drink a bit. Not a lot, but some. If she's impacted from dehydration, then she's going to need to get some water inside to help things move along."

Laken nodded, then took off for the house with the bucket in hand. In less than five minutes she was returning to the barn. Water sloshed as she set down the bucket, glancing at Cyler.

Margaret's legs were quivering, and she was leaning heavily on Cyler as she walked.

"C'mon, girl, you can just take a few more steps." He spoke softly, one hand still on the halter while the other braced her shoulder against his. Sweat trailed down his temples as he continued to shove against the horse, making her carry her own weight when she was reluctant.

"Damn, it's hotter than hades in here." Cyler used his shoulder to help Margaret's weight, and with his free hand, started to unbutton his shirt. With a quick toss, it landed on the barn floor and as he continued to walk in the wide circle.

Laken couldn't ignore the way his shoulders created the perfect V into his back, or the way his collarbone defined the hard planes of his chest, accentuating the perfectly sculpted abs that her fingers itched to touch. A smattering of chestnut hair added to the allure. Biting her lip, she forced herself to glance away.

Client's son, client's son, client's son! She reminded herself, only to have her gaze stray once more to watch as he carefully led the horse around and around.

"Eh, I looked better in my prime," Jack grumbled, giving a snort.

"You wish, old man," Cyler retorted.

Jack gave him a glare, though his gaze looked slightly surprised, as if he hadn't expected his son to hear.

"Not all of us are deaf," Cyler added, shooting a grin over his shoulder.

"Not deaf," Jack whispered then gave a narrowed gaze to his son, probably wondering if he heard that one.

Laken smirked, unable to help herself, yet as she glanced at Jack, she noted the change in his coloring and the increased sag of his shoulders. Pride was important to Jack, that much was clear, but how did she get him to rest without wounding that pride?

She pursed her lips, thinking. "Hey, Jack?" Laken pulled out her phone then held it out to him. "My phone is almost dead, and I don't want to miss any calls from the vet. Can you take it inside and plug it in? You'll have to stay by it though, just in case."

Jack took the phone tentatively; his blue eyes narrowed suspiciously. But to her surprise, he didn't argue. *He must be even more exhausted than he let on.* She'd have to remember that.

"Fine. Just come and get me if anything changes." He gave a quick nod to Cyler and slowly walked to the house.

Margaret made another loop before Cyler spoke. "He was dead on his feet. Good thinking."

Laken shrugged, not wanting to own up to her slight manipulation.

"Yeah, okay, play the game. I know what you did. You're not fooling anyone." He chuckled softly, his boots pounding the familiar rhythm.

"My phone was dying." Laken shrugged, thinking of a way to change the topic of conversation. "Is there anything I can to do help? I feel kinda useless just standing here." *Even if the view is amazing.*

"Bring that bucket over here. Let's see if she'll drink." Cyler pulled up on the halter, and Margaret happily stopped. The mare tried to tuck her legs under, but Cyler was quicker and jerked her halter so that she stood upright once again.

"Don't even think about it."

Laken lifted the bucket and took it to where Cyler and Margaret waited, careful not to spill any more of the water.

Cyler loosened his grip on the halter, and Margaret leaned down, sighing into the water, creating a ripple across the surface. A moment later, she dipped her muzzle in and slowly drank. Water dripped from her lips as she lifted her head, and Cyler patted her neck. "Good girl."

Laken smiled, thankful for Margaret's cooperation. "Is that a good sign?"

"Yeah, we don't want her drinking too much, but we don't want her dehydrated either."

"Is she hungry? Should I get some hay?" Laken started to walk toward the covered stack.

"No, no! The last thing she needs is more food. She's probably impacted, which means she's constipated, and the gas is filling her belly. That's why we need to move her around to get her body to work through the food that needs to finish digesting." Cyler started the circles again.

"Oh, okay." Laken stopped and turned back to Cyler. "So, we wait?"

"Yup. Pretty much."

Laken watched as they continued their circles, the only noise the plodding of Margaret's hooves and her occasional sigh.

"So, I was pretty shocked to—" Cyler was interrupted by the sound of gravel crushing under tires.

"The vet." Laken turned toward the barn doors, a mix of relief and annoyance filling her. Whatever Cyler had been going to say was long gone now.

Soon Cyler was working with the vet to put a nasogastric tube down Margaret's nose to relieve some of the gas built up in her stomach. Laken simply watched in wonder as the two men worked together to save the horse's life, seeing so many similarities and differences in the way one worked with animals versus people. Yet they all had the same goal: care. And it was so much more than simply medicine. It was a kind word, a gentle touch, all combined with the right mix of fluid and medicine to try and make the difference between life and death. Laken rubbed her arm absentmindedly as she watched, then she slowly backed out of the barn. She'd let the vet take care of the horse while she went inside and took care of the horse's owner.

Because while that horse needed the vet, she knew that right now, Jack needed her even more.

Chapter 11

Several hours later, Cyler shuffled toward the house, his shoulder aching from dealing with Margaret's weight, and his hands sore from pulling the lead rope each time she tried to lie down. It was a fight, and it wasn't over, but before Vince left, he'd said Margaret would probably pull through just fine. Cyler couldn't remember hearing sweeter words. Stupid horse meant the world to him, even if he hadn't seen the old girl in a decade till this past week. She was getting older, and this bout of colic had been a sober reminder, one that threw him off-balance.

He paused on his way to the house, studying it with a new perspective. For so long, he'd only saw that building as a place of pain and betrayal. Yet there were good memories too, ones of Margaret, ones of his mother, and recently, of Laken. He shook his head, wiping his hand down his face. Stupid girl had gotten under his skin, and as much as he had tried to forget her, it only made him remember her more. He'd already been trying to find a valid excuse to check in on the ranch when she called. Margaret being down wasn't exactly the excuse he was looking for, but it had gotten him here.

As he climbed the front steps, the acrid scent of something burning alerted him that Laken was in the kitchen. "Here we go again." He opened the screen door and strode to the kitchen.

Sure enough, as he drew closer he could see that smoke had created a light fog in the house. "Just what are you trying to burn now?"

Laken looked up and glared at him. "I'm not trying to burn anything."

"Could have fooled me."

"Be useful. Fix this. Again." She waved toward some charred burger buns on a broiler pan.

"Uh, do I want to know?" he asked as he walked forward.

"Sloppy Joes. I can usually handle that, but the broiler is super-hot in this oven and I, uh, didn't know that."

"Yeah…." Cyler drew out the word as he studied the buns that resembled hockey pucks. "That explains the smoke. And the smell. Do you have more?"

"Yes." Laken nodded then rummaged through a white plastic sack and pulled out another bag.

"Perfect. So, not to be an ass, but why don't you, uh, check on Jack? Or do something…really, anything else." He smiled, trying to soften his words.

"Gladly." She sighed in relief and disappeared out the door. He was just opening the bag of buns when she called to him once more. "And Cyler?" She popped back into the kitchen. "Thanks. I'm really glad you're here."

He watched her face flush with a pink blush before she escaped into the hall. His lips bent into a grin. Maybe, just maybe, he had gotten under her skin as well. He could think of several ways to find out.

His body responded to the simple thought with a powerful intensity creating a massive exodus of blood flow to his southern regions. With a shake of his head, he tried to focus on the mess of a meal that Laken had attempted. Yet the task at hand wasn't enough to distract him fully.

Fine ass? Check.

Sweet smile? Check.

Loves horses? Check.

Cook? *Hell no.*

Hates Jack? No.

Well, three out of five wasn't exactly a deal-breaker.

He opened the oven door and peeked in, checking out the progress of the bread. Perfectly golden, he turned off the broiler and used an old towel to pull out the pan. After setting it on the counter, he turned his attention to the simmering cast-iron skillet. He slid a spoon from the drawer nearby, and dipped it in the simmering tomato and beef sauce. Steam swirled as he blew across the spoon then took a tentative taste.

"Eh." He squinted, his lips puckering. Damn woman must have put a bottle of vinegar in the mix. Heaven only knew why. He shivered slightly and made quick worked of adding molasses, brown sugar, and ketchup into the mix. Once it tasted better, he started to put together three plates.

He was whistling when he heard soft footsteps from the hall. Glancing over his shoulder, he watched Laken approach the kitchen, her stocking feet quietly padding along the hardwood floors and her hair pulled up in a messy bun. She appeared more relaxed than before. He turned back to the plates, but he couldn't shake how much Laken *fit*. He forced the thought into the back of his mind.

"Smoke's clearing." Laken walked up beside him, her green eyes studying the food.

"You're welcome."

"Yeah, yeah." She made a dismissive gesture with her hand.

He chuckled, lifting two of the plates and walking them over to the kitchen table.

Laken picked up the last plate and set it beside the others. "I'll get Jack."

"Can't wait," Cyler muttered.

Laken arched a brow.

"Well, what's stopping you?" He arched his own brow, baiting her.

She placed a hand on her hip, and he waited for her to give him a set-down, reminding him that Jack was dying, giving him some guilt trip or holier-than-thou sermon.

But she didn't. Rather, she tilted her head slightly, gave a small smile, turned, and left down the hall.

Damn if that woman didn't ever do what he expected.

And damn it all if he didn't like that about her—a little too much.

Cyler went to grab a few forks when he heard Jack and Laken approaching.

"Are we having smoked, er, something?" Jack asked, and Cyler bit back a chuckle at the man's wary approach to dinner.

"Uh, no. I don't know how to use a smoker." He could hear Laken's answer as they stepped into the kitchen.

"Could have fooled me," Jack whispered to Cyler in passing then walked to the table.

"Could have fooled us both," Cyler muttered, but a grin teased his lips.

Laken huffed. "For your information, Cyler saved the food. Again."

"Damn it all, girl. I have to thank the boy twice in one day? You trying to kill me?" Jack grumbled.

"If only…" Cyler replied, shrugging as he took a seat. He could see Jack's glare from the corner of his eye.

"Gah, here we go again." Laken sighed. "How about them Mariners?"

Jack gave Laken a glare as well. "Cyler, what did Vince say about Margaret?"

Cyler swallowed then explained the vet's instructions. As Jack listened, Cyler studied him, really studied. Jack had lost weight. A lot. The man was a solid brick at 210 and only six feet tall. But by the looks of him, Jack had lost at least thirty pounds. His clothes were baggy, and the weathered lines of his face were no longer their usual sunbaked brown, but more of an orange tone that reminded him of the shade one gets from using cheap sunless tanning lotion.

Jack turned to Laken, and Cyler noticed that his hand was still bandaged from when he'd taken a swing at him. Then Jack lifted his cup to take a swig and started to cough, sloshing water on the table, but that wasn't what drew Cyler's attention. It was the spray of blood that covered Jack's hand as he covered his mouth.

Cyler's gaze shot to Laken.

It was like she was waiting for it to hit him, to really and fully grasp that Jack was dying. Really, truly dying.

As she met Cyler's gaze, he saw her nod softly, as if affirming his realization. A moment later, she handed Jack her napkin and left the kitchen. Cyler watched her leave then turned back to Jack, who was still coughing some.

Laken returned, a small device with a mask attached in hand. She set the machine on the table and quickly handed the mask to Jack. With a nod, he placed the mask on his face and inhaled deeply. A small whizzing noise came from the machine, and Jack sat back, his face relaxing as his breathing grew more regular and the coughing ceased completely.

"Take it easy now. A few more minutes and you're good to go, alright?" Laken spoke softly, her tone the perfect mix between compassion and reassurance.

"It'll get cold. Eat, you two." Jack's voice was muffled from the mask.

"Only because I'm starving, and I want to eat something that I didn't make," Laken joked, and Cyler shook his head.

She was good at what she did. He had to hand it to her. She didn't get wound up, and she kept things moving. He didn't realize how important it was, but it would be really easy, normal, to just sit there with Jack and stare at him while he took his breathing treatment, which would do nothing but make Jack more anxious. Damn it all, he *should* be staring at him, making the bastard as uncomfortable as possible. Yet, he found himself scooping up a forkful of ground beef and sticking it in his mouth.

Damn, he was getting soft.

Before long, the breathing treatment ended. The rest of the meal was uneventful, and Laken helped Jack to his room as soon as he'd eaten his last bite. His shoulders slumped, and Cyler tried to ignore the way the coughing fit had sapped nearly all of Jack's energy.

As Cyler collected the dishes, he tried to reconcile the man who had just left to the man who'd raised him.

They looked the same.

Sounded the same.

Had the same stubborn-ass streak.

But that was it. This Jack was almost a shell compared to the Jack he remembered. But that didn't change the fact that what the old man had done was unforgiveable.

Yet, the more he was around Jack, the more he wondered if that was still true.

"You wash, I'll dry?" Laken asked, picking up a towel and sliding him a grin.

He nodded, still lost in his own thoughts.

After silently handling the few dishes they had to clean, Cyler broke the silence. "Is Jack asleep?"

Laken shrugged. "Probably. He was pretty exhausted. Those coughing fits..."

She reached up to put away the plates, exposing a peek of toned peach skin. As quickly as he'd caught a glimpse, it was hidden once more under her shirt.

"You want to get out of here?" he asked, sliding a glance to her as he placed the forks back in the drawer.

She turned, her clear eyes studying him for a moment. "Is there coffee involved?"

He chuckled, shaking his head. "If that's what it takes."

"I'm in."

"Good, because I wasn't exactly taking no for an answer." He gave her a wicked grin.

Laken sighed dramatically. "So, you're saying I could have negotiated more than coffee. Noted."

"Probably."

She gave a soft laugh.

"C'mon." Cyler nodded his head toward the front door. "I'll drive."

"Because you want to, or you're afraid I drive like I cook?"

He chuckled, pausing to open the front door for her. "Both."

She gave a mock glare as she walked outside. "At least you're honest."

Cyler slid his hands in his pockets, and hesitated. "I'm going to quickly check on Margaret once more before we leave."

Laken nodded and watched as he ran to the barn, and moments later returned with a grin. "Doing well."

"Glad to hear it!" Laken replied as they walked to the truck. But rather than go to his side, he crossed over and opened the passenger door for her. "Ma'am."

"Thanks." She blushed slightly. "Pouring on the charm huh? What do you want?"

"Nothing too demanding, promise." He winked and shut the door. As he strode around the front of the truck, he tried to remember the last time he'd opened a car door for a woman. It had been a while—on purpose.

"So, coffee?" Laken asked as the engine purred to life.

"You ever seen those shirts that say, *But First, Coffee*?" he asked as he pulled out to the drive.

"Yeah, I have one."

"That's pretty much my answer to everything."

Laken's laughter echoed quietly in the cab, and he soaked it up, wanted more of it. "For example, building a house? But first, coffee. Or mountain climbing? You bet! But first, coffee."

"Ha! It's like those mad libs. I loved those as a kid. So basically just fill in the blank? Skydiving? But first, coffee," she announced.

"Grocery shopping? But first, coffee." He played along.

"African safari? But first, coffee."

"Save the world? But first coffee." Cyler winked.

Laken rolled her eyes and laughed. "Oh! I have one!" She clapped a few times. "Okay. Black Friday shopping? But first, coffee."

Cyler grinned. "Yeah, but I don't do the dangerous things. I keep it safe."

"Like saving the world, sky diving, mountain climbing."

"All safer than shopping on Black Friday. Amazon is my friend. I don't shop—traditionally, at least, like at the mall." He gave a shudder. "Me and Amazon are in an exclusive relationship."

Laken gave him a cute smile. "Amazon is mine."

"Whatever you say," he teased.

Cyler turned on the main road and watched as the sun started to arch toward the western horizon. Washington was far enough north that the summers had long daylight hours, and even though it was evening, the sun wouldn't fully set till nine to ten p.m.

Laken took in a breath, pausing as if about to say something, then released the breath and turned to the passenger side window.

"Out with it." Cyler clenched his teeth. Here it came, the sermon, the scolding, whatever the hell it was that had been brewing from day one.

"Heard that, did you?" She gave him a sheepish grin.

He twisted his hands on the steering wheel, waiting, accepting her words as confirmation.

"It's just that…well…I'm worried about Margaret. But, I know that you are probably more worried than me, and I thought better about asking because I didn't want to bring it up, and make you worry more." She completed in one breath, her lips twisting up on the side.

"Oh." Cyler blinked, flashed his eyes to her and then back to the road. "That's not where I thought you were going."

He cast a quick glance to her again, watching as her brow furrowed with confusion before it smoothed out in an understanding expression. "You're waiting for my talk."

"If by *talk*, you mean preach at me why I better let my bastard father die in peace, then yes."

Laken confused him by releasing a small chuckle.

"Yeah, well, basically it comes down to this. It's not my place. It's not about me. And me telling you what to do isn't going to make things better, or right, or even heal your relationship. It just won't. And honestly, right now, Cyler, you're not ready. I can see that, and basically, who am I tell you what to do? I haven't been in your shoes, boots, or whatever." She shrugged slightly. "This is something between you and Jack. Not you, me, and Jack."

Cyler narrowed his gaze at her, then shifted his focus back to the road. "So, that's it?"

Laken frowned slightly. "Do you want me to chew you out?"

"No—hell no. I just—well, my experience is that women don't usually mind their own business, if you know what I mean."

"In my experience, men are far more stubborn than they need to be, but I'm going to give you the benefit of the doubt, and I'd appreciate the same. Deal?" Laken reached out her hand, waiting.

Cyler tentatively reached over and shook it, curious about this mysterious woman beside him.

"To answer your question—" He released her hand and pulled into the Starbucks drive-through. "Margaret will probably be fine. We got her on her feet, and I'll check on her when we get back."

Laken sighed deeply. "That's good news."

"Yeah, it is." He pulled up the menu. "The usual?" he asked Laken.

"Yeah, that would be great."

Only a few minutes later, they were driving down the road toward the west side of Ellensburg.

"So, where are we going?" Laken asked, blowing across her coffee.

Cyler pulled onto a small dirt road, kicking up dust behind him. "Wait and see."

"I'm more of a plan-ahead type of girl."

"Live dangerously."

"But first, coffee," she teased.

"You're holding your coffee. Now trust me." He took a fork in the road and went up a sagebrush and cheatgrass-lined hill. They crested the top, and he smiled as Laken gasped softly.

"Wow." She breathed reverently.

He pulled off the narrow road and parked the truck, watching as she took in the scene before them. The hill looked over a hidden draw with a winding creek that trickled into the Yakima River not too far ahead. Wind machines dotted the horizon, their white arms rotating lazily in the breeze; it was a peaceful view and one of his favorites.

"C'mon." He opened his door and thought about running around the front of the pickup to open hers, but before his feet even hit the dirt, she had beaten him to the punch.

He settled for tucking his hands in his jeans and sauntering up to where she waited, overlooking the small valley below. The soft warm air teased a few strands of honey hair and brushed them across her cheek as she took in the expanse.

Beautiful.

He swallowed then reached out to grasp her hand, not asking for permission. Her warm fingers closed around his, and he bit back a grin of pleasure because she hadn't objected. He led the way down the hill, careful to avoid the more slippery areas, knowing from experience that one wrong step could send him—them both—sliding down. That was the deceptive nature of these hills. The sagebrush and bunch grass made them appear rolling, gentle and safe, when the angles were far steeper than often expected, and jagged basalt rocks made for a treacherous fall.

"You can smell the Russian olives." Laken broke through his concentration.

He inhaled deeply, the rich scent of warm resin and sage filling him. "It's that time of year. Thankfully, I'm not allergic. One of my old friends would sneeze from July to September, poor kid."

"Yeah, my dad was allergic, too, but I always loved the smell. It's the scent of summer." She shrugged, offering him a grin.

When she flushed a pink, he grinned, squeezing her hand as they made it down the final switchback to the draw.

"How'd you find this place?"

Cyler stepped over a large rock. "One of my escapes. Good hunting for grouse too. But mostly, it's just peaceful." He paused, listening to the gentle rippling of the creek as it tumbled over the smooth bedrocks. "But this is not somewhere you want to be in a rainstorm. This draw acts like a siphon, and this little creek here will turn into a swift river in no time flat."

"I can imagine." Laken slid her hand from his, pulled out her phone, and took a few pictures.

Immediately, he missed the contact, the sensation of her skin on his. His gaze shamelessly took in her silhouette against the evening sun, and he edged closer. Yet with each step, it wasn't enough. Rather like a magnet, she pulled him in, and he didn't want to fight the impulse.

Softly, he reached up and tucked a loose strand of hair behind her ear, his body heating as she met his gaze, then shyly diverted her eyes. He traced his fingertips down her neck then gently grasped her shoulder, encouraging her to turn and face him fully. Anticipation flooded him. Her breath quickened, and her pink tongue darted out to caress her lower lip, enticing him. Deliberately, he leaned forward, watching as her eyes widened, but quickly she stepped out from his hold, putting several feet of distance between them.

"No. I can't." She wrapped her arms around her waist, hugging herself. Her eyes were bright with suppressed excitement, encouraging him.

"Why?" he asked, stepping forward.

Laken edged back. "This is the very definition of conflict of interest." She arched a brow but grinned, her posture relaxing.

"I'm not going to take no for an answer." He gave a small grin in return, taking a step closer.

She laughed, rolling her green eyes. "Why am I not surprised?"

"Just being honest." He shrugged.

"Thank you. I think." She chuckled again, the sound slightly nervous.

"Unless you're not interested?" He let the question linger, closing the distance as he watched indecision, desire, and hesitancy flash across her face.

"That's beside the point—"

"That is the only point," he interrupted.

"I...I could lose my job." She spoke quietly.

"Are you on the clock right now?" Cyler reached up, tracing the line from her ear along her jaw, pausing at her full lips.

"It's complicated. But in short, no." she murmured, her expression softening.

"Good." Without giving her a chance to protest, he closed the final distance between them and sealed her lips with his.

At first contact, he realized the danger he'd just invited. It wasn't just a kiss; rather, each nerve had come alive, demanding more. Angling his head slightly, he was able to capture more of her kiss, deepening the exchange as his tongue ran along the seam of her lips, begging for entrance. He could feel her hesitation melt as she leaned into him, her lips caressing his, inviting, intoxicating him with each touch.

As she opened her mouth, her arms tentatively grasped his forearms before sliding up to his shoulders then pulling him in tight. Cyler's already-burning body smoldered deeper, demanding more than just a kiss. Yet he held himself in check, in spite of the pounding blood that seemed to overtake every other sense.

His hand slid up her back, mapping the delicate curve of her waist. Her tongue met his, stealing every other rational thought as he accepted her invitation and tasted the full flavor that was Laken. Her fingers slid up from his shoulders, threading through his hair and tugging, causing his heart to pound harder, his body to grow even harder as he pressed into her soft curves. He breathed in her soft gasp as he bit on her lower lip, pulling her in, leading her. He mated with her lips, fusing his with hers, searing his brand with each brush of his lips, each caress of his hand across her waist.

Abruptly she pulled away, her green eyes wild as they blinked up at him, staring deep into his soul. Naked in his eyes—yet fully clothed—she studied him, and the kiss had him off guard just enough that all the careful walls he'd constructed were still lowered.

Damn it all.

"So…that just happened," she whispered, a hand reaching up to touch her pink lips. "Whoa." She swallowed, his eyes capturing each minute movement, each tiny shift of her gaze.

Then she smiled.

"To be fair, I did warn you I wasn't taking no for an answer." He relaxed slightly, feeling less exposed and vulnerable.

"You did." Her gaze flickered to the ground as her lips tipped into a lopsided grin.

"And I'll be straight with you. I'm going to kiss you again."

Her gaze shot back to his, widening slightly. "So, you're saying I don't get a choice?" She flirted.

He chuckled. "I'm saying you don't really want one."

She rolled her eyes. "A little sure of yourself, aren't you?" She tucked her hands into her back pockets, regarding him.

He took a small step forward, leaning in to her before whispering, "You kissed me back."

Her pert nose scrunched up. "Caught that, did you?"

"Yup. Pretty much." He laughed softly, reaching out and tugging on her elbow, and she willingly released her hand from her back pocket.

"Fair warning?" she asked as he leaned in.

"Fair warning," he murmured before taking her lips once more, astounded at how her warmth captivated him, and how his blood went to an immediate boil.

He'd expected her to moderate the kiss, and he'd been fully prepared to tease her, to test the waters to see how far she'd let him push, but what he hadn't been prepared for was her response.

Rather than play hard to get, she returned the kiss with full force, biting his lower lip and fanning the already-burning flames. Her hands mapped his back, kneading, tracing, driving him crazy with each touch, reminding him that he could—should—be closer. He groaned as she tugged on his button-up shirt, sliding her hand up his chest, skin on skin.

He breathed in her sigh as he splayed his hands across her hips, pulling her closer then rocking her against him. He was taken by surprise when she kissed then bit him gently on the neck before quickly disentangling herself from his grasp and walking away.

Confused, he turned to watch as she glanced over her shoulder, giving him a teasing grin. "Fair warning."

Cyler's face broke into a wide smile, one that caused his cheeks to ache with an unfamiliar yet welcome pain as he watched her hike back up the hill.

"Are you just going to stand there and stare, or are you going to hurry up? Daylight's burning." She taunted as she continued her trek toward the truck.

Cyler rubbed the back of his neck with his hand, shaking his head, and grinning. "Is that how it's going to be?"

"Are you complaining?" Laken turned, taking a few steps backward on a flatter portion of the hike.

"No, ma'am," Cyler replied, starting toward her.

"Good." She giggled and finished the hike with him not far behind.

When Cyler reached Laken, he grasped her hand in his and kept it tight the whole way back to the ranch. The sunset's glow made her face appear even more flushed, and he couldn't help the smug satisfaction that he'd done that to her. It had been a long time since he'd felt that way, since he'd even wanted a woman to wear his kiss. It was disconcerting, yet electrifying all at once, but as much as he wanted to ride the wave of excitement, he felt the familiar suspicion creep in, the kind that made him question if this were truly real.

Because heaven only knew how he'd been fooled before.

Cyler glanced over to Laken, meeting her gaze and smiling before he went back to gazing out the window.

The past was the past. This was a chance for a new future.

Let that serve as fair warning…to his heart.

Chapter 12

Laken closed her eyes, listening to the phone ringing as she waited for Kessed to pick up. The crickets called as she sat on the back porch, close enough to hear if Jack needed her, but far enough away to have some semblance of privacy. Desperate to have some insight into her predicament, she impatiently waited.

"Hello, friend,"

Relief flooded Laken. "I'm so glad you answered," Laken replied.

There was a slight hesitation before Kessed spoke. "Because I usually avoid your calls," she sarcastically teased.

"No, it's just—yeah, I need help." Laken's pitch raised at the end, signaling her desperation.

"Uh-oh. What happened?" Kessed's tone went flat.

Laken sighed, closing her eyes and biting her lip before speaking. "I kissed him."

Silence. Laken started to count, making it to three before she heard her friend's laughter. "Okay…and the problem is…that he's bad at it?"

"No! That is *not* the problem. It's the opposite of the problem!"

"Did you sleep with him?"

"No! Of course not! Seriously?"

"Well, you're acting like you committed a crime, like you're confessing to someone's murder, so I was just wondering what you *weren't* saying." Kessed giggled.

"Gah, why did I call you?"

"Because you love me."

"Not right now, I don't," Laken mumbled.

"Whatever. Okay, so you kissed the hot guy who *I* saw first, mind you, and it wasn't a bad kiss, and we're upset because?"

Laken sighed. "Sometimes you're so dense! Because he's my client's son."

"Oh. Ethics. That's why I missed it."

Laken smacked her forehead gently. "Again, why am I calling you?"

"Listen, so is Cyler going to run off and tell everyone? Call your boss and complain? I mean, I've never kissed you, but I can't imagine you being *that* bad at it," Kessed joked.

"Really? That's the turn this conversation is taking?"

"Just sayin'. You need a little perspective. He kissed you, Laken. That means he *likes* you. He's not going to try and ruin your career from one kiss. So, stop the panic. Deep breaths. You're going to get wrinkles from the forehead creasing I know you're doing."

Laken rolled her eyes, but bit back a grin. "Fine. I get that point. But, what do I do now? I mean, how do I not kiss him again?"

"Wait, hold up. Why are you not kissing him again?"

"Because it's like playing with fire."

"Fire's good."

"Fire gets my ass burned and out of a job!"

"You've got some serious trust issues."

"I have some serious issues period, right now."

"Horror of horrors, a hotter-than-wasabi guy just rocked your world with a kiss. Your life sucks."

"That's not what I mean."

"It's what you sound like."

"What do I do?" Laken whined, glancing behind her to the door, listening for a moment to make sure she didn't hear Jack. Satisfied, she leaned forward on her knees, waiting.

"Well, where is he now?"

"He went to Lower Valley, but he's returning tomorrow. There's a problem with Margaret, the horse, and he's going to check back on her." At the mention of Margaret, Laken rose from her seat on the porch steps and walked toward the barn.

"I'm sure the horse is not the only reason he's coming back...but okay, so we have some privacy right now."

"You think I'd be calling you if he was right beside me?" Laken squeaked, peeking into the barn.

Margaret was standing up, sleeping, and no longer thrashing. Relief welled up within her.

"No, but I didn't know if you ran away scared. You...well, you don't exactly have a lot of history with this sort of thing."

"Exactly why I'm freaking out!"

"Calm down. Simmer. First things first. You just need to let it go. My gut tells me that this Cyler-guy is not going to pretend nothing happened."

"Right. Yeah, he said he wasn't taking no for an answer." Laken remembered.

"Wait, you missed that part. So...this wasn't just a spontaneous kiss? It was premeditated! That's good! He's all hot for you! Go, Laken!"

Laken's face heated with a blush that tingled the roots of her hair. "You're so romantic."

"Hey, that *is* romance! He totally gave you a heads-up. Took out the guesswork! Do you know how awesome *that is*? What did you say to him?"

Laken closed the barn door, kicking a bit of dust with her shoe. "I just said that didn't surprise me. And then we kissed. End of story."

"Yeah, that changes things though. You probably said no, didn't you?"

"Yeah, I did."

"Seriously. I've taught you nothing. Nothing! Why, for the love of all that's holy, did you say no? Gah! When the hot guy asks to kiss you—asks! Like a really great guy with manners, you say yes! You kiss him! I've failed you." Kessed lamented, and Laken shook her head.

"It's not like he listened to me," she replied.

"Okay, we're moving on. This whole idea is frustrating. So, what to do now?" After a moment, Kessed added decisively, "You let him lead."

"Oh..." Laken blinked. "That's actually a good idea."

"Don't be so shocked," Kessed retorted playfully.

"But what about Jack? I mean, he's my priority—"

"As he should be."

"But that's not exactly possible with—" Laken stopped before she gave away private patient information. It wasn't Kessed's business to know the rift between father and son.

"Stupid patient-nurse confidentiality," Kessed grumbled, picking up on the reason Laken had ended her sentence.

The evening was still, as if holding its breath as Laken worked through the situation at hand.

"Do you like him?" Kessed asked after a bit.

Laken glanced up at the darkening sky. "Yeah."

"A lot?"

"Enough to be kinda out of my element here," she answered honestly.

"Then get to know him. There is nothing wrong with that. You can check all your rulebooks, but getting to know someone isn't against any of your ethics. And once you become a little more familiar, let things take their natural progression. It sounds like they already are. If he's serious about this, he'll totally get that you're kinda freaked out. And chances are, you have that in common. Did you ever think of that?"

Laken arrived back at the house, listened for a moment at the door then sat back on the step, breathing deeply as she considered Kessed's words. "That would make sense. It's just, for me, I'm used to knowing how to navigate things. I mean, I help people deal with death, *death*, Kess."

"Sometimes death is simpler than life, honey."

Laken's brows rose at her friend's words. "You always know more about the book at the end than the beginning. You're right."

"So, write the book, Laken." Kessed started to giggle. "It sounds like it's going to be one hot, steamy romance. Just keep me posted, promise?"

"Fine." Laken felt a tingling in her cheeks and decided it was time to change the subject. "How's work?"

"You mean, do I have any coffee left?" Kessed sighed.

"Basically, yes."

"Needy tonight, aren't we? Well, you want to pick it up, or do you need me to drop it by? It's almost quitting time."

Laken considered the question. Jack was doing well, but she didn't feel comfortable leaving him again. "Can you drop it by? I'll text you the address."

"Sure. See you in a few. And don't panic when we end the call. You've got this. Look at it as one of life's many adventures. I mean, think of all the patients you've worked with. Some have had a lot of regrets; don't let this be one of yours. Bye!"

Kessed hung up before Laken could remark, but her friend was right.

How many patients had she spoken with, held their hands as they told stories of their lives, stories of their adventures, of failures, of chances not taken that still haunted them. Instinctively, Laken knew that if she brushed Cyler aside, she'd regret it. Always.

It was a risk.

One she was utterly terrified to take.

But she'd take it.

Lost in her thoughts, the minutes passed. Her phone buzzed in her hand, distracting her, and she glanced at the odd number. Heart stuttering, she slid the button to answer.

"Hello?"

"La-la Lake! How's my favorite sister?"

Laken grinned so wide her face ached. "Sterling! Aw! I miss you! How are you?"

"Good, good. I'm taking a break at Bagram Air Base. The food is amazing. I may never want to leave," he teased.

"Pretty sure anything is better than an MRE," she teased back.

"Truth. So, what are you up to? Saving the world?"

Laken breathed through a smile. "Nope, I'll leave that to you. But you would love where I am right now." She glanced about the ranch, the wide-open spaces, the safe, fresh feeling of home.

"Oh? Where's that?"

"I have a patient who requires live-in assistance. He owns a huge ranch just outside Ellensburg. I even got to ride a horse." She was thankful that her brother couldn't see the blush that flamed as she remembered who'd ridden the horse with her.

"Sweet! I bet you're loving that."

"I am. What about you? When's your next leave?" Laken glanced down the road, seeing headlights bob in the distance. Kessed had gotten here fast. Immediately she grinned, remembering the history between her brother and best friend.

"Not sure. I think I'll try to make it home for Christmas, but the deployment end isn't until March. I do have two weeks coming, but, yeah, I'm just saving it for now. Why? Miss me that much?"

"Always. You know that. Stupid brother always thinking he has to go and fix everything, make world peace."

Sterling chuckled. "Yeah. World peace. All about that."

Kessed parked beside Laken's car, and she slipped out with a Starbucks cardboard takeaway thermos. Laken's mouth watered.

"I'm looking at one of your favorite people," Laken teased her brother.

"Oh? Emma Watson. Wait, no, Jennifer Lawrence!"

"Nope, less famous, more notorious."

"Ah, how's little ladybug?" He used her hated nickname, and Laken could almost see his wicked grin.

"She's good. She's my dealer—Pike Place."

"I knew she'd make something of herself one day."

Kessed pointed to the phone and furrowed her brow then arched it suggestively at Laken.

"*Sterling*," Laken mouthed, watching as her friend narrowed her eyes.

"Hi, frog-lover." Kessed spoke loud enough for Sterling to hear.

"Yeah, some things never change." Sterling's tone was irritated, but he chuckled.

"Nope." Laken smirked as Kessed rolled her eyes.

"I'll let you go and chat with the monster. My time's up anyway. I love you."

"Aw, my heart. Saying that out loud and everything." She feigned a sob.

"Yeah, I'm getting soft in my old age."

"Thirty is old," Laken teased.

"It's the new twenty. Plus, my abs are way more chiseled now than at twenty, so I'm so much more badass."

"And we're done. I don't want to know about any of your anatomy."

"I do!" Kessed chimed in, giving Laken a conspiratorial grin.

"That's my cue. Talk with you soon, sis!"

"Bye." Laken waited till her brother disconnected before closing her eyes and saying a short prayer. *Please God, bring him home safe.*

"Still hiding his secret love for me?" Kessed asked.

Laken glanced to her, grinning. "He's seriously the only one who's ever been immune to your charms."

"That's because he knew me before I learned how to use them."

"Truth."

"Someday he'll wake up and love me. Until then, I'll play the field." She gave a small shrug and lifted the container.

"Bless you. I love you so much," Laken whimpered, taking it from her hands.

"I know you do."

"I almost thought you were talking to Bachelor Number One."

"I'm going to ignore that." Laken arched a brow.

"You're no fun." Kessed sighed. "I gotta run anyway. Hot date tonight." She winked.

"Netflix?" Laken guessed.

"You know it. Speaking of commitment, it's a relationship that's gone the distance."

"You're crazy." Laken shook her head. "Go on, I'll talk with you soon."

"You bet your sweet ass we will. I'll be waiting. This time, take better notes. I want to know the gory details, okay? I'm living vicariously through you, so make it worth my while." Kessed wagged her brows before turning and going to her car. As she made it to the door, she called over her shoulder. "And make the second kiss better than the first!"

Laken sighed, turned, and nearly stopped breathing. "Uh…hi, Jack."

Jack stood just inside the screen door, leaning against the doorframe, his brows arched in a question.

Laken slowly took a deep breath. *Why couldn't Kessed keep her mouth shut for once?*

"So, uh…I see you're going behind my back, bringing contraband into my house again." He jerked his chin to her cardboard thermos.

Laken released a pent-up breath. "I told you I wasn't woman enough for your coffee."

Jack shook his head, grinning. "How's Margaret doing?"

Thrilled to have a safe topic to discuss, Laken spoke in a rush. "She's doing well. I just checked on her, and she's upright. No more thrashing."

"Good, good." Jack nodded then opened the screen door for her.

"Thanks. How's the chest?" Laken asked, studying the slight tightness around his eyes.

"Painful, but nothing I can't survive." He shrugged. "When's Vince coming back?"

Laken made her way into the kitchen and set the coffee on the counter. She turned and leaned against the countertop, tilting her head as she regarded Jack. "Tomorrow morning. He said that her case wasn't as bad as a few others he's seen, and they all bounced right back. He didn't seem too concerned."

"Good, that's…well, that's damn good. Stupid horse," he muttered. "It's odd. I'm facing my own mortality, and I'm more concerned about my damn mare than myself. That's a warped perspective for ya." He rubbed his whiskery jaw with his fingers, his expression bemused.

"Priorities," Laken replied. "Margaret is important to you. It would be painful to deal with her loss, and honestly, you're dealing with enough pain. It's understandable why you wouldn't want to deal with more."

"You're far too wise for one so young. Kinda gets on my nerves." He arched a gray brow.

"Someone's gotta keep you in line."

"Speaking of in line." He shuffled his boot a bit. "Hold up, I need to move to my recliner. My legs are protesting all this standing around."

"By the way, Paige is coming the day after tomorrow. I just wanted to remind you." Laken followed him into the living room, taking a seat across from his chair.

"Joy." Jack grumbled.

"She's an excellent nurse."

"She's boring."

"Boring is good for you."

Jack arched a brow, but rather than argue further, he switched topics. "Would you happen to know if Cyler has plans on coming back anytime soon?" Jack asked hesitantly.

Laken glanced at her lap, keeping her facial expression under strict control. "I believe he's coming back tomorrow. He mentioned keeping an eye on Margaret."

Jack nodded, frowning a bit. "Good. I'm...I'm glad. He needs to be here. She's as much his horse as mine, loath as I am to admit it. And don't you ever tell him either. Got me, girl?" He pointed a finger, though his lips curled into a crooked smile.

"Your secret's safe with me," Laken affirmed.

Jack nodded once then speared her with a thoughtful gaze. "He likes you, you know."

Face blooming with a painful blush, Laken glanced to the ground before meeting Jack's amused grin.

"Don't get your panties in a twist, girl. It's not like I'm scolding you for it. Just...checking to see the way the land lies, if you get my meaning. And judging by the way your face just turned red like a tomato, I'm betting I'm not the only one who's noticed Cyler's interest." He chuckled. "Was that who your friend was talking about when she said to kiss him better the second time?"

Wanting to melt into the carpet, Laken forced a calm she didn't feel. "I...I really don't know what to say." She closed her eyes, feeling out of her element, and all kinds of stupid for even hinting that he was close in his assumption. But what choice did she have? Lie? *That* would go over well.

"Don't let me stop you, girl." He gave his head a quick shake. "Lord knows, that's happened before, and with God as my witness, that won't happen again. I'm sure you're worried about your job or something like that. You're too levelheaded for your own good." He mumbled the last part, making Laken give an awkward giggle.

"Jack, I—"

"No. You listen here, missy"—he pointed at her—"it's been a long— and I do mean *long*—time since I've seen my son laugh, or smile. Really, anything that resembles something other than anger, and there's not a chance in hell that I'm going to ruin that for him by some misbegotten idea that you can't give him a chance since he's my son and you're my nurse. Got me?" Emphatically, Jack nodded once.

Laken blinked, digesting everything that had just tumbled out of his mouth.

"I did him wrong, honey. And honestly, not to put any pressure on you, but I'm looking at this as God's way of allowing me to make it right. Okay? So, don't take that away from me, unless your heart's leading you a different way. But in my bones, I can see that it's not. You look at him the same way he looks at you when you both think I'm not paying attention."

"He's only been here a few days—"

"Honey, when you know, you know. I'm not saying you have to get it all figured out, but I'm trying to explain that you shouldn't be afraid to try." Jack leaned back into his recliner, sighing. "Now all this emotional fluff has me tuckered out, and I want to go fall asleep to *Die Hard* or *Rocky*, so I can feel like a man again, so if you'll excuse me..." He gave her a quick wink and left toward his room.

Even with her mind spinning, Laken noted the way he didn't pick up his feet like he had a week ago, and she made a mental note to have a walker on standby; he'd likely need it in another week.

She took a big breath and blew it out slowly, thinking over everything Jack had said. It was a lot, it was loaded, and it was all startlingly accurate. Such an odd reversal of roles and one that she found slightly awkward to categorize. Usually she was helping others, and Jack had just helped her tremendously by giving her a gift.

Latitude.

Odd, but that was what she needed—room to grow, room to learn, room to discover—and with Cyler's recent words, that was going to be necessary.

The prospect both thrilled and scared her. Jack was right. Kessed was right. They had both ganged up on her without even knowing it. She at least needed to try. Just try.

Remembering Jack's slowed gait, Laken strode to her room and opened her laptop. After signing into her company login, she scanned for new emails from the system. Jack's blood analysis was due back any day, and it was crucial for them to use it as a mile-marker for treatment of pain and other developing symptoms.

Sure enough, Interpath had given her the secured email, and she clicked it open.

Her eyes scanned the numbers, her heart growing heavy.

Cancer was a monster that played in multiplication. Cells didn't just divide, one plus one, they would exponentially divide and conquer, and Jack's weren't exactly being lazy. They were reproducing at an alarming rate, faster than she or his doctor had anticipated. She noted that the email had also been sent to Dr. Wills and went back to her inbox to check for any further instructions from him.

As she refreshed the page, she noticed a new email at the top. Opening it, she twisted her lips as she read.

Nurse Garlington,

Due to the increase in detected cancer cells in Jack Myer's blood, we can expect to see an increase in his psychological and somatic pain. As such, protocol requires different medication to keep him at a comfortable level. I expect an increase in his chest pressure to likely occur, if it already hasn't presented itself. I'm recommending that we switch from the anti-steroidal and anti-inflammatory meds to codeine. When that no longer manages the pain, we will make the progression to either morphine or oxycodone. Currently, I've sent in a prescription for codeine to his pharmacy on file, and in a week, we'll take another blood sample. But, if the pain isn't manageable, please let me know before then, and we'll move toward the morphine route.

Based on the replication of his cancer cells, I believe that the outlook of three months was optimistic. Because of the replication rate we're seeing, two months is a better timeframe. I'll be speaking with Jack concerning this information on our next appointment, Friday, August 9th.

Regards,
Dr. Wills

Laken closed her laptop. Taking a deep breath, she stared at the gray computer, not really seeing anything, her mind flipping through a thousand words, a thousand moments, a thousand memories.

How many times had she read that same email, only about a different person? A different life?

It still hit her hard each time. Part of her saw the words clinically, yet her heart still was vested. This was someone's life—Jack's life.

Three months wasn't very long.

Two was even shorter.

And they were already about a week in.

She exhaled a deep breath just as she heard Jack's coughing from across the hall.

Rising from her chair, she forced a smile. "Jack?" she called, walking toward his room.

"I'm here...honey. Not...dead yet," he called out, his words interrupted by sporadic coughs.

"Let's get ahead of it and start the nebulizer. No need to wait till you're suffering."

She pulled out the tube and started the albuterol treatment. Soon Jack's chest relaxed into easy breathing, and he drifted off to sleep.

After taking care that he was propped up, she covered him with another quilt and walked into the living room. She turned off the TV and the lights, and checked the doors before going to bed.

It was a juxtaposition that never ceased to amaze her. Life while facing death. Just because one loomed on the horizon didn't mean that the other had lost the battle yet. Most of the time, people believed that life and death were separate, when in truth, they often co-existed. Death could start while a person was still breathing, still fighting. And sometimes, life's most beautiful moments were not when death won, but when death set them free. As she closed her eyes, sinking into her pillow on Cyler's old bed, she said a prayer, hoping, praying, wishing that the latter would be true for Jack.

Would be true for Cyler.

That death wouldn't steal anything from them.

But be the ultimate gift.

Chapter 13

The ride back to the ranch had Cyler in a bundle of nerves. He tapped the steering wheel of his truck impatiently, his mind speeding ahead to the ranch, wondering. He'd all but laid out his hand and shot his poker-face to hell with one kiss. His gut said that Laken was worth it, but experience said that a pretty face could be a seasoned liar. Not that he really believed that about her, but it still gave him pause.

He'd hated leaving yesterday—ha, that was a new one—but had known it was necessary. The housing development was clipping along, and he'd needed to check on a few details. If they were going to be on the market within the month, the houses had to be perfect, every seam caulked, every roll of sod laid. It wasn't his favorite part of the job, but he was good at it, and it was rewarding seeing all the details finally fall together to make the blueprints a reality.

Cyler took the exit from the interstate and glanced at the clock. It was late afternoon, with the sun still arched high in the aqua-blue sky, giving him plenty of time for some maintenance in the barn. When he'd been in with Margaret, he'd noticed several issues that needed to be addressed, especially if the mare was going to need a little more hands-on care. He'd packed some tools and lumber in the back of his truck and would arrive at the ranch in time to get a good start. He wasn't heading back home till next week. Taking the next few days off gave him an awkward sensation in his chest, but he reasoned that a few of those days were part of the weekend.

After navigating the main street through the small town, he passed by Central Washington University with its large red brick buildings and took a left, leading him out of the heart of Ellensburg and into the wide-open spaces. Inhaling deeply, he noticed how his chest expanded as if he were releasing a tension he hadn't known he'd been holding till it dissipated. The expanse of sky and miles of rolling hills had a soothing effect, and he welcomed it.

He turned down the ranch drive, and his nerves returned. Would Laken be there? He had no reason to expect her to be anywhere else, but certainly she had some time off? And like a whipped puppy, he wondered all the stupid things he'd sworn to never think.

Does she miss me?

Does she regret the kiss?

What did she say to Jack?

A million thoughts flickered through his mind, and he chased them all away with a low growl of frustration.

The house grew larger as he closed the distance, and pretty soon he was putting the truck in park and glancing between the house and barn, vacillating between going to one or the other first.

His mind was made up for him when Laken slipped out the side door, her hand sweeping her hair from her face at the near-constant breeze as she made her way toward the barn.

Desire burned the edges of his mind while he watched her hips sway teasingly, innocently as she walked. His hands burned with the memory of those curves under his fingertips, the shape of her pressed against him when they kissed. The memory was stronger than he anticipated, and he had to adjust his jeans before exiting the pickup.

When his door shut, she jumped slightly, turning toward the sound. She was far enough away that he couldn't read her expression clearly, which wasn't helpful, so he closed the distance between them, offering a wide grin.

"Afternoon." He nodded once.

"Hey." Laken's face warmed to a delicate pink as she grinned shyly, glancing down for a moment before meeting his gaze with a brave one of her own.

"How's Margaret?" he asked, needing to put her at ease.

Laken's expression brightened. "Fantastic! Vince was here earlier, and she's already doing far better than he'd expected. There shouldn't be any further complications."

"That's great to hear." His grin widened. "I noticed last time that there were a few things than needed some repair." He gestured to the barn and used the perfect segue to let her know he was planning on being around. "I have a few days off, so I'll be working out there."

Laken nodded, glancing from the pickup to him, a flash of intuition brightening her expression. "Giving me a heads-up?"

"Basically."

"So, I'll need to put up with you till..." She let the question linger.

"Monday. If you're lucky."

"I'm not usually lucky," she teased, starting to walk toward the barn again.

"That's okay, I usually am." He flirted.

He earned a laugh from Laken. "I bet." She arched a brow. "So, what's all needing repair?"

He opened the sliding barn door for her and waited till she walked through, sneaking a glance at her butt as she walked ahead.

"Uh..." He cleared his throat, glancing around the dimly lit room. With the door fully open, the sun streamed in, filling the room with golden light. "For one, Margaret's stall got kind of torn up from her thrashing." He jerked his chin to the bungee cord that held the door closed and the gouged wood beside it.

"I was pretty proud of my idea." She unhooked the cord and walked into the stall. Margaret nickered as she approached. The mare placed her head on Laken's shoulder then sniffed her pockets, searching for a treat.

"She's got you figured out."

"I'm not exactly complicated," Laken replied dryly, reaching into her pocket then pulling out a sugar cube. "Fine, take it. You're so impatient," she scolded the mare gently.

"Pushover." Cyler coughed, hiding the words poorly.

Laken gave him a mock glare.

"Just sayin'." He held up his hands in surrender.

"You're just jealous that I brought her a treat and you forgot," she shot back. "I think she loves me more now."

Cyler chuckled. "Is that so?" He glanced down, wondering if he should press the subject. *To hell with it.* He gave a high whistle.

Margaret's ears perked, and she lifted her head abruptly, nickering softly.

Laken narrowed her eyes, glancing between the horse and Cyler.

Cyler clicked his tongue three times, and Margaret gently nudged Laken aside and then used her head to press open the stall door. Laken watched in amazement as the mare passed through the opening, slowly turned, and then used her nose to close the door behind her.

"What the..." Laken watched, wonder evident on her face.

But Cyler wasn't done. He whistled lowly, making a circular motion with his finger. The mare nodded her head and started to circle him, her big brown eyes trained on him, waiting for the next signal. In all honesty, Cyler was pretty amazed she remembered everything. It had been at least a decade since they'd gone through the routine. He nodded once and gave a quick, piercing whistle. Margaret halted, frozen. He whistled again, and this time she marched in place, shaking her head and nickering as if enjoying the chance to perform.

"Impressed yet?" Cyler crossed his arms, regarding Laken's still shocked expression.

"You win."

"I thought you might say that." He chuckled then whistled the halt for Margaret. She stopped, waiting for the next command. "Go on, take a bow." He made a sweeping gesture and couldn't hold back a bark of laughter when Laken gasped as Margaret knelt very gently then rose back to her feet.

Laken started to clap slowly, her eyes giving a quick roll of defeat as she glanced between the two. "So, what you're saying is that rather than train a dog, you trained a horse."

Cyler nodded. "Pretty much."

"I'm impressed."

Margaret bumped her head against his back. "I know. I know. Hold up." He went to the tack room and came back with a handful of oats. "Just a little bit. Your stomach's still a bit ginger, girl," he murmured softly as Margaret's velvet lips tickled his callused palm. He slowly rubbed the star on her forehead.

When he glanced up, Laken was watching him with an expression that was intimate, deep, and pierced down to his very bones. She tried to shutter it but failed. She'd shown her hand, just like he'd shown his the day before. It wasn't just him. She was every bit as far-gone, and the realization flooded him with anticipation and relief.

"I, uh...I need to check on Jack."

She is running scared. Cyler reached back, patting Margaret's hindquarters, and the mare started toward her stall once more, trapping Laken within.

Her gaze widened then narrowed as she took in the grin he couldn't hide.

"I'm not quite finished with you yet." He shrugged, answering her silent question. He walked over to the stall and opened the door wide then gestured for her to walk through.

"Should have seen that coming," she muttered under her breath.

"Come help me." He turned his back on her and headed to the pickup.

She didn't reply, but he heard the crunching of her shoes on gravel, and soon they were unloading the supplies and setting everything in the barn.

"One more thing," he called out to Laken just as she tried to escape back to the house.

She turned and watched him with a wary expression.

"This is going to take a few days, and since you're in my old room, I thought I'd take the guest room"—he took a few strides toward her—"unless you want to share." He gave a quick and gentle tug on one of her curls and added a wink for good measure. As he hoped, her face flushed with pink.

"Maybe another time," she replied, shocking the hell out of him just before she walked away, glancing over her shoulder and grinning.

Shaking his head and laughing at the mystery that was Laken, he regarded the barn and got to work.

Several hours later, Cyler shed his shirt and hung it on a stray nail. His muscles ached with the wonderful sensation of working with his two hands. He'd missed that feeling of working hard, of doing something physical rather than mental. He swiped his hand across his forehead then finished nailing a board back into place. He assessed his handiwork. Most of the repairs had been completed. The upgrades would have to wait till tomorrow, but Lord only knew how much the old barn needed some work. After all, it would be his responsibility soon.

His mind wandered to Jack. That area of his life was like an old scratched CD that kept going around and around on repeat, unable to find a way to resolve. The anger and the resentment were still there, but somehow, he was able to think around them. It didn't change the reality, just the way he was responding to it. He sighed. Cyler didn't want to give his father a chance; he didn't deserve it. While he hated how he felt like an ass for standing on his principles, a man had to pay for his actions, didn't he?

If he just walked away, forgave Jack—his stomach clenched at the thought—then what consequences did the old man have from his decisions? None? How the hell was that fair? Cyler thought back over how he'd suffered, how Jack's actions had destroyed the most precious aspects of his life, cold and calculating.

Yet, as Cyler turned to glance at the house, the heat of the anger was less. And he hated Jack more for it. While Cyler knew life wasn't fair, that didn't mean that justice was irrelevant.

But the whole situation was turning shades of gray, rather than black and white. Part of him wanted to blame Laken, but the greater part of his heart rejected the idea. Regardless, he didn't care. She was the only reason he was here, and that was enough of a risk for him without adding in the issues with Jack.

With that, he shoved the thoughts to the back of his mind and picked up a pine two-by-four and placed it on two sawhorses. After measuring, he made two marks and started to saw the board to fit the sliding barn door to reinforce it. It wasn't until he turned off the power saw that he noticed Laken's approach.

"Hey." Her face lit in a warm smile. "You hungry yet?"

Cyler nodded, setting down the saw. "Sure thing. I'm at a good stopping point anyway."

"Good." She turned to walk away but not before he noticed how her gaze lingered on his chest.

"Wait." He reached out, holding his breath as she paused then slowly turned. "I was wondering something on my way up here." He closed the distance. "When exactly do you get time off?"

Her expression was mildly surprised. "Paige is the on call for Jack. She'll be here tomorrow so that I can take a day off."

"Do you have plans tomorrow?" he asked, reaching for her hand then turning it over in his and tracing the lines in her palm.

"N-no," she answered, taking a deep breath.

"And tonight...after Jack is all tucked in nice and tight..." he murmured.

"I'll be on call, but he's usually fine till earlier in the morning," she answered, a bit of her sass returning as she gave him a grin.

"Then we'll have plenty of time to make plans for tomorrow. I have a few ideas. And, of course, all of them start with coffee." He grinned before he took her palm and rested it on his shoulder, freeing his hands to pull her into the lee of his body.

Her breath caught at the contact, and slowly she traced her palms over his shoulders then down farther over his back. The sensation of her exploration had him fighting for control over his reaction. He wanted to push her gently back till she was flush against the barn wall and explore her as she explored him. He took a step, but she reached up on her tiptoes and brushed a kiss against his lips, inviting him as her tongue grazed his lower lip enticingly. It was a wrestle for control as he leaned into her kiss, and she pressed back, giving as much as he gave, marking him every bit as much as he was marking her. Her lips angled across, her teeth nipping, her tongue caressing while her fingers arched into his skin, creating an odd mix of pain and pleasure. With a growl, he slid his hands down from her shoulders to the tempting curve of her hips then pulled them in tightly against his, wanting—needing—her to be closer.

"Laken, honey! There's smoke!" Jack's voice held a slightly panicked edge, and Laken pulled back abruptly, her lips swollen, her face flushed with desire.

"I-I, oh shit." She groaned and took off to the house at a dead run.

"Is something on fire?" Laken called out, and Cyler couldn't help the grin.

Yeah, *something* was burning. Him. And like ice water, Jack had effectively put out that fire.

Some things never change.

But this time, Jack wouldn't interfere. He'd make sure of it. Because Laken was his.

She just didn't quite know it yet.

Chapter 14

As Laken pulled out the store-bought lasagna, she wasn't sure if she'd been saved by the smoke, or if the smoke had ruined everything. Well, so maybe not everything. She glared at the oven, biting back a curse as the wisps from the overflowed lasagna burning on the bottom filled the air.

She sighed.

And here she thought she'd been so brilliant by buying something pre-made again.

She should have stuck with takeout.

"Everything okay, honey?" Jack called from behind her.

"Yeah, yeah. Just overflowed and burned on the bottom. That's going to be fun to clean"—she blew out a breath—"but the lasagna isn't ruined or burned even." She studied the pan. "In fact, I think it's still half-frozen."

"That's why God made microwaves. We'll dish some out, zap it, and boom! We'll be good to go. Don't worry, honey. Can't be perfect at everything." Jack clapped once, rubbed his hands together, and went to pull down some plates. His steps were slow and unsteady, so Laken intercepted him.

"I'll tell you what. You just boss me around from that chair over there, and I'll pour you some coffee. Sound good?"

He narrowed his eyes and allowed her to lead him to the chair, but not before muttering, "Who's bossing whom?"

"Heard that."

"Don't care."

"I'm putting sugar in your coffee to sweeten you up."

"Won't work. I'm tougher than rawhide and just as mean." He nodded emphatically.

Laken rolled her eyes. "Sure, sure. Your secret's safe with me." She bit her lip and turned, but not before noticing his wry grin.

"So, I'm assuming we don't need the fire department. Unless Jack wants to go down in a blaze of glory instead." Cyler's voice carried from the hall as he strode into the kitchen.

"You wish," Jack replied.

"Nah, no heroics for you," Cyler shot back.

"And again, done. And no, no fire department. I didn't actually even burn the lasagna."

"Nope, it's still frozen."

"Thanks, Jack. Helpful." Laken gave a sarcastic smile.

"Anytime, sweetheart. Just making sure he knows what he's getting into." He chuckled.

Laken froze, then closed her eyes. *Thanks again, Jack.*

Cyler's laughter had her eyes snapping open. "That obvious, huh? Well, I never was one to beat around the bush." Cyler strode the rest of the way into the kitchen and pulled down the plates. "Hey, Laken? You're only cuter when you blush."

She took a deep breath through her nose and shook her head. She was surrounded. "Between the two of you, this might kill me."

"Nah, I'm the one with a timetable to work with. You're young, sweetheart. Act like it. I'm putting myself to bed, but not till after dinner. Kinda hungry, you understand. Then you two can—honestly, I don't want to know." Jack held up his two hands, his grin becoming more of a smirk.

"Just when you thought it couldn't get more awkward," Cyler stage-whispered.

"Not helping."

"Wasn't trying to."

"Gah!" Laken groaned.

"Anytime tonight, sweetheart." Jack called out, and as Laken turned to glare, he pointed to the lasagna.

"Fine." She cut through the still chilly middle of the lasagna and handed a plateful to Cyler, who placed it in the microwave.

"So, since Jack's being helpful and all, putting himself to bed…" He gave teasing grin.

Laken rolled her eyes as anticipation filled her.

"Come with me tonight." Cyler hitched a broad shoulder, his blue eyes burning through her.

"Where?" she asked as she placed a portion of the lasagna into the microwave.

"That's for me to know and you to find out."

"Then no." Laken turned, hiding her smirk.

"Playing hard to get?" Cyler flirted, reaching around her as the microwave dinged. He opened it and pulled out the plate. His masculine scent overpowered the aroma of the food and had her body tightening, remembering the sensation of his lips on hers.

"Just seeing if you'll take no for an answer," she shot back, curving a brow in challenge as she swiped the plate from him and walked over to where Jack waited.

"Dinner and a show. Keep going." He lifted a fork and grinned, watching them.

"Lovely," Laken grumbled.

"Actually, I didn't really ask, so…" Cyler leaned against the counter, a cocky grin on his face.

"Then I didn't really answer," Laken challenged, grinning in spite of herself.

"Better than HBO," Jack murmured from the table.

Laken gave him a glare.

He grinned wider.

"Please?" Cyler interrupted her scolding of Jack, and she turned to him.

"There's something I want to show you, and I promise you'll enjoy it. It's stargazing, and Jack, so help me, if you make any smart-ass remark—"

"Whoa there. Ding-ding-ding. We have a winner! Hell has officially frozen over and—"

"Eat your damn lasagna," Cyler replied, his tone exasperated. He turned his gaze to Laken. "Please, Laken?"

Laken took a deep breath, knowing she was powerless to say anything but yes, but enjoying the opportunity to mess with him a bit. "Yes."

"You better bring your *A*-game, boy," Jack remarked around a full mouth of lasagna.

"I promise not to disappoint." Cyler leveled his blue gaze at her, making her body tingle.

Nodding, Laken made a plate of lasagna for herself as well, and soon, after dinner, she walked Jack to his room, making sure he didn't need anything.

In short work, she was changing into jean shorts and a T-shirt before nervously returning to the kitchen.

"You ready?" Cyler asked. Everything about him screamed sexy, from his faded jeans to the way he filled out his black T-shirt.

Laken nodded, her stomach full of butterflies as he pushed away from the counter and walked toward the door.

"It'll start getting dark soon," he remarked as he opened the back door for her, leading to the driveway.

"I don't think I've ever actually been stargazing." Laken spoke, walking to his truck.

Cyler opened the truck door for her as well. "I used to do it all the time as a kid. The city lights don't interfere if you go down by the canyon." With a grin, he closed the door behind her and circled around the front of the truck before hopping in on his side. Soon they were driving behind the ranch on an old dirt road with rye grass growing between the wheel ruts.

"Is it on the ranch property?" Laken asked, holding on to the armrest as they hit a large bump.

"Yeah, it's out where Jack used to run the cattle during the spring. He sold everything but a few old longhorns when he was diagnosed. Those last steers were sold yesterday. Bo called this past week and caught me up on everything. Bo is his lawyer."

"Oh, I actually kinda wondered about that." Laken turned to Cyler.

"Well, it was just wiser to keep things simple," Cyler remarked, pulling the truck left down a narrow path.

"I can understand that."

"Here we are." Cyler put the truck in park and flashed a quick grin. "Stay put."

Laken unbuckled her seatbelt, and Cyler opened the door then held out his hand for her.

"Thanks." She blushed as his warm hand held hers then slowly let go as he opened the second door to the back of the cab. He pulled out a few quilts and then shut both doors.

"Because the truck bed is great for lumber but sucks for stargazing, these will help a bit." He tossed the quilts in the back of the truck bed then lowered the gate. After extending his hand, he helped Laken as she climbed onto the bumper then the tailgate to walk into the truck bed.

Cyler one-arm-hurdled into the truck bed and picked up the quilts from where he'd tossed them. He laid them out one by one.

Once he was finished, Laken took a seat on the wheel well, thankful for the warm evening to combat her nerves.

"I love it out here," Cyler remarked, sitting down on the quilts, his back resting against the cab.

"It's quiet," Laken whispered.

"You can hear yourself think." Cyler closed his eyes, and Laken watched as he took a slow breath.

"You can." She listened to the silence, her whole body slowly relaxing.

"The first star will be the north star. It will be visible just above where the sun sets. It's pretty bright, so we should be able to see it in a few minutes since the sun's starting to set over the ridge." Cyler opened his eyes and met her gaze, grinning.

"So, we really are stargazing?" Laken half teased.

Cyler grinned mischievously. "What else would we be doing?"

"No idea," Laken answered too quickly.

"Honestly, Laken, I just wanted to spend time with you. Is that so hard to believe?" He hitched a shoulder.

"Nah, I'm pretty amazing."

Cyler laughed, the sound echoing around them. "Yes, yes you are. So, while we're discussing how amazing you are, would you be open to spending more time with me tomorrow?"

Laken's face burned with a blush. "Again? Hmmm. It's my day off, so I'll have to check my calendar," she teased. "Are you sure? I mean you might be sick of me after stargazing."

"Damn, I gotta stop asking," Cyler shot back with a grin. "Tomorrow. Spend it with me."

"That's still a question," Laken flirted.

"Sorry, I was raised right."

"I'll tell Jack you said that."

"He'll give credit to my mom."

"You're probably right."

"It's true." Cyler shrugged, waiting.

"Fine."

"Fine..."

"Fine. I'll spend tomorrow with you. But I need coffee." Laken pointed at him.

"Done." Cyler gave her a warm smile, his mouth drawing her attention, and she licked her lips instinctively.

Then she remembered.

"I completely forgot. Okay, not forgot. You kinda had me a little distracted—"

Cyler's chuckle interrupted her, and she would have laughed had her stomach not tightened with the foreboding about the doctor's appointment tomorrow.

His smile faded, his eyes tightening as she studied her face.

"What is it, honey?"

"Sorry, it's just that tomorrow I'm open all afternoon, but in the morning, I need to take Jack to his doctor's appointment." She put on her best *nurse* face, hoping it gave nothing away.

"Oh, well, that's fine." He studied her further, his gaze intent. "There's something else," he stated as his gaze narrowed.

"It's important that I'm there so I can ask any questions that maybe Jack wouldn't think of and can get the best idea for his care," Laken answered, leaving out the part where she'd need to help Jack work through the bad news.

"What time is the appointment?" Cyler asked, leaning back on the truck bed, his hands tucked behind his head.

"Ten."

"And you'll be free after that?"

Laken bit her lip. Technically, yes, she would be. But with Jack getting an update on his cancer's progress, he might need her. Normally, it wasn't an issue to lose potential time off, but this time it wasn't so easy to ignore the chance at a break.

Not a break—a date—a chance to explore this...thing...with Cyler.

"That doesn't exactly sound like a yes." Cyler's voice broke through her deep thoughts.

"It's complicated."

"Complicated like you don't want to go, or complicated like you are torn between Jack's needs and yours?"

Her gaze flickered to his, her brows drawing as she replayed his words in her head. Her needs? No...well...*huh.* She twisted her lips.

"There's more to the appointment than just a checkup, isn't there?" he asked softly.

She couldn't answer; it wasn't professional. It wasn't ethical.

"You can't tell me, can you?" Cyler rose on his elbow, regarding her.

"No, I can't." Lake answered honestly.

"I can respect that. I'll tell you what. I'll be working on the back shelter of the barn. The roof needs patching from that windstorm last spring. If you feel comfortable taking some time to yourself, come find me."

Laken nodded. "Thank you...for understanding."

It meant more to her than she could quite articulate. Whomever she was with, he needed to respect, to encourage her in her passion, in her work. If Cyler felt that she was picking work over him, then that didn't bode well for any future in their relationship. That he was able to understand—when the person in question wasn't one he particularly liked—was impressive.

Then he shocked her completely. "Do you want me to go to the appointment with you?"

She blinked. "Uh, that would actually be up to Jack. You'd have to ask him," she answered automatically, her mind spinning with the idea that Cyler would choose to be in the same, small, confined room as his father. Did this mean part of the rift was beginning to mend?

"Don't let your hopes run away wild, Laken. I'd be there for you, not him," Cyler replied dryly, apparently reading her mind.

She arched a brow. "Still up to Jack."

"Enough about Jack. Gives me indigestion to talk about that pain in the ass." He gave a quirk of his lips, taking a bit of the heat from his remark. "Tell me about yourself. I figure I've learned a bit just though observation, but that's not enough."

Laken slipped from her seat on the truck bed wheel and lay back on the quilt beside Cyler, watching the stars growing brighter. "What do you want to know? Just a heads-up, whatever you ask, I'll be turning right back around on you," she teased.

"Wouldn't expect anything less," he joked. "Hmmm. Family. Mom, dad, siblings..."

Laken took a break. "Dad's a plastic surgeon in Seattle. Mom is a preschool teacher at a small classical school. They've been remarried for six years." She smiled to herself.

"Re-married?"

"Yeah, they got a divorce when I was about eleven. But neither of them really got over the other, and my dad decided that he wanted my mom back. He pursued—my mother calls it chased—her for a year-and-a-half, and then they remarried when I was about eighteen."

"Huh, I don't think I've ever heard of that actually happening."

"I know. I was pretty thankful. Divorce sucks," Laken whispered.

"Yeah, yeah it does," Cyler answered quietly.

"Sterling is almost thirty. He actually called yesterday! He's coming home for Christmas, I think. We'll see. I don't really take anything he says about leave seriously till I actually see him with my own eyes."

"A few false alarms?" Cyler asked, a twinkle in his eye.

"Yeah, a few. He loves being a marine though. He's good at it." She sighed a laugh. "I tell him he's saving the world one day at a time."

"In a way, he is," Cyler replied kindly.

"I miss him," she admitted softly.

Cyler's hand wrapped around hers, enveloping her in warmth. "I'm sure you do, honey."

"What about you? Your family? I mean, I know *Jack*, but your mom?" Laken let the words linger, suspecting that his story didn't have a happy ending.

Cyler took a deep breath then blew it out deliberately. "Mom was amazing. I loved her. She was beautiful from the inside out and loyal to a fault. She didn't believe in divorce, hated it. Her parents were divorced, and she swore she'd never do that to her kid. But Jack didn't have the same convictions." His grip tightened on her hand, and she waited patiently for him to continue.

"I was engaged to Breelee when things between my parents hit the volatile stage." He paused again, and as she glanced over, she could see the tightening of his jaw. "My mom thought Jack was seeing another woman, and I came over to have a chat, man-to-man about it. But that chat turned into a brawl when I discovered the other woman was my fiancée."

The crickets were the only sound as Laken closed her eyes against the onslaught of despair she felt for Cyler, for Jack, for his mom. "That's horrible."

"We broke things off, as you can imagine, and less than a week later, Jack was in Mexico with Breelee, and my mother called me to let me know she had been served divorce papers. I—I couldn't come home. Too many memories, and I was hurting too, but that didn't excuse the fact that I'd all but cut things off with my mom as well, only to get a call a month later from the sheriff's office. The autopsy said she had alcohol poisoning."

Laken exhaled, considering just how much alcohol one needed to consume to get to that point. "I'm sorry." It seemed so inadequate, but there wasn't a word—or any number of words—that could communicate the depth of the pain.

"It was a long time ago," Cyler replied, his tone kind, as if trying to comfort *her*.

"Still."

"At least you can kinda see why Jack and I aren't on friendly terms."

Laken nodded, not trusting her voice. She understood, and it didn't change her acceptance or friendship toward Jack, but she could see the flipside of the coin and struggled with the depth of the canyon between father and son.

"Boyfriends?"

Laken frowned, turning to Cyler with a questioning expression.

"I figured that as long as we're letting everything air out, I'd get the dirt on you too." He grinned.

"Well, my past isn't nearly as exciting as yours."

"Yeah, let's call it exciting. Sounds much less depressing," he replied dryly.

"Not much to tell. I was dedicated to my studies, which didn't leave time for anything else. I graduated early, went into my specialized field, and did as many internships as they'd allow. Lots of late nights, more than my share of studying, and a few hot flings with Netflix when I had a day or two off." She bit her lip, giggling as Cyler rolled his eyes.

"What a sordid past."

"Told you it was boring."

"Yeah, you are pretty boring. I wonder what I see in you?" he teased, rolling over and reaching out to pull her closer to his side, his warm breath tickling her nose a moment before he kissed it.

"No idea," she teased back, her whole body warming. Her lips searched for his, but he pulled back.

"Overeager. I'm not done figuring you out yet." He ducked his head down and nipped at her neck, playing. "Childhood pets."

Laken took a shaky breath, feeling his warm body pressed against hers. "Hmm, I had a golden retriever, and a goldfish that I won at the fair. That's it. You have Margaret and—"

"Ha, yeah well…as you know, Margaret counts as a dog and horse so…"

"Show off."

"How else am I supposed to impress girls?" he questioned.

"Because all this isn't enough." She pressed against his chest then slid her hands down suggestively.

"Hedging my bets," he replied.

She rolled her eyes. "Fine. Anything else?"

"I had a few dogs, several barn cats, but with the coyotes…let's just say the cats didn't stick around for long."

"Ah."

"Mostly it was Margaret."

"And you went to school…"

"At SPU. Seattle Pacific University. Majored in business, worked summers at a construction company and loved it. Jack and I had never seen eye to eye on, well, anything, so I didn't expect or want to take over the ranch. So, I went into construction and built up a company. It didn't really take off till after the fallout with Breelee and my mom's funeral. Pouring myself into the job was what saved me from going crazy. It's solid now, though."

"I've been to SPU. Hills everywhere."

"It's on Queen Anne Hill. Walking to class counted as intense cardio."

"I bet."

"Your turn."

Laken grinned as they continued to chat. For the next hour, they exchanged questions and learned about the other. Cyler's hands never strayed from her body, only changed positions. From tugging on a loose strand of hair to tracing the outline of her lips, he'd caress up and down her arm, only to return to hold her hand. It was magical and crazy-romantic in ways she'd only read about, never actually experienced. The stars slowly moved across the sky, a few shooting down to earth as the night went on.

"Almost done?" Laken asked after a few moments of silence.

"Nope."

She giggled then froze as his finger traced her lip once more but with more pressure than before as his other arm banded around her waist and pulled her in close. His lips met hers, searching, and she willingly leaned into the kiss. Her mind flashed back to the barn, to the way his bare chest was highlighted by the expanse of his shoulders. Her fingers burned with the memory of the feel of his skin beneath her hands.

His lips nipped hers playfully. She smiled against his mouth, earning a mock growl as his hand moved to her hair and drew her mouth against his with a powerful demand. She willingly met his kiss, deepening the exchange, and she caressed his tongue with hers, memorizing the spicy flavor that was all his own. She slid her knee between his legs, inching herself closer as they lay side by side.

Cyler's breath was hot against her mouth. He peppered her lips, her jaw, her neck with kisses that made her heart pound. In one smooth motion, he rolled over her, resting his weight on his elbows as nearly every inch of her aligned with him. Heat coiled then burst through her as she pressed her hips into his, instinctively needing more. His lips traveled down her neck, then nipped her earlobe, the sound of his breathing and the pounding of her heart drowning out the cricket's song. He nudged her chin up with his nose, and she willingly obeyed when her body caught fire as his lips traveled from her throat to her collarbone then lower, tugging her shirt out of the way with his teeth.

Her hands moved without conscious thought, traveling from their mapping of the hills and valleys of his back, to tugging on his dark brown hair, pressing into him deeper.

He shifted to one elbow, freeing his hand to trace from her hip to slide under her shirt till his fingers teased the edge of her bra, tempting her, flirting with the fire that was threatening to consume her.

"Laken," he murmured against her neck.

She couldn't find her voice, only nodded, trying to catch her breath.

He pulled back, his blue eyes black in the darkness. His chest moved with each panting breath.

"Come here," Laken replied, tugging his head back to hers, and with a groan, he surrendered.

His hand grasped her breast, kneading the soft flesh, earning a gasp of pleasure as Laken almost forgot to breathe. The pleasure surged through her, burning through any rational thought as to why they should stop. Arching into him, she gave him the chance to unhook her bra, and after fumbling for a moment, the offending garment loosened. He pulled at her shirt, removing it in one smooth motion. Her hands tugged at his clothing as well.

With frenzied movements, Cyler obeyed her request, and soon his shirt and jeans were in a pile somewhere in the truck bed. The thick quilt protected Laken's bare back from the cool metal of the pickup bed, and fleetingly, she was shocked at her behavior, but just as the idea flickered through, Cyler's hot mouth traveled from one breast to the other, stealing every thought she'd ever had. She arched her back and slid her jeans from her body. Cyler rose from her, and immediately she shivered from the absence of his heat. He gently tugged her pants off the rest of the way then located his jeans. Her lips were tender from his adoring assault, and she bit down gently and watched as he pulled something from one pocket of his discarded jeans. The full implication of what that package held slammed into her as he tore it open and removed its contents.

Is this really going to happen?

She never did things like this! Yet as Cyler slowly met his body with hers, every hesitation melted away in the midst of the searing heat his body gave. Slowly he kissed her lips, melding into her then pulling away, flirting with the edge of her sanity as she gripped his shoulders trying to force him closer. At his amused chuckle, she smiled, enjoying the moment, living for it. Then her breath was stolen as he granted her wish, filling her.

Time paused, and she held her breath, watching his gaze open completely as he watched her. Then slowly he moved. Each glide created a tension that built upon itself, till the intensity was so powerful she could no longer think around it. As she reached the edge of the cliff, she felt his shoulders tremble, a slick sheen of perspiration covering them. She arched her fingers deep, anchoring herself to him, and flew over the edge, her body singing with the release of passion that they'd built together. As she slowly came to reality, her body tightened again, this time meeting Cyler's release, matching it, cresting the wave with him. He groaned, his breath irregular and hard as he panted against her neck, his body shaking with the power of his release.

Heart pounding, she watched with unabashed amazement as Cyler's gaze roamed her features, his own breathing ragged, his heartbeat surging through her. He pressed his forehead to hers. Closing her eyes, Laken forced away all the rational thoughts that threatened to steal this perfect moment and just focused on the warmth of his skin on hers, the memory of his kiss, the sweet passion of making love.

Cyler leaned back, a devastatingly alluring grin on his face. His blue eyes seemed black in the dim light. Placing a kiss to her lips, he then groaned as he rolled off her and to his side.

Laken bit her lip, her body achingly tender, but in the most perfect way. She racked her brain for something to say and came up with nothing.

"Speechless?" Cyler asked, winking as he reached for his clothing.

Laken grinned. "Close."

"I'll admit. I didn't exactly bring my *A*-game. I'll do better next time." He chuckled. "I'm man enough to admit it's been a while for me, and that didn't do my stamina any favors."

Laken gulped. Heaven help her if the sex got better. Yet she continued to smile, thinking of his promise that there would be a next time. "I wasn't complaining."

"Didn't think you were. Just felt the need to be upfront, Laken." He shrugged into his shirt then handed her clothing over, setting it on her lap as she rose into a sitting position. "You know my history. I'm pretty jaded. But this—you're worth the risk."

Laken nodded, slipping into her clothing as she thought over his words. If anyone had a reason to be skeptical about any sort of relationship, it was Cyler. Yet that hadn't scared him off, and he still wanted her, wanted this. The amazement of it was fresh and powerful.

"Yeah well, I don't stargaze with just anyone so…" she offered, lightening the mood yet still conveying her own sentiments.

Cyler chuckled.

"…you're worth the risk too."

"I'm glad. I'm not a mysterious or smoke-and-mirrors, talk-in-circles guy, Laken. Be upfront with me. I like you. A lot"—he rubbed the back of his neck—"as I hope was very apparent."

Laken grinned.

"Just tell me the truth of it, always. And we'll make this work. Deal?" He held out his hand, waiting.

Laken reached out and grasped his warm hand, the same hand that had branded his mark all over her body, and shook it. "Deal."

Cyler's answering smile was startling in its glory, causing fresh desire to slam into her.

He released her and hopped down from the tailgate. He extended his hand to her. "We probably should get back to the ranch. I'm betting you want to check on Jack, and as much as I'd love to keep you out here in bed, I'd rather keep you in a more comfortable one."

Laken shook her head in amusement at his joke, smiling in spite of herself. "Probably a good idea."

"I'm usually right."

"Oh really? You wanted honesty, right? Well, you'll be getting it. Be prepared," she shot back, taking his hand, and jumping to the ground.

"Wouldn't want it any other way."

She tilted her head, regarding him. "You might change your mind."

"I usually make my mind up and stick with it."

"We'll see," she challenged.

"We sure will," he replied with a devilish grin, not releasing her hand. He led her to the passenger side of his truck and opened the door.

"Thanks." She spoke quietly, gasping as she felt his touch circle her waist and pull her close then seared her lips with his.

Laken willingly answered his kiss, her body responding with building heat. As he gentled the exchange, she pulled back reluctantly. "That's going to be a problem."

"How so?" he asked, tickling her hip as he grinned.

"Keeping my hands off you."

Cyler winked. "Yeah, at least it will be a struggle for us both. Now quit distracting me and hop in." He stepped back, Laken slid into the truck, and Cyler closed the door behind her.

The way back to the ranch was quiet. Cyler's hand wrapped tightly around hers, and she happily watched the dark world pass by, denying thoughts about tomorrow or the next day. Because tonight? Tonight was perfect. And she refused to neglect the moment, to move past it, when moments like this in life were so few and far between. She closed her eyes and laid her head back, savoring each second, knowing that tomorrow—and the challenges it would bring—would be there soon enough.

But that was tomorrow.

And she was living for each moment today.

Chapter 15

The pale dawn was just starting to illuminate the guest room as Cyler rolled over, the odd feeling that something was missing.

He tried to go back to sleep, but the sensation nagged at him, and as he pulled from the fuzziness of deep sleep, he realized that some*thing* wasn't missing.

It was some*one.*

He grinned, stretching his legs and twisting his ankles, hearing the familiar popping noise. Yeah, sure as hell someone was missing, but not for long.

When they'd arrived back at the ranch from stargazing, he'd been prepared to kidnap her and go for round two. But Jack was coughing in his sleep, and as much as Cyler wanted to ignore him, he knew Laken never could. It was both aggravating and endearing. Her passion for her profession humbled him, and he respected her for it. She shouldn't have to choose between him or her job. It wouldn't be fair. In a way, it would be like asking her to separate a part of her soul. Being a nurse was as much a facet of her character as it was her profession, and Cyler realized that. So rather than haul her off to his bed, he'd kissed her goodnight and made sure she didn't need any help.

Help.

Like he'd bloody lost his mind because that *help* was for his son of a bitch father.

He was going soft.

Yet he couldn't find the heat from his anger anymore; he'd started to pity Jack. Not for the cancer—though that sucked—but for his life.

Because he'd had a family, a loving wife, a home, and he'd spat on it. And what was he left with now? A son who all but hated him, a money-grabbing ex-wife, and a dead wife, so in a nutshell, nothing. He had nothing.

And no one to blame for it but himself.

Cyler mulled over things, wondering if he could actually deal with being in the doctor's office with Jack. He didn't want to ask the old man unless he was sure he could curb his resentment. Laken seemed to take it in stride, but he doubted the doctor would.

After rolling from bed, he stretched again and pulled on his jeans. He found a clean shirt from his duffel bag. The scent of coffee called to him, and he considered drinking a cup of Jack's sludge, just to tide him over till he could make a Starbucks run. Padding toward the kitchen, he passed Laken's room. The door was cracked open, and he pushed it just a few inches farther, smiling at the sleeping beauty. Her blond hair was splayed all over the pillow, her clothes from last night scattered on the floor, and a pair of short shorts barely covered her perfectly round ass.

Her eyes flickered as if dreaming, and Cyler's gaze traveled down her back to the skin exposed at her waist. His hands burned with the memory of her skin's softness under his fingertips, the way she'd responded to each touch, each kiss. He bit back a groan, and his body hardened at the thought. He closed the door softly and forced his thoughts into line as he continued his way to the kitchen. He glanced behind him, noticing Jack's door closed as well, signaling that the man was still asleep.

As he walked through the kitchen and picked up the coffee carafe, he sighed at the brew's thick coating of the glass.

Maybe he wouldn't brave Jack's sludge.

He glanced to the clock. Seven-thirty. Surely, he had time to get to Starbucks and back before anyone else got up. It had been after midnight when he returned with Laken, and he guessed she'd been up for at least another hour or two after that, so perhaps she'd sleep in a bit.

Nodding to himself, he grabbed his keys from the counter and left quietly, cringing as his truck roared to life. The drive to Starbucks was short, and after taking his customary parking spot across the street, he jogged over to the building.

"Hello, stranger," Kessed called as soon as he walked in.

"Hello, yourself," he answered, strolling toward the counter then waiting behind another customer.

When it was his turn, he started to order but was interrupted. "I got this one, Grant," Kessed called to the other barista. And with a grin, she handed him a carrying tray with two venti cups. He took it, arching a brow.

"You are going back to the ranch, right?" Kessed asked with an impatient tone.

"Sure am."

"Then do our girl a favor." She winked.

Cyler grinned. "Was already planning on it."

"Speaking of Laken"—she jerked her chin to the left, signaling him to follow—"it's on the house. Now come here, slick." She walked out from behind the counter to a vacant table then motioned for him to join her as she pulled out a chair.

"What's up?" Cyler asked, setting the tray down and regarding Laken's friend with wariness.

"What are your intentions toward Laken?" Kessed asked, folding her arms over her chest and giving him a challenging stare.

Cyler bit back a grin. "Well…" He thought over the last night, pretty sure he'd made his intentions quite clear. But Kessed didn't know that. "I like her," he answered plainly.

"What are we, in junior high? I didn't exactly pass you a note and ask you to circle an answer here. *Like* doesn't cut it," she replied, sarcasm thick in her tone and expression.

Chuckling, Cyler shook his head. "Isn't that between Laken and me?"

"Nope."

"Really?" Cyler challenged.

"Yup."

"There's no guarantees in life, but I'm not playing with her, if that's what you mean."

"Okay then." Kessed nodded, seeming satisfied. "You're free to go. Just one thing." She leaned across the table, her brows raised, her petite form attempting to be threatening. "You break her heart, I'll cut you." She gave an evil grin. "Good talk." She patted his shoulder and walked away.

Cyler blinked "And that is why I will never understand women," he muttered under his breath then took the tray and left.

He arrived back at the ranch and opened the door quietly then realized it wasn't necessary. The TV was on, the news filtering through the air, the smell of burnt toast dominant.

Yup. They were both awake.

The smoky scent told him Laken was in the kitchen, so he quietly passed through to the living room. He needed to talk with Jack, alone.

"Hey, old man." He nodded, earning a glare.

"You still here?"

"Huh, I was just thinking the same thing," Cyler answered.

"Walked right into that one," Jack muttered.

"Pretty much." Cyler took a seat and stared at the TV, not making eye contact with Jack. "So, you have an appointment today, right?"

"What's it to you?" Jack shot back.

"I want to be there. But I need to ask your dumb ass before I can go, so, this is me asking."

As the silence stretched on for more than a few seconds, Cyler turned his attention to Jack. His father was regarding him shrewdly.

"Why?"

"Laken," Cyler answered honestly.

"Figures," Jack retorted. "Fine. I don't care."

"Thanks for the welcome." Cyler lifted a cup from the tray he held and took a sip.

"It's about time you pulled your head from your ass. That girl in there's gold. You know it. I know it. Learn from my stupidity and don't mess this up. You hear me?"

Jack's tone had Cyler turning back, meeting his gaze.

"For once, we agree on something," Cyler replied then left for the kitchen.

"Good."

Cyler let Jack have the last word and strode into the kitchen, already wondering what attempt at breakfast Laken had tried. He grinned as he watched her bend over and peek in the oven, giving him a prime view of her ass in those tight jeans.

"Good morning," he called out, knowing the sound of his boots would let her know he was coming.

She set the dish on the stove then turned. Her face lit up into a welcoming grin. "Good morning to—oh, please tell me that's mine." She glanced to the tray.

"Compliments of your friend, who may or may not have done prison time," he teased.

"Do I want to know?" Laken asked, her eyes narrowing as she pulled out a cup from the tray he extended.

He opened his mouth then shook his head instead.

"Yeah, with Kess, less is more. God put a huge amount of attitude in such a small person."

"You can say that again."

"Oh, where have you been all my life?" Laken whispered to the coffee before taking a sip.

"Should I be jealous?"

"No competition." She winked.

Cyler started to close the distance between them. "Good to know."

"Coffee will always be first in my heart," Laken added, flirting.

"Oh? Is that how it is?" he replied, pulling her against him, taking her mouth in a searing yet quick kiss.

"You're a close second, but that's all I can promise. And, I'm on the clock so..." She pulled away, but not before giving him a daring grin.

"Yeah, I'm not so great at keeping my hands to myself." As she turned around he reached out and grabbed her ass.

At her squeal, he chuckled. Laken whirled around and glared at him, and he laughed harder.

"Hands off. This is my place of work. Thank you. I think that qualifies as sexual harassment?" she challenged.

Cyler placed his hands on his hips. "Soon I'll be the management, and I'll take all the complaints you want to give me. In fact, let's go and have a private meeting to discuss those concerns you have. My office is just down the hall."

Laken rolled her eyes, but she grinned as well. "You're trouble."

"In every way, ma'am."

"Are you two done flirting, or do I need to wait longer for breakfast?" Jack called from the hall. "Laken, honey, what time do we need to leave? Cyler here is driving us."

Laken's gaze shot to Cyler's, a hundred emotions flashing through before she closed them off. "We need to leave about nine-thirty," she answered slowly.

"Good. Now, about breakfast? Man can't live by coffee alone, sweetheart. I've tried," Jack replied.

"It's all ready. I actually made a quiche! And it didn't burn! Granted, it was a frozen quiche I just warmed up, but it counts."

"And the burning smell?" Cyler asked, goading her.

She glared. "Was the leftover burnt lasagna on the bottom of the oven."

Cyler clapped. "I'm proud."

Laken glared daggers.

"Okay, let's eat before there's bloodshed." Jack stepped into the kitchen and clapped his hands once before shuffling over to the table.

Breakfast was finished quickly, and before long, Cyler was playing the chauffeur as he drove to the doctor's office for Jack. Laken was in the back of the quad cab, and as he caught glimpses of her in his rearview mirror, he noted the tension in her expression.

This wasn't going to be good.

"Okay, Jack. Let's get this over with." He pulled into the parking lot, his gaze continually straying to Laken.

But she was in full nurse-mode, no longer displaying any traces of the previous tension. She was all calm smiles as they walked into the office.

To the doctor's credit, they didn't wait long, and soon they were in the small examination room, posters of medical research, vaccination information, and flu-symptom charts decorating the pale green walls.

"Why are doctors' offices always painted some sickly color? It's kinda twisted," Cyler commented, his own nerves starting to grow tighter.

"Psychology," Laken answered, turning to him. "The cooler and more neutral the tone, the more relaxing. It's much better to have a pale green or blue than a vibrant red or orange. It helps the patient relax."

"The only thing I'm feeling is irritated."

Jack snorted. "Because it's your appointment?"

Cyler glared at his father but kept his mouth shut. As much as he hated to admit it, the man had a point. He didn't even have to be here. Yet here he was, staring at the rack of outdated magazines.

All this for a girl.

Oh, how the mighty have fallen. He smirked to himself and shook his head.

"The nurse should be in soon. She'll take your vitals, and then you'll see the doctor."

"Same ol', same ol'." Jack shrugged, adjusting his position on the patient table, the tissue-paper barrier beneath him crinkling with each movement.

A knock at the door had Cyler stepping out of the way as a petite older woman scurried in, her face pinched as she took in the crowded room. "If you'll excuse me, I need a few vitals, Mr. Myer."

In short order, she'd taken his temperature, his blood pressure, and asked several questions about sleep, appetite, and pain, and depression. With a quick nod, she was out the door.

"Why didn't you just do that, honey?" Jack turned to Laken as he asked the question.

"Because it's her job, she's in the system, and it's much easier for her to chart the details than me," she answered succinctly, though her calming smile softened the business-like tone.

Cyler could feel the tension in the room. The way Laken kept her distance from him was both amusing and irritating. He understood the need for it, and how she was determined to separate Laken-the-nurse from Laken-the-lover—he bit back a grin at his stupid phrasing—and right now, he had to admit it was necessary.

Another knock on the door stole his attention, and an older gentleman strode in, his bifocals low on his nose as he studied the chart in front of him. "Mr. Myer, good to see you." He spoke without looking up. As he closed the folder, he scanned the room, his eyes pausing on Cyler. "I'm afraid we haven't met." He extended his hand. "I'm Dr. Wills."

Cyler took his extended hand and shook, noting the doctor wasn't afraid to give a solid shake. "Cyler Myer. Jack's my fa-ther." He darn-near choked on the word.

"Ah, I see. Pleased to meet you Cyler." He turned to Laken. "Nurse Garlington." He gave a firm nod.

"Dr. Wills." She offered him a warm smile, and Cyler was thankful the doctor was old enough to be her grandfather.

"Well, it looks like you and I need to have a discussion, Jack. Would you like to have that in private?" He let the question linger as he took a seat on the swivel stool.

Jack nodded. "No need, Doc. I'm pretty sure I know what's coming and I've got nothing to hide."

Dr. Wills nodded, then opened his mouth to speak.

Jack interrupted. "Before you start, just...just save all the technical jumbo for Laken here. I just want it cut and dry, okay? I'm a simple man, don't sugarcoat it or use fancy words, just...lay it out." The tissue cover on the medical bench tore slightly as Jack shifted again, yet his gaze was focused on the doctor, waiting.

"I can respect that, Jack." Dr. Wills took a deep breath. "While every patient is different, in my experience, you've got about six-to-eight weeks left, and it's going to go downhill fast. Laken and I are going to set up a different string of pain meds, and she's already arranged for you to have a walker and a wheelchair. Walking will get harder because breathing will become more difficult. Your lungs can't absorb the oxygen like they need to, making you weak and feeble. If you have any final affairs to take care of, I suggest doing those in the next week or so."

Jack nodded, folding his hands as he regarded the doctor. "Guessed as much. Well, at least I'm under good care." He gave a wink to Laken.

Cyler glanced to her, noticing a sheen of moisture in her eyes, yet she didn't break but gave a firm nod to Jack and patted his shoulder gently.

It was hard to watch, to hear, to simply be a part of it all. And damn it, he hated how he had a growing respect for how Jack was facing death. How difficult would that be to hear that only weeks were left? He couldn't imagine, yet Jack was smiling, winking at the beautiful girl across the room, and now was comforting her.

"It's going to be just fine. You'll see." He winked again at Laken and turned to the doctor. "If that's all?"

Dr. Wills's eyebrows shot up, but he cleared his throat as if trying to hide his surprise. "You always were tougher than rawhide, Jack. I'll be available for you, and Nurse Garlington has been keeping me in the loop. The important thing is to keep on top of the pain. It's better to manage it than to let it get too much to bear then try to tamp it back down. So don't be a hero, Jack. Just tell her if you need more medication, alright?"

"Fine, fine." Jack waved off the doctor's advice.

Dr. Wills glanced to Laken as if communicating the need to watch him. Laken nodded, a grin tipping her lips.

"Well, it was a pleasure to see you all again, and meet you, Cyler. Hope you enjoy that great sunshine we've been having." And with a soft click of the door, the doctor was gone.

"Well, that could have been worse." Jack shrugged.

Laken gave him a bemused smile. "Yup, find that silver lining, Jack," she teased.

"Let's get home." Jack stood slowly, his frame stooping as he started to shuffle from the room.

Laken opened the door for him, and in a few minutes, they were back in the truck on the way home.

"Laken, honey. You have the rest of the day off, right. I've got that other woman comin'?" Jack asked, his eyes closed as he leaned back.

"Nothing's wrong with your memory."

"Like a steel trap." Jack pointed to his head.

"With rusty teeth," Cyler muttered.

"Heard that."

"Hearing's good, too."

"I've already established that. Now, what was I saying? Oh, yes. Laken, honey? Go and get out a bit. If what the doc says is true, then you're going to have less time off in the future, and I want you to take some time to yourself while you can, alright? And know this is a sacrifice for me."

"Jack, I—"

"Quit arguing. It makes me tired and grumpy."

Cyler watched Laken grin in the rearview mirror. "Fine," she answered.

"Good. You'd think I was asking you to do something terrible."

Laken met Cyler's gaze in the mirror, and he had to force himself to break the eye contact to watch the road. "So, you want to work in the barn or"—he grinned to himself, having a great idea—"we can float in the river."

"I vote plan B," Jack mumbled. "It's low this time of year, and if you take the canyon, you'll have a pretty great view."

Cyler waited for Laken's reply.

"Manual labor or floating on a river in the sunshine. Hard one," she joked. "I vote plan B too. As long as there's food involved."

Chuckling to himself, he couldn't resist the opportunity to tease. "What? You don't want to cook us something up for the trip?"

"Mean," she shot back.

"Can't be good at everything, honey." Jack tried to smooth her ruffled feathers.

Laken arched a brow as Cyler glanced at her in the mirror again. "It will take me a few minutes to check the old tubes in the barn, but they should still be okay. In the meantime, you can get Jack all situated. Sound good?"

"Sounds good," she answered as they pulled in to the ranch.

Cyler helped Laken from the pickup and waited as she took Jack's arm and helped him walk to the house. As soon as they disappeared inside, he turned to the barn. A green sedan pulled up, and he assumed it was the on-call nurse, Paige. He headed to the barn, thinking.

Floating the river was great idea, and he was pretty sure Laken would love it. Plus, it would give them some privacy, his body all too aware of what that could imply. Margaret nickered as he passed her stall, and he paused a moment to pet her nose then moved on to the back room. It was crazy how a million memories could live in one place. And just like he'd left them years ago, the deflated tubes and rafts were stacked neatly, collecting dust. With a flip of the air compressor switch, he was pumping them up and checking for holes. This would be his first real date with Laken, and he wanted it perfect.

He knew she was struggling with the news from Jack's doctor; the moisture in her eyes gave away her deep emotions. Hopefully, this would be a way to escape, if only for a moment. If he were guessing, Laken didn't get to escape much, and she was so busy taking care of others, she rarely thought of taking care of herself. But that was then, this was now. And now, she had him. So, come hell or high water, she was going to have the time of her life.

He'd see to it.

Chapter 16

The sun was arcing over the Yakima Canyon as the river lazily tugged her raft along. A soft breeze made the heat more bearable, and just for good measure, she pulled the cap off the sunscreen and sprayed another layer.

"Having fun yet?" Cyler asked from his massive black tube, tied to her raft.

She grinned. "Yup! I can't believe I've never done this before!" And it was true. When Jack said they could float the river, she kinda knew what to expect, but she didn't think it would be so…therapeutic. Out here, there was nothing demanding her time or attention. She didn't feel guilty about not being productive with her time, and cell service was sketchy at best. She could just be. The sound of the flowing water was a relaxing background to the shifting scenery.

"Tell me you've at least driven the canyon?" Cyler asked.

"I don't think so. I usually take the freeway."

Cyler's chest glistened from the spray of water that he was constantly splashing on himself to keep cool. His walnut-colored hair was covered by an old baseball cap, shielding his bright blue eyes and making them a deeper color as he regarded her. "We'll drive it sometime. You can see bighorn sheep, and the cliffs are breathtaking."

"Not such a fan of heights," Laken replied.

"If you fell, you'd just hit water. No big deal," he answered with a smile.

"How about I admire the cliffs from the river-level," she countered.

"That works too."

And that was how the past few hours had gone. A little bit of conversation, a little bit of silence—truly fantastic to just be comfortable in her own skin with another person. Yet, in thinking of skin, her mind took a turn down memory lane as she mulled over last night. Truly, she'd never, ever,

ever slept with a guy that quickly after meeting him! It was not her usual behavior, yet she couldn't muster up enough shock to be sorry. Rather, she'd been wondering—hoping, really—he'd kiss her again, or even that she'd have the chance to initiate the kiss, just as long as the kissing happened! They were alone and, well, with the diagnosis from Dr. Wills, that alone time was going to be in short supply.

A wave of guilt washed over her as she thought about how selfish that sounded. But she didn't resent Jack needing more of her time; she regretted it because that meant that time was getting cut short. She hated it, wanting more, yet time never stopped moving forward, pressing onward, not respecting those with quickly filtering sand through the hourglass.

"You're not relaxed anymore. Why?" Cyler tugged on the rope connecting them and pulled himself closer.

Laken gave him a sidelong glance. "Noticed that, did you?"

"Yup, like an open book."

"Shoot. I was just thinking about time."

"And how it passes really quickly?" he asked.

"Yeah, it always does. Sometimes I feel older than I actually am." She offered a small smile.

"Old soul," Cyler remarked, reaching to lace his fingers through hers.

"You could say that."

"Life is full of things that can either give us joy or steal it. But Laken, that's part of its beauty. So, enjoy it. Leave the rest of the tension, the worry, leave it behind. Because right now, it's just you and me…and this really lazy river. And there's nowhere else I'd rather be than here with you." Cyler gave a quick grin that turned mischievous.

Laken narrowed her gaze, all melancholy gone. "What?"

"Nothing." Cyler blinked innocently then splashed her, making a huge wave of chilly water wash over her.

"Ah!" Laken squealed, covering her face. As she glanced up to glare at Cyler, he splashed her again. "Why?" she shouted, covering her face.

"Because there's a time to be serious, and there's a time to cut loose and enjoy life. And just in case there's confusion, this is one of the times to enjoy life." He laughed.

"I'll show you enjoying life," Laken threatened before creating a huge splash that washed over Cyler, his laugher echoing around the canyon.

"Is that all you've got? Weak!"

Laken growled and turned her raft, slipping her feet into the water and kicking her feet so that it splashed water all over him as well.

"I've seen better!" Cyler called out in the middle of the onslaught.

Fine. Laken grinned and made a huge splash with her feet then slid off her tube quickly. She ducked under the water and popped up behind Cyler. He was leaning forward, watching for her to appear in front of him.

"How about this?" she asked before pushing down on the rear of his tube, making him somersault backward into the water beside her.

His eyes crested the surface just as his hat floated by. Laken reached up and grabbed it, grinning widely as she placed the soggy thing back on his head.

"Is that better?"

"Eh, it'll do," Cyler teased, reaching out for the rope that connected their tubes.

"But I have a better idea." He arched a brow, standing up in the semi-shallow water.

"Oh?" Laken asked, finding her footing as well on the slippery rocks beneath.

"Yeah," he whispered then reached out and pulled her in, her feet slipping but finding solid rock as he pressed his lips to hers. Immediately the cold water was forgotten as the warmth of his kiss seared through her. Familiar, exciting, the passion caused her to lose herself to the sensation of his slick skin pressing against hers, her body remembering last night. But a moment later, she was being lifted.

"Hold your breath," Cyler warned before throwing her into the water, her legs kicking just before she hit the surface.

"Not fair," she sputtered as she spat a mouthful of water on him.

"All's fair in love and war, sweetheart."

"I'll remember that," she shot back, laughing as she waded to her tethered raft that Cyler held for her.

As she sat back down, Cyler leaned over, searing her lips with a kiss. "All's fair in love and war, but I promise that the war will be fun, and the love part will be even more so," he whispered against her lips then backed away, holding her gaze before he turned to hop onto his tube.

"Shall we?" he asked as he held out his hand to her.

Laken grinned, taking his hand. His warm gaze melted her from the inside out.

And she knew that he wasn't just holding her hand.

He was holding her heart.

Chapter 17

The next few weeks passed quickly. Cyler made the necessary arrangements so that he could spend three-day weekends at the ranch, which not only gave him the time he needed to be with Laken but also allowed him to keep up with Margaret's care and the rest of the ranch. Each week saw a marked decline in Jack, and consequently, his resolve to hate the old man was crumbling faster and faster.

It had been a long work week and was finally time for him to head to the ranch, to head home. It was odd, having it feel like home now, but he had to give credit to Laken. She was the difference, and he'd never loved anyone more.

The nights he'd spent away had been torturous, and he'd missed the soft warmth of her body snuggled next to his and the way she woke up with her hair splayed all over her face and pillow.

It had been a struggle, coaxing her into his bed at first. She'd fought tooth-and-nail, saying how it wasn't at all *professional* behavior. But he'd kiss her into silence, and when she'd come up for air, he'd threaten to wake up Jack.

It had worked like a charm.

One night last weekend, Cyler had woken in the guest room with Laken's side of the bed cold. After padding quietly to Jack's room, he'd found her asleep on the chair. After giving a quick glance to Jack to make sure he was asleep, he gathered her up in his arms and carried her back to his bed.

That was the first night he'd told her he loved her.

Of course, he'd also assumed she was still asleep.

Which she wasn't.

Still drowsy, she'd stretched on the bed, reaching for him. As she wound her fingers through his hair, she'd whispered the sweet words back, setting his world on fire and calming it at the same time.

I love you.

Three little words that could change the world.

His world.

It might be quick, but like he always reminded himself, *when I know, I'll know.*

And he knew.

And soon she'd have the ring to prove it.

The thought alone had him pushing the truck past the speed limit as he passed through the Manastash Ridge and into Ellensburg. From the top, the town looked like one of his grandmother's quilts, pieces of different shapes, sizes, and colors all connected and making a beautiful piece of art. After descending the hill and taking the exit into the town, he grew impatient with each closing mile. Soon he was crunching down the gravel driveway, his heart slowing its pace as he caught sight of the house.

In short work, he was opening the front door and grinning wildly. Hurrying down the hall, he glanced into the kitchen to see Laken sitting with Jack at the table, her usual welcoming smile traded for worry lines around her green eyes.

As soon as she saw him, the expression melted into relief then slowly grew tense once more. That was when he noticed that Jack was on the phone.

"No—" He bit the word off in a gruff tone. "I don't think that's a good idea."

Cyler mouthed, *"Who?"* to Laken.

She rose from her chair and patted Jack's shoulder.

As she walked over to Cyler, he pulled her into a deep hug. "What's going on, sweetheart?" he murmured into her ear, his body relaxing when he inhaled her warm scent.

Laken glanced to Jack as he answered something else. "Well, today he got a phone call from his lawyer. It looks like Breelee is back in town." She paused, glancing to Jack briefly. "She knows about Jack's condition and is threatening to hire a lawyer."

Breelee's name sent a cold chill down Cyler's back and set his teeth on edge. "What does she want?" he ground out.

"Jack's talking with her now, so I'm not sure. But he's pretty stressed." Laken tilted her head, motioning to the way Jack's fist was clenching and unclenching at his side.

"She always did bring out the best in people."

"I can see that," Laken replied softly without heat.

"The answer is no." Jack growled, slammed the phone on the table, then picked it back up before fumbling as he tried to end the call.

Silently, Laken walked over and took it from him. She ended the call calmly and set the phone back down.

Jack laid his head in his hands, groaning. "You know, what's a man gotta do to die in peace?"

"She after money or the ranch?" Cyler asked, taking a seat. His jaw was ticking from residual anger.

"Anything and everything she can try to get her hands on. Bo says she can't do anything, but she's a crafty bitch, and I don't like her sniffing around," Jack answered.

"Fantastic," Cyler snapped.

"You think *I'm* happy about this? Woman was a thorn in my side from day one!"

Cyler snorted. "Woman was my fiancée, Jack. Remember?"

"And I did you a favor."

"You did what? How in the hell does sleeping with my bride-to-be add up to doing me any favors?" Cyler shoved back from the table, anger feeding off the tension in the room.

"Son, have you no sense in that pea-brain of yours?" Jack gave him a condescending glare. "I'll admit, I was an opportunist and dumber than a box of rocks, but I didn't seduce her. She came over and propositioned me! Now, I'll admit I should have said no, but well, I didn't, and that's when you came over. When you left, I figured I had nothing left to lose. You'd go and tell your mom, and that would be the end of that. I knew I'd most certainly lost you. All I had was Breelee. So, we hopped it to Mexico and—"

"What in the hell? Do you know how warped you are?"

Jack rolled his eyes, adding insult to his tone. "Son, are you honestly still busted up about the idea that your engagement with Breelee broke off?"

Cyler pulled up short. "No, she's a conniving bitch." He spat.

"Then, you're welcome. In a way, I saved you. You thought she was so perfect." He snorted. "Remember the first night you brought her over to meet us? What you didn't know was that she was flirting with me the whole night, whenever you turned your back. At first I didn't get it, but she, uh, made that distinction later."

Cyler held up his hand. "I don't want to know."

"I don't want to tell you," Jack answered.

"But—" Cyler rubbed the back of his neck, processing everything. "But, okay, let's just say I can see past the Breelee incident, as twisted as that is. What about the divorce papers for Mom? The way you didn't even go to her funeral—"

"Wait right there." Jack held up his hand. "First things first. Your mom deserved better than an old tomcat like me. I gave her the option. *Option.* She didn't have to go through the divorce—"

"But you married Breelee."

"How in the hell could I have married Breelee if I was still married to your mother?" he asked, shaking his head in confusion. "Think about it, son. I couldn't have. That was just something Breelee wanted you, and everyone else, to believe. I didn't hear about it till much later, and it was too late by then to fix." He shrugged.

Cyler's mind was spinning. "But…the funeral." It was all he had left.

Jack took a deep breath then released it. "Your grandfather, Red?"

Cyler nodded.

"He said he'd disinherit you if I darkened the door of his daughter's funeral. So, I stayed away. It was a good thing too. Bastard died a few months later, and you inherited quite a pretty penny, didn't you?" Jack asked.

Cyler swallowed, his world spinning out of control. "It started the bankroll for my construction company. It made all the difference," he answered honestly.

"Then, you see why I didn't go. You know, it wasn't about me as much as it was about you, son. I told Laken—" Jack paused, searching the room as if suddenly remembering she was present.

Cyler searched too, noticing that somehow, she'd snuck out of the room, giving them privacy.

"Damn woman." Jack swore under his breath but grinned. "What I was going to say, was that I told Laken that all your anger toward me was a reaction. I had to do something to warrant that reaction. And I did. And I deserve the entire wrath and then some. But I'm glad that I could set the record straight on a few things. Now maybe you'll get some closure too. Lord knows you need it, Cyler."

"I—" Cyler rubbed his hand down his face. "I don't know what to say."

"There's a first time for everything."

"Pain in the ass," Cyler shot back but without heat.

"Takes one to know one," Jack retorted.

"True, true," Cyler conceded.

"But, I don't get how Breelee can come after you if she wasn't ever married to you? What entitlement does she have?" Cyler asked.

"I'm not sure. Honestly, she probably just thinks she can charm her way into something. You'll want to watch your back, son."

"I don't want to be in a ten-mile radius of that she-devil."

"You and me both."

Cyler stared at the table for a moment. "I better find Laken." He frowned. "Jack?"

"Yeah?"

"Thanks. I, uh, I needed to know those things. And in some sordid way, I can see what you mean when you said you did me a favor. It's still sick and abnormal...but I think I get it now. Thanks." He nodded once, and with a hesitant hand, patted Jack's shoulder.

"You have no idea how long I've wanted to hear that, son. And for what it's worth, I'm sorry."

Cyler nodded then walked down the hall, his mind flipping through memories but reversing them, like reading something backwards and using a mirror to understand it. If you try to read it without the reflection, it's jacked-up, but look in the reflection and suddenly it makes more sense.

"Laken?" he called out as he walked into the living room. She was nowhere to be seen. Next, he checked the laundry room and their bedroom. Finally, he walked out to the barn, and as he slid open the door, he saw her talking softly to Margaret.

"There you are." He strode up to her, his tension melting away.

"I thought you two needed a moment." Laken gave him a wink.

"A few moments actually."

"Is there blood?" she asked cautiously.

"Nope. Not this time. But no promises for the future. You understand."

"What's a good family discussion if no one bleeds, right?"

"You get me."

"I'm learning too," she teased. "How did it go?"

Cyler trailed his hand down Margaret's face, taking a deep breath. "Well, we talked about the stuff we needed to talk about, and my world was pretty much hung up to dry, and now I'm re-evaluating my life."

Laken blinked then grinned. "Sounds like it was an enlightening talk."

"It was. Jack's still a twisted son of a bitch, but oddly enough, I can see why he did some of what he did, and how in some demented way, he thought he was doing the right thing."

"I'm glad. I'm not saying any of his actions were right, but I'm glad you were able to talk. That's—that's really important, Cyler. Because someday soon, you won't have this opportunity."

"I know. Sucks. Whoever knew the devil was flesh and bones, huh?" He sighed.

"Who knew?"

"Laken, I, uh, want to talk to you about Breelee." Cyler approached the topic with more than a share of hesitancy. It wasn't like he was divulging some shadowy secret, but the topic brought him to a dark place, one he didn't want to explore unless necessary.

And damn the woman, her presence made it necessary.

Laken turned to him, seeming to give her full attention as she leaned against the stall door.

His eyes strayed to the way her hip curved out, and he forced his gaze to meet hers. "You probably already know this, but hear me out."

Laken nodded.

"I don't trust her, and if I'm not here, and she comes prowling around, I want you to call me immediately. Then call the police. It's trespassing, you understand? I'm not wanting to be that overbearing and jackass of a boyfriend, but so help me, if she lays one stilettoed heel on this property—"

Laken interrupted, "Give me a little credit. I think I can handle her."

"I don't doubt you. I just don't trust her." Cyler wrapped a hand around her waist, drawing her close.

"Well, when you put it that way," Laken replied, her eyes twinkling as she wrapped her arm around his waist and hugged him tightly.

Cyler kissed the top of her head, her coconut-scented shampoo reminding him of falling asleep beside her. "You're kind of important, you know," he murmured into her hair, kissing it again.

"Eh, I'm kinda fond of you too."

He tickled her hip, and she tried to jerk out of his embrace, but he held her tightly, squeezing till she squealed and giggled. His answering grin was wide and unhindered while she wrestled within his grasp, tempting his body, and securing the hold she had on his heart.

"Mean," she grumbled when he stopped and pulled her back into a hug.

"Never implied that I wasn't."

"Valid."

"Just as long as we're clear."

"Crystal," she murmured into his shirt, her head just at his heart.

He rested his chin on her head, enjoying the moment. But something else was bothering him. "How was this past week? Anything I need to know about Jack?" It was the usual conversation they'd had once Jack was in bed, but now seemed like a good time. Get it over and done with.

Laken tensed beneath his grasp. "He had a rough week. Today is his best day, actually. Tuesday and Thursday, he didn't even get up from bed. Yesterday, he did for a few hours, but only made it as far as the living room. Today, he made it to the kitchen. That's when you came in."

Cyler nodded. Jack's face was drawn; his angular cheeks had grown sharper each time Cyler had come back to the ranch.

"How's his pain?" he asked, remembering the doctor's visit.

"Dr. Wills has balanced the medication well. Right now, Jack's good on that end."

"At least there's one good thing," Cyler encouraged.

"For now," Laken answered, her tone solemn.

"For now," Cyler affirmed. Damn it, he was starting to worry about Jack. A hell of a lot of good it would do, but the old devil was kinda growing on him. Damn, that left a bitter taste in his mouth just thinking it.

"I'm glad you cleared the air, Cyler. Honestly, I'm going to shift into palliative-nurse mode for a second, okay?" She disengaged from his arms and took a step back, her expression soft and compassionate.

"Fine, but be quick about it. I want the girlfriend back." He tried to tease, but judging by the look on her face, his efforts had fallen short.

"Based on the timeline from Dr. Wills, this last month is going to be rough. Right now, you're seeing the best. Jack's going to start spiraling, and with each loop of the spiral, it will go quicker. Next week when you come back, he won't be leaving his room. The week after, he won't be breathing on his own. The week after that, he'll be under heavy sedation to manage his pain, and the week after that, you'll be saying your final goodbye. What I'm saying is that if you have anything else to speak about with Jack, do it now. Each day is a new chance, and those chances are numbered." Laken lifted her chin, as if putting on a brave face, for him.

"I realize that." Cyler nodded. "You know, death really sucks." He sighed. "Steals your dignity and your chances. But I think Jack and I have a truce of some sort, so don't worry your pretty little head, alright? And I'll be sure that if I need to pick a fight with the old man, I'll do it now. Wouldn't want an unfair fight. That's unsporting." He tried to lighten the mood again.

This time his efforts were rewarded with a small tip of Laken's lips into a grin. "Wouldn't want an unfair fight."

"Nope."

With a shake of her head, she walked back into his waiting arms. "We should go inside. Jack will need help getting to his room."

"Getting cockblocked by the old man. Damn it," Cyler teased.

Laken pinched his ass, and he jumped, glaring as she giggled and released him.

"And you said I was mean."

"Never said I wasn't," she shot back, using his words against him as she strode from the barn and into the evening sun.

"Well, as long as we're on the same page." Cyler shook his head and followed her to the house.

"Jack?" Laken called.

"Here, here. It's about time you guys came back inside. I need help getting to my room. Damn walker," Jack grumbled from the table in the kitchen.

"Sorry, I was getting bossed around by your son. You should really work on him, Jack," Laken teased as she entered the kitchen. Rather than grab the walker to the side, she rolled out a folded wheelchair from corner and set it up. "Let's try this instead."

Jack's glare was cold as ice. "I'm not using that damn thing."

Cyler quickly jumped in, unable to resist. "What? You have something against a beautiful woman pushing you around?"

"Ass." Jack directed his glare to him.

"What?" Cyler raised his hands innocently.

"Both of you..." Laken arched a brow. "C'mon, Jack. I won't be pushy. I'll even let you boss me around and tell me where to go," she encouraged.

"Because there are so many places to go around here," Jack muttered. "Fine. Just, get it over with. I'm tired anyway and need my nap. Gotta keep my wits about me with you two around. Lord knows what this one's planning." He jabbed his thumb toward Cyler.

"Fair enough," Cyler answered.

Laken rolled her eyes but was quick to pounce on Jack's agreement. In short work, she was wheeling him down the hall toward his room.

Cyler glanced around the kitchen, noting that nothing was out for dinner. After checking the fridge, he started to make some spaghetti. As he was browning the beef on the range, a warm hand snaked around his stomach.

"Hungry?" he asked, glancing down to the hand at his waist. Manicured, blood-red nails flexed into his stomach and gently clawed away. His body locked down in cold dread.

"Miss me?"

He'd recognize that voice anywhere; it had haunted his nightmares long enough. Stepping from her clutches, he sidestepped and bit back a shiver of revulsion at the woman before him. A moment later, his brain snapped into gear.

"How the hell did you get in here?" His nostrils flared as he glared at her. He quickly shut off the gas to the burner and put more distance between them.

Breelee swept a length of long brunette hair behind her shoulder as she popped a hip suggestively. "The door was open, and I knocked." She shrugged delicately.

"In that order?" He cut in.

She sighed dramatically. "Knowing Jack's condition, I figured the kind thing to do was let myself in and check on him. But I must say, I'm surprised to see you here." She arched a brow, her gaze narrowing as it trailed from his boots to the top of his head. "Cyler Myer, I must say, you might be a lot of things, but hard to look at isn't one of them."

He flexed his fists, feeling his forearms tighten, his blood pounding with fury, but he held his ground. "Sure was a damn-quiet knock."

"Delicate hands." She lifted one as if proving her point.

A tic started in his jaw as he studied her. Little had changed about Breelee. Although still attractive, her beauty was of a harsh nature, all hard lines and fake warmth. Her dark brown hair was still the same espresso color, her legs apparently still her favorite asset to flaunt in her cut-off shorts, leaving little to the imagination. Rather than entice him, the very sight of her caused a revulsion to rise in his stomach. All the beauty in the world couldn't hide such a black heart.

"If that's all, you can rest assured you did the *kind* thing and can now show yourself the door. I'm here and have everything under control." He'd purposefully left out any mention of Laken, hoping to get rid of the she-devil before Laken had to deal with her.

"But surely you need some help." She tilted her head innocently.

"No, that's where I come in." Laken breezed into the kitchen, her face hosting a beatific grin that had Cyler narrowing his eyes. It was too innocent, too perfectly masked.

"Oh." Breelee turned toward the voice and did a quick onceover of Laken then dismissed her. "And who might you be?"

"She's—"

"Palliative care nurse for HCEW." Laken interrupted his attempt to direct the attention back to himself. She held out her hand to Breelee, her expression open and welcoming.

Breelee relaxed and took her hand, giving one of those weak-ass handshakes that reminded him of an old lady at a country club, afraid to get her hands dirty.

"And you are?" Laken asked, disengaging her hand.

"Breelee Hampton. I'm an old family friend."

Cyler snickered. "Sure, you are."

"Lovely, I've heard so much about you," Laken added. "So, you'll understand if I ask you to respect my patient's request that only family be present. Can I show you the door, Miss Hampton?"

Breelee narrowed her eyes, studying Laken, probably trying to figure out if the nurse standing before her was as innocent as she looked, and if she had any chance of manipulating her.

"Well, it is late. It might be better if I come by a different time." Breelee spoke carefully, her gaze never leaving Laken, testing the waters likely.

"You're more than welcome to call and make arrangements. In fact, here's my number." Laken walked over to the counter beside Cyler, picked up her purse, and withdrew a card. Before she turned, she gave him a quick wink and walked back to Breelee. "Here you are. It was great to put a face with the name, and I hope you have a great evening. It's beautiful outside, isn't it?"

Laken gestured to the hall, and Breelee's brow furrowed, but she followed. Laken escorted her to the door then closed and locked it. Soon he was standing behind her, pulling her back against his chest as he watched Breelee drive away.

"Ok, so I figured you had a plan, but would you mind telling me what the hell that was?" he murmured into her hair, holding her close, finally relaxing knowing that Breelee was putting distance between them.

"She's not the first nor the last person with selfish intentions who's tried to rebuild a relationship with one of my patients. Honestly, they come out of the woodwork once they hear that someone is passing, and when that person has any sort of monetary value..." She let the words linger, a lamenting tone to her voice. "It's easy to pick them out from the rest who, honestly, are only trying to make things right for the sake of making peace. People like that"—she nodded toward the window—"are only after what they can do to benefit themselves."

Cyler rubbed his nose along her head, taking a deep breath. "Well, you got rid of her faster than I was able to," he admitted, "and with less violence."

At that, Laken giggled. "Yeah, I figured. You were in full fight-mode. You should have seen yourself when I walked into the kitchen." She shook her head. "Basically, I was thinking how do I keep him from prison?" she teased.

"That's not too far from the truth."

"People like her will only rise to the occasion to fight. They use it as justification. I mean, if you're an ass to her, then she will use that to quantify her reasoning to be here. I mean, if you're an ass to her, surely you're an ass to Jack, and someone needs to help." She sighed. "You see, don't you? People always have reasons, and they'll twist them as much as possible to make themselves look good. Even if the only person they look good to is themselves." She took a deep breath through her nose, her head lowering as if weighed down by the truth of it all.

"I hadn't thought of it that way."

"Yeah, I've seen a lot." She drew out the words. "But with the bad there's always the good." She turned in his embrace, wrapped her arms around his neck then pulled him down into a kiss. "Also, one more thing. The card I gave her is for people who tend to be problematic. It will connect her to a division of our company that deals with grief and personal growth."

"Hmm." He tasted her lips once more, savoring the sensation and the rightness of the moment before pulling away just slightly. "Brilliant *and* beautiful. It's kinda sexy." He nipped at her lower lip, his body hardening as she traced her tongue along the seam of his lips in return. "Ready for bed? I'm exhausted." He feigned a yawn then pulled her up so that she straddled his hips as he hooked his hands under her sweet ass.

"It's not even six p.m.," she shot back, grinning against his lips before meeting his kiss once more.

"I woke up early."

"Sure, you did."

Cyler stood and started carrying her toward their room, but Jack's coughs sliced through the air like ice water, effectively halting his progress. With one glance, he saw Laken's eyes tighten as she glanced toward the sound. Sighing in resignation, he simply carried her to Jack's room and set her down before kissing her nose.

"I'm not going anywhere," he murmured softly, trailing his fingertips down her arm before turning to head back to the kitchen. If he wasn't getting laid, he might as well restart dinner.

He heard Laken speak softly to Jack, and he couldn't help but see the twist to what he had said to her. Sure, he wasn't going anywhere, but Jack? The same wasn't true for him. Time was sifting away, and in moments like these, an acute realization hit him with the force of a crashing wave. Time was running out.

And Breelee was lurking around.

And life seemed damn complicated.

And unfair.

Closing his eyes, he leaned against the counter. In a way, he'd just forgiven his father, and now that he'd finally released that burden, he felt like he'd been slapped with the reality that his father truly was leaving.

And this time it wasn't because it was his choice.

Death sucked.

He'd said it once; he'd say it a million times more.

And it never lost its truth.

The hatred and resentment for Jack had defended Cyler like a shield, protecting him from the truth while he was distracted with anger. But with that anger fading, all that was left was raw pain. Never had Cyler felt so helpless, so at a loss. As a man, he wanted to step in, fix it, do something, but it was impossible to fight death.

Eventually, it was one battle everyone lost.

Cyler took in a deep breath, focusing on the sound of the ticking clock in the kitchen, the way the floor creaked slightly from him shifting his feet, things that reminded him of anything other than the demons he couldn't fight.

"You okay?" Laken broke through his weak moment, and he stood straight, shrugging the weight off and into the darker recesses of his mind.

"I'm good."

"You suck at lying. I love that about you." She gave him a soft smile, her gaze understanding. "I'll be back in a few minutes. I just need to get some water for Jack."

Cyler moved over to the side, letting her grab a glass from the cabinet beside him. He watched as she filled it with cool water, his gaze using her as a lifeline. It was a vulnerable position, relying on someone else's experience, but there was no one else he'd rather trust with his father—or with his heart—than Laken.

She gave a squeeze to his arm and turned back toward Jack's room.

How did she remain so strong? To see death after death, to deal with families broken, to see lives end, and witness how others have to pick up the pieces and move on. It was astounding.

It was humbling.

But damn it all, it was nice that she at least had one flaw, horrible as that sounded.

With a self-deprecating grin, he turned to the stove.

Woman could do everything else...but cook.

Chapter 18

Blood stained the gauze as Laken helped Jack turn his head so that he wouldn't aspirate. The steroids he was on tended to make the blood thinner, and that wasn't doing him any favors. On the flipside, the steroids were allowing him clear airways, so that he could breathe. It was a fighting battle, one they were losing day by day, and each one broke her heart a little more.

"Stop giving me that pitying look, girl," Jack choked out. "I'm not dying yet, in spite of how I feel. Good Lord, why am I taking all these damn pills if I still feel like shit?"

Laken gave a weak smile. "Just think of how you'd feel if you didn't take them."

"Well, when you put it that way—" Jack started another coughing fit.

"Why don't you just quit arguing with me? Let's just operate under the premise that I'm always right," Laken teased, knowing that was often the best way to deal with a hard situation.

Jack glared, but didn't reply.

"See? Isn't that easier?" Laken winked.

Jack rolled his eyes.

"I'm going to set up an IV drip with some morphine. It will help with the pain so you can sleep tonight. Sound good? Thumbs-up?" Laken held up a thumb.

Jack twisted his lips but gave thumbs-up reluctantly.

"See? Always right." Laken walked over to her medical supplies on the other end of the room and pulled out a series of needles, lines, and the morphine drip. In short work, she had everything situated and soon was wrapping Jack's arm in a tourniquet and checking for a vein. His blood pressure was low, and he was dehydrated, so it took a little longer to find the best option. After a few minutes, she'd successfully inserted the needle and had taped his IV to his wrist and checked the drip.

"Why does it always feel so damn cold?" Jack whispered softly, holding up his hand and studying the needle below it.

"Because it *is* cold," Laken replied turning to him. "You're a toasty ninety-eight-point-six degrees. The fluid is about seventy-two."

"Dumb question," Jack muttered softly.

"Get some rest. Are you hungry?" Laken asked, but she was pretty sure she knew the answer. His appetite had waned, and it was to be expected.

"Not if you're cooking." Jack gave a tired grin and sunk into his pillows.

"Ha, ha. Funny." Laken arched a brow. "I think your son is taking care of it, so does that change your mind?" she asked, hopeful.

"Nah, I'm bushed. Save some for me tomorrow?" he asked.

Laken nodded once, watching as he closed his eyes and seemed to rest. She listened for a few moments, making sure his breathing sounded relaxed, but not too relaxed, before she closed the door partway, and headed down the hall.

Her stomach rumbled as she inhaled appreciatively the aromatic scent coming from the kitchen. "You know, I think I'll keep you around. As long as you feed me," Laken announced as she walked toward Cyler. She halted her steps as she studied the table.

Cyler had covered the table with a lace cloth, and a sputtering and slightly bent candle burned in a glass-holder in the middle. Two plates of spaghetti waited with steam curling around the top.

"Yup. Definitely keeping you around," Laken repeated, only more quietly as she met Cyler's gaze.

"Glad to know I can be of some use," he teased. "We can't exactly go out, and even if we could, you'd be worried about Jack the whole time. So, I figured I could just make it nice for us here." He hitched a shoulder.

Laken felt her cheeks ache from her wide smile as she flung herself into Cyler's arms, hugging him tightly. "Thank you."

"You're welcome. You know, if this is the response I get, I might have to do this every night." He flashed her a wink.

"It smells so good and I'm starving." Laken released him and walked over to the table.

Cyler beat her to the chair and pulled it out for her.

She grinned a thank you and sat down.

After taking his place across from her, he lifted his fork. "After dinner, I need to make a quick run to the grocery. All this was just to butter you up so you'd do dishes." He twirled the spaghetti around the tines and shoved it in his mouth, grinning at her all the while.

"Should have known," Laken teased before taking a bite. After swallowing, she shrugged. "Fine. I can do dishes. But tell me that you're meal planning for the next few days."

"Maybe, or maybe I have something else planned," he replied ambiguously before taking another bite.

"Hmm, a man of mystery. Just so you know, I prefer my men as cooks. Just saying. Mystery is totally overrated."

Cyler simply rolled his eyes.

It was a perfect moment. The day hadn't exactly been easy, and Laken guessed that seeing Breelee had been difficult for Cyler. Yet here he was, making the world stand still for the two of them. It was odd how he knew exactly what she needed, when she didn't even know she needed it herself. But this quiet, intimate dinner in the middle of the kitchen was perfect.

Laken thought about how people always talked about love, but few ever actually experienced it in all its glory. Sometimes there had been hints and glimpses of it, but to truly experience it was nothing like Laken had ever known. Love was terrifying and wonderful, and so much deeper than she'd ever expected.

"Something on your mind, sweetheart?" Cyler asked, pulling her from her thoughts.

She lifted a shoulder. "Just thinking about life. You know, it's kinda beautiful."

"Kinda, huh?" he teased.

"You know what I mean. It's just…I'm really glad you're here. I *kinda* like you."

"*Like*, huh? Well I kinda *love* you, Laken. Weeks ago, when I all but chased after you for that kiss, I told you I wouldn't take no for an answer." He chuckled. "You should have seen your face though. You'd have thought I had you at the end of my gun barrel."

"Hey! I was a little terrified."

"Maybe so. But you warmed up real quick." He winked.

Her face burned, remembering the pickup and the stargazing that didn't really happen. "Too quick."

"Life's uncertain. I'm learning that more and more. But there are a few things I'm sure about, and one of them is you, honey."

His blue eyes seared his words on her very soul as she met his gaze.

"I love you too."

"Good. I wasn't exactly giving you an option," Cyler teased, standing from his chair.

"You killed my moment."

"Nah, I'm just making you a new one."

He held out his hand, and she took it, rising from her chair. He met her lips with a searing kiss, nipping, teasing, loving her with each caress before breaking the exchange.

"I don't want to leave, but I know you'll love what I have planned. So, I'm going to step away, get in my truck, and be back in an hour. Oh, and I know you haven't had Paige out here for a while, so I asked Jack for her number. She's coming out in about an hour to give you a break."

"Wow, that's nice of her."

"She was more than happy to do it." He kissed the top of her forehead then backed away. "Damn, I hate leaving you, even for an hour." He gave her a broad grin, causing his blue eyes to crinkle before he gave a quick wave and darted out of the kitchen.

Laken sighed, watching him leave.

"I hate it when you leave too," she murmured as she heard the front door shut quietly. She took a deep breath. "Well, let's get this done."

In short work, she saved the remaining spaghetti for Jack, just in case, and cleaned the dishes. A knock on the door signal's Paige's arrival, and Laken greeted her with a hug. "I had no idea until Cyler just told me. Thanks for coming out."

"We all need a break sometimes. I'll just sit with Jack for a while and you go and have some fun." Paige nodded kindly, and disappeared down the hall.

Laken was setting a large quilt on the kitchen table when she heard Cyler's truck rumble up the drive.

As she went to the front porch, he waved her over to the truck. "Give me a hand? But no peeking."

"Sure." Laken lifted her crossed fingers.

"Funny."

"I thought so. At least I'm honest about my dishonesty."

"Yeah, you're a regular saint, Laken."

"I've been called worse."

"Just carry that bag. If you peek in there, I'll get rewarded." He handed her a paper sack.

She couldn't resist and glanced inside. A big grin covered her face. "Yes! Bless you." It was a twelve-ounce bag of Starbucks Pike Place roast. "I'm sure Kessed is taking good care of you, but I also know you're not going to be making your coffee runs as often, so…" He hitched a shoulder.

And Laken fell a little more in love.

"But first, coffee?" she joked.

"That's my girl," Cyler replied over his shoulder as they walked into the house.

Laken listened, but Jack was still sleeping quietly, so she headed to the kitchen to put the coffee away with Cyler and the mystery bag behind her.

"Don't peek," he warned then paused. "You know what, I don't trust you. Go outside and wait for me." He set his bags down and nodded toward the door.

"What?"

"You heard me. Outside." Cyler pointed and waited, giving her a steady stare.

"You don't scare me." Laken crossed her arms.

Cyler strode over to the counter and picked up the coffee, arching a brow in challenge.

"Fine! That was low," Laken grumbled, trying to hide her grin as she left the kitchen.

"Here." Cyler called quietly, and she turned.

The thick quilt landed against her chest. Instinctively, she held out her hands and caught it.

"Nice catch."

"Good reflexes," she shot back but turned to go out the screen door.

The summer temperature was still steady, and when she looked to the horizon, Laken could see the heat mirage distorting where the land ended and the sky began. Not much grass was left, and most of it was more brown than green, but she found a patch that seemed more welcoming than the rest and laid out the quilt.

"Alright, close your eyes," Cyler asked from the porch.

"Closing them," she answered.

Laken heard his boots crunch the brown grass as he walked over. The rustling of paper and a low curse had her grinning, wondering what he'd tipped over or messed up. "Everything okay?"

"Yeah, keep 'em closed," he murmured, and the sound of glass clinking softly had her curiosity growing. "Is there blood? I hear glass?" she teased.

"No blood. I'm starting to get a complex. You've asked that twice today. I don't know if that makes me sound like a badass or a walking disaster."

"It's a tossup."

"You know how to build a man up, Laken."

"I know. Another one of my many talents."

"Annoying talents."

"I never said they were good talents." She bit her lip as she grinned. "Can I open my eyes yet?"

"So impatient."

"So slow," she whined.

"Okay, you can open them now."

A battery-operated candle flickered its glow against a plate of grapes, sliced apples, and what looked like honeycomb. Next was a plate of various cheeses, some soft while others crumbling or slivers of a harder variety. Two wine glasses were sitting precariously on the bumpy quilt beside a bottle of wine. Another plate had dark chocolate sprinkled with pink sea salt, as well a lighter version that hinted at a sweeter taste.

"Whoa. Totally worth the wait." Laken glanced up, meeting Cyler's almost-wary expression.

"I'm glad you like it. Being romantic takes a huge effort on my part, and I wanted to make sure I got it right." His lips tipped into a lopsided grin, one that made his dimple deepen on that side. His blue eyes twinkled in the orange sunlight, and he glanced away as if slightly unsure.

Odd.

Her brow furrowed as she regarded him.

"Stop staring. I—I just wanted it to be right."

"Because I'm really picky," she taunted, reaching for a grape.

He lightly smacked her hand. "Hey, not yet." He held up a finger. "You've been winetasting, right?"

Laken shook her head. "Nope. I know, I know. It's like a sin, living here and not going to the local wineries, but I—I don't exactly have much free time and, well, Starbucks is closer?" She smiled like a kid trying to be pardoned from something wrong.

"What am I going to do with you?" Cyler muttered. "Okay, so let me explain all this." He sat up on his knees and started to point to the various things. "The grapes will bring out a different flavor in the wine versus the cheese. It's amazing. I went with a red blend, rather than, say, a cab. It's a little friendlier of a wine."

"You realize you just called wine friendly." Laken tilted her head, giving a sly grin.

"Pay attention." Cyler feigned a mock glare.

"Yes, sir." She saluted and watched as he picked up the bottle.

"This is from Gard Vintners. It's local and one of my favorites. You'll like it because it has a cocoa powder note and—"

"Note?"

"I have so much to teach you." Cyler closed his eyes and muttered, "Yes. *Notes*. It's the"—he twisted his lips as he thought—"subtle hints that come out in the wine. And it will change and highlight different flavors with different food pairings."

"Food. Now we're talking." Laken nodded her approval.

"You're killing me."

"In the best way possible."

"Sure." Cyler nodded, his tone heavy with sarcasm as he poured two glasses of wine. The deep red color swirled like a burgundy whirlpool around the glass till it settled. He held out a stem to her.

"Thanks." She took the glass and gently tilted it back and forth.

"Smell it first. Like this." He eddied the wine, like he had before, but tipped the glass slightly as he held it up to the sunlight. "See the streams of wine coming down the side? Those are the legs."

"Friendly wines with legs. You know, this is starting to sound less like winetasting and more like—"

"Just swirl your damn glass," Cyler interrupted, rolling his eyes. "The legs are the alcohol content."

"Friendly legs of alcohol." Laken smiled and swirled her glass as well, watching as the sunlight highlighted little streams. "Wow, that is kinda cool."

"Took you long enough. Okay. Now one more time then smell it." Cyler started swirling again and sniffed, closing his eyes. "Everything you smell is the bouquet, and with each rotation, different nuances come to the surface, changing the scent slightly."

Laken mirrored his actions, inhaling deeply. The hint of something dark and fruity hit her with a vague familiarity. "What is that? I can't think of what it smells like, but it's familiar."

"It gets easier as you practice. You're picking up plum and the cocoa powder I mentioned earlier," Cyler said.

"Yeah, that's it. Wow. I'm kinda impressed."

"That was *kinda* the plan. You're just making it really easy."

Laken rolled her eyes. "Yeah, well, it's the least I can do."

"Ok, swirl it again, take another deep inhale, and tell me what you think now."

Laken followed his directions, only this time the fruity scent was weaker, and a smoky note came to the surface. "Okay, I'm officially into this. Something's smoky? Tea-like? How does it do that?" She blinked at her wine glass, amazed she'd learned so much without even tasting it.

"I knew you'd love it. What you're smelling is a black tea note, and if you swirl it again, you might pick up olive or bay leaf."

Laken swirled the wine once more, this time trying to pick up the olive or bay-leaf note. Sure enough, it was there in the distant background.

"Take a sip now, just a small one," Cyler instructed, tipping his glass back.

Laken followed suit, the flavor practically assaulting her as she picked up the notes of fruity mixed with the dark cocoa and something deeper. Cherry?

"How many bottles did you bring?" Laken asked, smiling as Cyler rolled his eyes.

"Easy. I only brought one. That's more than enough."

"For you."

"For us both." Cyler shook his head as amusement danced in his gaze. "Alright, now take a grape and then take another sip. See if it changes."

"So now I have permission to eat?"

"Yes, unless you annoy me. Then you're cut off."

Laken made a lock-and-key motion on her lips and picked up a grape. She popped it in her mouth; the sweetness was even more powerful than she'd expected.

"Nice to know I can control you with food."

"You do know how I cook, right?" Laken asked after swallowing.

"Yeah, I see your point." Cyler chuckled. "Take a sip, and tell me what you think."

Laken sipped the wine again; this time the red blend seemed almost sour before blooming to a bold flavor that highlighted the grape's lingering sweetness. "I think I understand why people eat wine with their meals. It makes food taste better."

"Exactly. Give me a steak and a cabernet sauvignon, and I'm one happy man."

"Rancher that eats steak. Shocker."

"You know, you're the one who said that mystery was overrated."

"Nothing wrong with your memory," Laken remarked, taking another sip.

Cyler walked her through several other pairings. The harder cheese made the wine seem almost buttery, whereas the honeycomb gave the wine a bright floral flavor. The sun slowly set over the horizon, and soon they'd finished the bottle.

"You need to check on Jack?" Cyler interrupted her thoughts on the very same topic.

Laken glanced to her watch. It had been more than two hours, and Paige was probably getting ready to leave.

"I'll be right back." Laken gave a quick smile before disappearing into the house.

Her body glowed with warmth, both from the sunshine and the wine. It had been a perfect evening, and she didn't want it to end. Thankfully, Cyler didn't have to go back for a few days. She'd noticed how she was living for those times when he was home with her. Biting her lip, she pushed those thoughts to back of her mind and gently pushed open Jack's door and walked to his bed, glancing over to where Paige sat.

Paige looked up from her book, greeting her with a smile. Lifting a finger to her lips to signal quiet, she collected her purse and gave a quick finger wave before patting Laken's shoulder, and leaving.

Laken smiled softly, but it was from a heart that felt heavy. As she turned back to Jack, she noticed that his pulse was regular, but his breathing was a little shallower than she'd liked. His oxygen levels weren't too low, but she wished they were higher.

Wished.

Hoped.

Prayed.

Really, those three things were all that remained for them, but with the same ending. Nothing could change that; the only thing remaining now was how that time was spent. When Jack was up and around, teasing her, it was easier to ignore the hourglass of life's sand. But in the quiet, it was harder to disregard.

Bruises lined his arms as he lay on his back, and a few bandages covered his fingers. It was a shame that people usually didn't realize what a miracle it was to simply heal, until that blessing was taken away.

Jack stirred slightly, his heartbeat spiking before returning to its usual cadence on the silent, flashing monitor. Laken kissed her fingertips then placed them on his arm before quietly leaving the room. She left the door slightly ajar to hear him if he needed her. She glanced down the hall to where she could see the living room clock. She probably had about three hours till Jack would likely start coughing, needing more care.

"Everything alright?" Cyler walked toward her from the hall.

"Yeah, he's sleeping."

"Good." Cyler reached out, pulling her into an embrace. "So, I was thinking…"

"The struggle is real." Laken flirted, looking up to meet his glare.

"For some," he shot back.

"Ouch."

"How about I just show you. I'm more of an action-type guy." He grinned and pressed into her then leaned down to nip at the edge of her neck. "Good Lord, woman. I've missed you," he murmured against her neck.

Laken nestled into his strong frame, her fears melting away against his inviting heat. As his lips trailed along her jawline, her heart stuttered. He ran his nose along her the lines of her neck, before nibbling at her ear.

"I think I missed you more," she replied, grasping his head and encouraging his angle so that she could meet his lips to taste his full flavor, now highlighted by the wine. If possible, he tasted even better.

Abruptly, he pulled her into his arms and wrapped her legs around him, never once breaking the kiss. His hands gripped her ass tightly before slowly leaning away, carrying her down the hall.

Laken massaged her fingers into his shoulders suggestively.

His blue eyes blazed as she brushed her breasts against his chest, biting her lip. Before she could torture him further, he all but tossed her onto the bed, covering her with his body shortly after.

"What was that for?" she asked, giggling as she trailed her fingers under his shirt, tickling his back.

"Do I need a reason?" he replied, kissing her deeply, pressing his hips against hers, making her blood rush, her heart pound in mad anticipation.

"Never," she replied, forgetting the question as she arched her back.

He slipped his hands beneath her T-shirt, trailing a hand along her navel before traveling down to grasp her hips tightly. His lips caressed hers gently, tempting, teasing, seeming to savor each taste.

Laken leaned forward, encouraging him to lift the fabric of her shirt, and he quickly obeyed. Without invitation, she slipped her hands under his shirt and lifted it over his shoulders, breaking the kiss only long enough to remove the offending item. His chest was hard lines, and warm planes as he pressed into her soft curves. A warm hand slowly slid between their bodies, tugging at her jeans, and she raised her hips, allowing him to slip them down. His mouth was hot and demanding on hers as he slowly explored each uncovered inch with his hand.

Gasping, she felt her heart pounding with each new sensation he created, her body awake and sensitive under his touch. He chuckled against her lips, pulling way slightly, watching her as he tickled her inner thigh, grinning.

"Mean," she breathed, but couldn't help the smile.

"Gotta mix it up a bit," he taunted, continuing the tickling torment.

"That's it," she challenged and used her hips to try and swing on top, but he held her fast.

"Say please," he whispered then flicked his hot tongue against her neck as his other hand slowly pulled her bra to the side to explore.

"Please, wait. No, keep doing that." She gasped, arching into his touch.

"Whatever you say," he whispered before lowering his head.

Her hips bucked off the bed, and she closed her eyes, seeing stars, needing more. "Cyler." She gripped his hair, tugging as she continued to arch beneath him.

"Not going anywhere." He spoke softly against her chest, before lifting his head, meeting her lips, sealing his promise with a kiss. Though the words had been spoken easily enough, the intensity of his kiss communicated something deeper. He rolled on to his back, pulling her over so that she straddled his hips. "Damn, the view just gets better and better." He grinned, his blue eyes wild with excitement, his body hard as he reached around and unhooked her bra.

"So that's how it's going to be, huh? Me naked, you not? I should make this harder for you," Laken teased, tiptoeing her fingers up his chest.

"I'll even up the playing field." He arched his back and quickly slid out of his jeans. He swiftly opened his side drawer and pulled out a square package. After making quick work of it, pulled her head down to meet his kiss. With gently exploring fingers, he made sure she was ready for him, then he tenderly slid into her.

Making love with Cyler was like coming home, like creating a masterpiece, like writing a symphony. Each stroke pulled her in deeper, each touch setting her on fire. When he whispered her name, her heart pounded with the power of it. His shoulders bunched as he drove deeper, her body tightening, meeting him the sweet release that called to her, that demanded she surrender to its grasp. With a final gasp, she submitted to its command. Like the tide, she crested then fell, only to be gathered up into a new wave even higher than the first as she called out his name.

He met her then, his grip tightening as he found his own release, his shoulders shuddering with the power of it. Her heart pounded from the intensity, and her fingers tingled with a slow relaxation that seeped through her. Cyler's lips pressed into her neck, kissing her softly as he whispered her name. Slowly, he raised his head to meet her gaze. With deliberate passion, he found her lips again, caressing, worshiping them with each move, each flick of his tongue. It wasn't a building type of kiss, rather a benediction, a whisper of a prayer breathed into her as she joined him, pouring her love out through each kiss.

She missed his warmth as he drew away, caressing her nose with his before sliding to the side, his breathing leisurely returning to normal.

"Every night I'm away, this is all I dream about."

Laken sighed softly, knowing exactly what he'd meant. He turned to smile at her, his expression open, unguarded. He tickled her ribs, earning a mock glare from her.

"Sex?" Laken leaned on her elbow, blowing a strand of blond hair from her face.

"That too." Cyler chuckled, rising as well, facing her. "But I was talking about this." He pulled her closer, kissing the top of her head. "You, in my arms. Waking up and seeing you there—or waking up and not seeing you, which means you're getting coffee," he teased, earning a jab in the side.

"But first, coffee." Laken rolled her eyes.

"You know what? I think I'd take you before coffee."

"I almost don't know what to say." Laken gasped dramatically, widening her eyes.

"Almost," Cyler clarified.

"Oh, glad we're not getting too crazy."

"Never that. We're totally sane here. Nothing crazy ever," Cyler replied with heavy sarcasm.

Laken giggled against his chest. "Keeps life interesting."

"It does indeed."

"It also makes you appreciate the moments when life is peaceful or especially beautiful. You don't take advantage of it as quickly, you know?"

"Yeah." He set his head on hers, pulling her in tighter. "It does. Life's a lot more beautiful when you actually stop to pay attention to it."

"Look who's being poetic."

"Yeah, well, you're wearing off on me."

"You're welcome."

"I wasn't saying thank you," Cyler replied, his tone thick with a smile.

Laken pulled her head away, meeting his gaze. "I'm sure you meant to say thank you."

"I was more thinking more along the lines of...I love you." Cyler kissed her nose.

"I'll take that."

"Figured."

"I love you too." Laken snuggled back into his arms, but as she tried to push the rest of the world into the background, the ticking of time grew louder and louder in her mind.

Jack would need her soon.

"You're getting tense," Cyler murmured.

"It's time." She hated saying it, wanting—no, needing—to just fall asleep in his arms.

Cyler hugged her tightly, then released her. He rose from bed, giving her a glorious view of his naked body. She bit her lip, memorizing each line.

"C'mon, honey. Like I said, I'm not going anywhere," he offered, saving her from the internal battle.

What he'd said was both terrifying and fantastic. Terrifying because she didn't know what would happen to her heart if he ever did leave.

Fantastic because deep in her heart, she knew he was telling the truth.

And that gave her hope in the middle of a time when she felt anything but.

Chapter 19

Cyler closed his eyes, instinctively knowing that Laken hadn't ever come back to bed. He tried not to think about what that probably meant, knowing that time was running low.

Damn it all, when had time become such a determining factor in his life? It was like he couldn't do anything without being aware of it, of the way it ticked past, moment by moment. Never had he even thought about it, but now it was all he noticed.

"Shit." Cyler swore under his breath, opening his eyes to stare at the ceiling. The sun was just starting to rise, and he guessed it was about six in the morning. Reluctantly, he stood from bed and dressed, half-afraid of what scene would greet him once he left the room. The fact that Laken hadn't come to bed was a sure sign that it had been a rough night for both Jack and her.

Guilt nagged at him for sleeping when Laken had been up, no doubt helping Jack breathe through the night. But what would he have been able to do? This was her area of expertise. No. He would have been useless, but that didn't stop the feeling of helplessness or lingering guilt.

Cyler stepped into the hall and walked into the living room, orange sunshine splashing color through the windows. He scanned the couch and chair, but Laken wasn't anywhere to be seen. As he made his way to the hallway that led to Jack's room, he heard Laken's soft voice. He couldn't quite make out the words, so he padded down the hall in an attempt to hear.

"In and out. Yes. Good work. It's perfectly normal. Usually the morphine takes care of the dyspnea, your shortness of breath, but the dose was too small. I've adjusted it, so it won't be long. Just in…and out…one breath at a time," she coached gently.

Through the almost-closed door, he could hear Jack's struggle, shallow breath after breath. Cyler found himself breathing deeper as if that would help.

"Like that. Good work. Yes. Your oxygen levels are getting better. In…out…" Laken paused, probably calmly breathing with Jack.

"Damn—"

"Shh, don't talk, Jack. Save your breath. Literally," she offered in a teasing tone.

Cyler shook his head. Even in the middle of it, Laken was still able to give Jack a hard time.

"Is it getting easier? It sounds like it. Just nod if it is." Laken asked.

Cyler stopped breathing, listening intently to Jack's respiration. It did sound better, less of a gasp and more of a calm, yet still-shallow breath. Cyler exhaled quietly in relief.

"Good, good. Now keep focused on your breath. It will only get easier. See? You're doing great." Laken's tone was encouraging, soft.

Cyler glanced to the kitchen. He wouldn't be any help here, probably just piss Jack off and make his breathing suffer.

Huh, to think I'd have jumped at that opportunity earlier. He was shamed. Yet the past was the past and he was resolved to focus on the future.

With a tense sigh, he decided food might be a better help. He left the hall and crossed to the fridge. After pulling out the fixings for breakfast burritos, he set the eggs, cheese, frozen hash browns, and a couple other items on the counter. Then he spotted the coffee pot.

Empty.

Curious, he lifted the carafe and looked inside. A brown ring of burnt coffee stained the bottom. Had it never started? He knew it was always programed to brew at five a.m. Had they forgotten to fill it the night before?

No, he remembered Laken filling the reservoir.

Unless it had already brewed.

And Laken had drunk it all.

Good Lord, she'd drunk the whole pot. Good thing it was the Pike Place blend he'd brought home. Heaven help her if she'd drank Jack's tractor oil.

Damn, it must have been one hell of a night.

Helplessness washed over him once again, a now-familiar emotion that he'd rather forget. Biting back a curse, he filled the pot with cool water and tossed out the grounds, feeling their warmth and confirming his suspicion. After filling its basket with fresh grounds, he pressed the brew button and started on the burritos.

In less than a half hour, breakfast was finished, but no sign of Laken. The room was filled with the sweet and smoky scent of crisp bacon and buttery eggs. If she wasn't coming down the hall, that meant that she couldn't leave Jack. Torn as to whether he should interrupt them or just keep the food warm, he opted to interrupt. As he lifted his hand to knock, the door opened, revealing a startled Laken.

"Holy cow! Hi?" She placed a hand over her heart, a tired smile spreading across her face.

"Hey." He scanned her features, noticing dark shadows under her eyes. "Hungry, or do you want to wait?"

She gave a quick glance behind her and then walked into the hall, closing the door behind her. "Starving, but I think I need to wait. Would there happen to be any more coffee?" she asked, her eyes pitifully hopeful.

"I'll do one better. I'll bring you a breakfast burrito—easy to eat quickly in the hall—and I'll run to Starbucks for you, okay? Anything else you need while I'm out?"

Laken closed her eyes, leaning forward, and resting her head against his chest. "This." She took a deep breath.

He tugged her in tighter, holding her in the strength of his arms, wishing he could do more.

"Thank you," she murmured into his heart. "No, I've got this. We're through the worst of it, I think. I'll explain later, but I'd love that coffee." She pulled back, giving him a brave smile.

"You've got it. I'll be right back with breakfast."

"A man who feeds me. I'll keep you," she whispered as he walked down the hall.

He glanced over his shoulder. "You didn't really have a choice."

"Get me my burrito." She gave a sweet, quiet laugh that belied her demanding words.

"Stop bossing me, and I might." Cyler disappeared into the kitchen. Soon he was back, handing over a napkin with a delicious-smelling breakfast wrapped inside of a warm flour tortilla.

"Bless you." Laken took a quick bite. "Hot, hot." She opened her mouth, breathing in quickly to try to cool the food.

"Take it easy. Do I need to stay to make sure you actually chew your food rather than try to swallow it whole?" Cyler leaned against the hall wall with a raised brow.

"Bite me," Laken retorted around a mouthful of burrito.

"I did." Cyler leaned forward and kissed her cheek. "You taste better."

"And we're done. You, make yourself useful and get me some coffee."
Laken rolled her eyes.

Cyler gave a quick salute and strode down the hall before swiping his
keys from the table by the door. The sun was just cresting the hills by
the time he swung open the door to the Starbucks restaurant.

"Aw, if it isn't my favorite customer's boy-toy," Kessed teased as Cyler
walked up to the counter.

"I'm insulted."

"No, you're not. Just calling it like I see it."

"Well, your favorite customer needs an IV of caffeine. Whatcha got?"
Kessed's teasing expression shifted to concern. "Jack?"

"Failing."

"I'm sorry. Wait, or are you still waiting for the old man to
kick the bucket?"

Cyler rubbed the back of his neck in chagrin. "Kinda mended that
fence, at least a little bit."

"Good. Laken doesn't need to deal with your sorry ass if you're going
to be a grudge-holder."

"Nice to know you have my back."

"Hey, no offense. I'm sure it's a damn sexy back. It's just that, well,
bros over hoes, you know?" She picked up a venti cup and wrote on it.

"I—never mind. Not going there." He held up his hands in a
futility. "Coffee?"

"I'm all over it. Ah, shit." Kessed shifted her gaze to the door behind him.

"Pardon?" Cyler narrowed his eyes and then followed her gaze.

"Damn it all to hell," he muttered as Breelee strode in.

"Friend of yours?" Kessed asked, acid in her tone.

"Nope. Pretty sure her summer house is somewhere in hell. Does that
give you an idea of my opinion of her?"

"Whoa, and just when we had all that hope from you mending
fences with Jack."

"This is different."

"Cyler. Imagine finding you here." Her voice was husky, and it grated on
his nerves rather than have the sultry quality she was probably attempting.

"Satan." He nodded then turned to Kessed. "To go, like fast."

"A little demanding, aren't we?" Breelee commented, coming to stand
beside him, a little too close for comfort.

"I don't mind," Kessed answered with a tight smile. "What can I start for you?" she asked Breelee.

"Skinny vanilla."

Cyler smirked as he heard Kessed whisper, "One skinny-bitch latte," just quietly enough for him to hear.

He glanced to Breelee, thankful she was looking in her purse and apparently oblivious to Kessed's jibe.

"Three forty-five." Kessed smiled sweetly to Breelee.

Cyler took a step back. Nothing good could come from Kessed smiling like that.

"What about him?" Breelee's gaze cut to Cyler.

"His is on the house," Kessed answered clearly.

"Oh." Breelee glanced between the two of them. "I guess that's one way to get your coffee." She arched a brow suggestively.

Cyler took another step back as Kessed's almond-shaped eyes narrowed, making her look more Asian than usual. "Your coffee will be ready shortly. I suggest you wait over there." Kessed bit out each word.

With a shrug, Breelee walked to the other end of the counter. As she waited, she tapped her manicured nails on the counter.

The second barista eyed her with what could only be described as venom-filled annoyance. "You. Wait over there." She pointed Cyler to a table.

"My girl's gonna need this too." Kessed filled up a to-go tote with coffee, then picked out several blueberry muffins and one chocolate donut. "How many hours?" she asked as she glanced at the espresso machine.

"Of?" Cyler asked.

"Sleep," Kessed replied with impatient sarcasm.

He held up his fingers in a big zero.

Kessed blew out a breath and twisted her lips. "You're going to need more then." She nodded then proceeded to set up another coffee tote.

"I didn't realize that Starbucks catered," Breelee remarked as she took off her lid and blew across the top of her just-delivered latte.

"Only occasionally," Kessed called out. "We're medicating the sleep deprived." Kessed set all the stuff on the counter in front of Cyler. "Next time tell her to text me ahead of time. I'm totally out of Pike Place, so don't let her pitch a hissy fit since she had to have Sumatra, okay? Tell her to stop being a little bitch and add some creamer or something if it's too much for her." Kessed's face relaxed into a grin.

"Who?" Breelee walked over, her brown eyes sharply regarding Kessed.

"His girlfriend. You know, sexy little blond that practically bleeds coffee." Kessed shook her head.

Cyler held his breath, hoping that maybe Breelee wouldn't make the connection. The last thing Laken needed was to deal with her again.

"Nurse Nancy with the fake number? No shit." Breelee's gaze took on a wicked glint. "Nice to know, thanks, er, Kessed, is it?" She regarded the barista with a false warmth.

"What's it to you?" Kessed dared her.

"Nothing, just…hmmm. That's an interesting conflict of interest, isn't it?" She slowly circled Cyler. "How did you meet her? I'm sure it was a pre-existing relationship, not one that started while—oh, never mind." Breelee's red lips stretched into a wide smile. "Your face says it all."

"Leave her alone," Cyler ground out, his fists clenching. He wasn't one to hit a woman, but he was thinking of all the reasons he should make an exception.

"Listen." Kessed stood in front of him, facing Breelee, giving him a moment to pause his knee-jerk reaction. "I think it's time you left. And I wouldn't mess with cowboy back there"—she nodded behind her—"but feel free to tangle with me. I'd love to see how you'd deal with someone your own size."

Cyler rolled his eyes, taking Kessed by the shoulders and moving her to the side. "Breelee is too smart to deal with your kind of crazy. Right?" He tilted his chin to Breelee, looking for her agreement. He didn't want to call Laken and tell her he was bailing her best friend out of jail.

Breelee gave a small shrug. "My coffee is getting cold. I'll see you around, Cyler." With a wink, she left.

"One swing. That's all it would take." Kessed narrowed her eyes.

"Easy, killer. Let's not get tossed in jail, alright? Save some fun for tomorrow."

"Ex of yours?" She turned and glared at him.

"Unfortunately," Cyler admitted.

"You know how to pick 'em." Kessed gave him a onceover before lifting the bag of baked treats and one coffee tote from the table. "Let's go. I'll help you take it out."

"Thanks." Cyler sighed, lifted the last tote and hurried ahead to open the door for Kessed.

As he drove back to the ranch, he held one hand over the coffee containers to make sure they didn't topple forward at the few stop signs.

Keeping an eye out for Breelee's car, he sighed in relief as he parked at the ranch and didn't see it. He carried one tote to the kitchen, noticing that there was a half-eaten burrito on the counter. He grinned, thankful that at least he'd done something to help Laken, and in turn, help Jack.

After he brought everything in, he walked to Jack's room and knocked softly.

"Come in," Jack called, surprising him.

"Hey, old man," Cyler replied as he opened the door. Swallowing his reaction, he kept his face at what he hoped looked impassive as he took in the oxygen tubes attached to Jack's nose and the monitors all hooked up to screen his blood pressure, his heartbeat, and his oxygen levels.

"I told her to go to bed, but she wouldn't listen. After I threatened to hold my breath if she didn't sit down, she finally took a seat, and less than minute later, she fell asleep." Jack lifted a hand and pointed to the other end of his room.

Laken was lying back against the armchair, her hands wrapped around her body as if chilled.

"I'm glad she finally gave up," Cyler whispered, turning back to Jack.

"Me too. It kills me that I need her. It makes a man feel weak, Cyler. I hate every moment, yet I'm so damn grateful for her. She, she—" Jack coughed, but it was a weak sound, not the body-wracking fits that usually overtook him. "She doesn't just talk me through it. She makes me believe I can make it to the next breath."

"How are you doing now?" Cyler asked, not sure if he could do any good if Jack needed help.

"Better. But"—Jack took a shallow breath—"take a seat, son."

Cyler nodded, glancing around and finally choosing to just sit on the edge of Jack's bed. His eyes scanned the room that should be so familiar, yet wasn't. So much equipment, the scent of medication, nothing about it reminded him of the room of his memories.

"I'm ready." Jack spoke decisively, nodding once to emphasis his point.

Cyler instinctively knew what he was saying, but he revolted against it. "For?"

"The end, death, whatever you want to call it. Last night, I made my peace with God, and the other day I made my peace—for lack of a better word—with you, and damn it all, I'm just so tired, Cyler. So damn tired." He closed his eyes, turning his head into his pillow, taking a few labored breaths. "Each breath, so hard. I never realized how easy breathing was...." His words faded as he pulled in another breath. "I'm ready. I just...I want to make sure you're ready too." Jack opened his eyes, regarding Cyler.

Breaking eye contact, Cyler glanced to his hands. "I'm not sure. It's—it's pretty final, Jack. And while you're not my favorite person"—Cyler gave a small chuckle as he turned to Jack—"you've kinda grown on me."

"Took you long enough," Jack remarked, a chuckle turning into a cough.

"You made it a little difficult," Cyler shot back without heat.

"Eh, details." Jack made a dismissive but weak wave with his hand. "But, I want you to know that...when the time comes...I'm ready. And like I said yesterday, I'm sorry. Because...while most of my life I was an ass to you, I don't want to finish that way. You deserve better than that. I'm only sorry I didn't try to start sooner." Jack's gaze grew misty as his gaze bore into Cyler's. "I have lot of regrets, but that's the biggest one."

Cyler glanced away, fighting every emotion that threatened to surface. "Yeah, well. We all have regrets." Cyler fisted his hands. One of those regrets had made an appearance not even a half hour ago. It was easier to focus on the anger rather than face what his father was saying.

Wasn't that always the case? Be angry, blame someone else, justify wrong feelings and hope for absolution, but what good did it do in the end?

None.

Because no one ever won.

But he was thankful that he'd at least given himself the chance to find some measure of healing with Jack. And as much as it sucked, if he had to say goodbye to Jack, then at least they made peace.

Cyler took a deep breath through his nose. "You know, if we would have had this conversation a few weeks ago, it would have been a bit different."

"We started to have this conversation a few weeks ago, and I ended up popping you in the nose, and you didn't even have the sense to dent the coffee table. I always thought your head was harder than that. You're surely stubborn enough."

"Aw, just as our conversation was becoming so heartwarming." Cyler chuckled.

"Yeah, well, I'm being honest. I'm not going to blow smoke up your ass."

"I probably should be thankful."

"Yup. You're welcome."

"You're an arrogant son of a bitch."

"Takes one to know one."

"Hey, for one who has a hard time breathing, you're sure talking a lot," Cyler challenged.

"You bring out the best in me."

"Touched, really. And now we're back to being heartwarming."

Jack shook his head, grinning as his gaze shifted to where Laken still slept.

"You going to marry her?"

Cyler furrowed his brow. "That came out of nowhere."

"Not really. We're talking about living without regrets. Not marrying her? Yeah, you'd regret that, I'm betting. So, have you thought about it?"

"Yeah, I'm marrying her. But you can't say anything to her. She thinks I'm demanding enough." Cyler slid a smile to his father.

"Ha! She thinks *you're* demanding. I don't think I've met a bossier woman."

"I know. She doesn't see it. It's part of her charm."

Jack nodded. "Yeah, it is." He shifted in his bed, changing his position a bit. "You have the ring yet?"

"How is that any of your business?" Cyler regarded his father with a narrowed gaze.

"It's not. But I'm asking, regardless. You should expect this by now."

"You have a point." Cyler rubbed the back of his neck, debating on how much to tell. "I had mom's ring reworked. But I...I don't know if I want to give it to her. I mean, it wasn't exactly a symbol of a great marriage," Cyler confessed. He glanced to Jack, who was regarding him.

"You're right, but my legacy isn't yours, son. You're not me."

"Damn straight, I'm not." Cyler couldn't help saying it.

"And you're going to write your own story. That ring? It doesn't determine your future. You do. If you want to give it to her, do it. It's the symbol of it all. It's a ring, never-ending. Do me a favor and redeem it for me." Jack leaned back in his pillow, his gaze shifting away as the moisture built before spilling down in a lonely tear.

Cyler swallowed. He'd never seen Jack cry before.

Hell, he wasn't sure *he* even knew how.

"Stop looking at me like I've committed a crime. Real men feel things," Jack grumbled.

Cyler cleared his throat and cast his gaze away, giving Jack a moment to collect himself.

"Can I ask one thing?" Jack inquired, and Cyler turned back to him.

"Probably," Cyler replied, slightly suspicious. *Old habits die hard.*

"Do it before I kick the bucket. I want to see her be settled, happy, know that you're not going anywhere."

Cyler grinned, shaking his head. "Why do I get the feeling that you like her more than you like me?"

"Because that's the damn truth. I put up with you, but I love that girl." Jack jerked his chin toward Laken.

"Nice to know where I rank."

"Behind Margaret."

"I would be behind the horse. Some things never change."

"I made peace. I didn't become a different person." Jack arched a brow with a grin.

"Fair enough."

Cyler took a deep breath, relaxing even with the heavy emotional atmosphere of the room.

After a few moments of peaceful silence, Cyler turned to Jack. "You hungry?"

"A little. I could really go for some coffee though. Damn, I want a donut now."

Cyler chuckled. "Coffee and a donut. You're not demanding at all. Let me see what I can do, old man."

"I believe in you."

"Yeah, you're cut off from the pain meds. I think you're starting to get high."

"Nah, I know what high feels like. I lived through the sixties, son." Jack chuckled softly.

"And that's my cue to leave." Cyler lifted a hand in defense.

"Your mother did too, mind you."

"Don't want to know!" Cyler whisper-shouted as he started down the hall.

Jack's soft laughter followed him, making him grin in spite of himself. Crazy old man.

When Cyler reached the kitchen, he sifted through the snacks that Kessed had packed and found one old-fashioned donut. After pouring a cup of Jack's sludge masquerading as coffee, he took the paper sack and mug down the hall.

"You should have woken me up!" Laken's raspy voice carried down the hall.

He grinned, anticipating her sleepy gaze, a soft smile on her face.

As he opened the door, Jack struggled to sit up, and Laken helped.

"Donut?" the old man asked with a pitifully hopeful expression.

"Maybe," Cyler teased, handing over the bag.

Jack opened the paper sack and grinned widely, pulling out the frosted treat.

"Really. A donut." Laken tilted her head, scolding.

"Let a dying man have his junk food," Jack replied before taking a bite.

"Here's your coffee." Cyler handed it over, shaking his head as Jack ate the donut with reckless abandon.

"Apparently, I need to feed you more often," Laken remarked, a delicate smile spreading across her features. Her lips were slightly swollen from sleeping, her expressive eyes slightly glassy from her short nap.

"I take back everything bad I ever said about Starbucks," Jack remarked as he finished the old-fashioned.

"Whoa. That must have been some donut," Laken teased.

"It was life-changing," Jack said, lifting his mug of coffee to his lips.

"Donuts usually are." Cyler nodded.

Laken yawned, and Cyler held out a hand to her. "I'll hold down the fort."

"By fort...he means me," Jack said between sips of coffee.

Cyler grasped Laken's hand and tugged her toward the door. "You need to sleep."

"But Jack—"

"Will need you to be on your game. Not a sleep-deprived zombie," Cyler finished.

"True story," Jack called from his room as Cyler and Laken made their way down the hall.

"Drink your coffee, old man," Cyler shot over his shoulder to Jack, earning a middle-finger salute.

"He's feeling good. You need to take advantage of it and get some rest. I'll wake you if he needs something that I can't handle, okay?" Cyler led her to their room. "Sleep."

"Fine, but you need to wake me in an hour." She grumbled, already half asleep as she all but fell into the bed.

"Is there a specific reason? Will he need more medication?" Cyler asked as he pulled the blanket over her curled up frame.

"No, I just—I'll check his vitals."

"Alright, you rest." Cyler backed from the room, the soft sound of her breath signaling her quick drift toward sleep.

He paused by the door, simply watching as her shoulders shifted with her breathing, thankful that he could take care of her. She needed that, more than she realized.

His gaze strayed to his bag draped over a chair in the corner. Silently, he strode over to it and pulled out the royal-blue box tucked carefully in the outside pocket. With a tug, the top slid off the box and inside nestled his mother's ring. It was a Black Hills gold band, almost the rose-gold color that was so popular currently. An emerald-cut diamond was mounted between two smaller versions of itself, reflecting every speck of light in the room since the jeweler had cleaned and adjusted the tines on the setting. He wasn't sure how he was going to propose, but intuition said he needed to act soon.

He had one more day before he'd usually head back to the Yakima Valley for work.

An idea started to form, and a grin stretched across his face at the thought. With a glance at Laken's sleeping form, he made up his mind.

Good thing she was sleeping now.

Life was going to get a little more interesting.

Chapter 20

Laken rolled over, stretching. The sweet fog of sleep was swept away as she shot up in bed, glancing to the old analog clock beside the bed. "Of course he didn't wake me up. Gah!" She tossed the covers back and yanked her ponytail band from her hair then quickly wrapped it up in a messy bun. Three hours!

Softly, she padded down the hall, just in case Jack was asleep. She carefully peeked into the room, frowning as both Cyler and Jack grinned at her.

"Hey there, sleeping beauty." Jack nodded, setting down a hand of cards. "Read 'em and weep." He coughed then cackled as Cyler groaned, tossing his cards on the bed. "Poor kid can't win for losin'." Jack jabbed a thumb in his son's direction.

Cyler's answer was a glower.

"What are you playing?" Laken asked as she picked up her iPad and started taking notes from the monitor's readings.

"Five card draw. He wanted to play for money, but I said whatever I had was going to him anyway. Took the fun out of it. So, we're playing for bragging rights. I can use those."

"He's using them already." Cyler gave a frustrated grin to Laken as she finished up her notes.

"It's the gift that keeps on giving," Laken teased. "I'd rather play for bragging rights than money any day. You can spend money, but bragging rights? You can use those for years." Laken's smile faltered as she considered how Jack didn't have years. Weeks maybe, if they were lucky.

"Stop moping. Cyler says he's fine with me dying. You should be too!" Jack gave a grin.

"I—" Cyler paused, twisting his lips. "Yeah, I did say that. But in my defense, you'd just won six games in a row. I still think you're cheating."

"Nah, it's a dying man's luck. That's irony for you."

Cyler rolled his eyes. "Whatever it is, you've got it."

"Has there been any change in your pain? Any increase in pressure in your chest? How's breathing?" Laken asked, regarding Jack.

His color wasn't great, but it wasn't the sallow bluish color of earlier. He coughed before answering, and she noted the way it sounded, much shallower than usual.

"I'm alive. That's about as good as it's going to get right now," Jack answered. "And whooping his ass has made me tired. I think I earned a nap. So, if you two want to go out and take a ride or something, I promise not to die on you before dinner. Sound good?"

"You think so you're so funny." Laken narrowed her eyes, glaring.

"I am!" Jack leaned back, settling in bed and pulling up the thick quilt that covered him. "No arguing. Get out of here. You're disturbing my peace." He closed his eyes.

"I think we've been dismissed." Cyler chuckled, the sound warm and inviting.

Laken faced him, noticing how the usual tension in his shoulders from being around Jack was absent. Maybe they'd talked more. She could only hope, because while Jack talked big, her gut told her time wasn't their friend.

"C'mon, let the old man rest."

"Who you calling old?" Jack grumbled, his eyes still closed.

"Exactly. Let's go." Cyler took her elbow gently and guided her down the hall. "I'm going to go out on a limb and say you're hungry?" he teased.

"I'm always hungry," Laken answered.

"Well good. I planned something while you were sleeping."

"Great movie."

"Huh?" Cyler turned to her, frowning in confusion.

"*While You Were Sleeping*. It's a great movie. I watch it every Christmas along with *White Christmas*. Classics."

"Random thought of the day." He shook his head good-naturedly.

"Wait, what did you plan?" Laken asked, curious.

"A picnic. Because I'm awesome. Go ahead, tell me."

"You're awesome."

"Thank you."

"And annoying."

"I'll take that too. I learned from the best."

"Me?" Laken asked, chuckling.

"Nope. Jack."

"That explains the hint of *Jack*ass in the air."

"Caught on to that, did you?"

"Are you going to feed me or not?" Laken popped a hip.

"Are you going to stop playing twenty questions?" Cyler returned.

She thought about continuing, just to piss him off, and gave a grin. "Probably not. But I am hungry." She gave her most pitiful look.

"Not fair. Plus, I'm totally immune to your attempts at manipulation." Cyler shrugged and walked into the kitchen. He picked up a basket and held it to the side.

"Whatever, you aren't immune at all." Laken walked up to him and slid her arm around his waist. She rose on her tiptoes and kissed along his jaw.

"So, that's not manipulation. That's seduction. And I'm totally into that. Don't stop." He smiled, leaning down to kiss her.

She pulled away, winking and walking to the door. "Nah, hungry."

"Cruel," Cyler muttered, though his tone was amused.

"Don't you forget it." Laken glanced over her shoulder. "Are you coming or not?"

Chuckling, Cyler caught up, taking her hand while holding the basket's handles with the other. "I figured we'd ride. Margaret is fine now, and I know it's been a while since she's been out."

Laken nodded. "I'd like that. Are you sure she's okay, though? I mean, you, me, the food. That's a lot of weight."

"She's a lot of horse."

Laken giggled. "Yeah, she is. Alright. I see your point." With a slide of the barn door, they spilled the early afternoon sun into the barn, and Margaret nickered in welcome.

"Hey you." Laken released Cyler's hand and walked up to her. She smoothed the soft velvet of Margaret's muzzle. "Miss me?"

Margaret pressed farther into her hand, nipping at her fingers tenderly. "I'll take that as a yes."

"Why don't you give her a treat while I go and get her saddle?"

Laken crossed over to the tack room and pulled the box of sugar cubes from the shelf where she'd left them. She took two out and fed them to Margaret, smiling as the mare's lips tickled her hand.

"Satisfied?" she asked, stroking the horse's white star on her forehead.

"Probably not," Cyler commented, opening the stall and laying a saddle blanket across Margaret's back.

The mare huffed, as if irritated.

"Don't you dare bite me." Cyler cut a glare to her.

Margaret sighed and turned back to Laken as if seeking comfort.

"Big baby."

"Spoiled baby," Cyler corrected.

In short work, Margaret was saddled, bridled, and ready. Her head bobbed with each step out of the barn, ears perked, listening to the world around them.

Cyler handed the reins over to Laken then swung a leg over the saddle.

Margaret huffed, turning her head and giving a look to Cyler.

After reaching out a hand, Laken handed him both the reins and the basket from the ground where he'd set it. He put both in one hand and held out the other for her.

"I think I can manage." Laken arched a brow. Grabbing the back of the saddle, she placed her foot in the stirrup, and as she swung onto Margaret's back, she wrapped her hand around Cyler's waist and held on. "See?"

"Maybe I offered help because I wanted to touch you, not because I thought you were incapable." Cyler glanced back at her, grinning.

"Let's go." Laken held him tightly, immediately remembering their first ride.

It hadn't been that long ago, yet felt like a lifetime. It was such sweet torture, wrapping her arms around him, feeling the solid nature of his body, its warmth, and trying to distance herself from it at the same time.

"Remember our first ride?" Cyler broke the silence.

"I was just thinking about that."

Cyler chuckled. "You about killed me."

Laken tilted her head. "How?"

"You were pressed so tight against my back I could feel ever curve of your body, even your breathing. Your perfume permeated my air, and your hips...damn. They moved against me with every step. I about lost my mind."

Laken bit her lip. "Really? That's...funny, actually. It wasn't exactly easy for me either. I kept repeating, 'Patient's son. He's my patient's son... so hands off.'"

"I'm glad you didn't listen to your own advice."

"Me too."

"Look." Cyler jerked his chin to the west. A herd of mule deer were grazing along a shadowed hill, their long ears twitching as they watched from several yards away.

"Beautiful," Laken whispered.

"They love it up here. Get pretty big too."

After winding around a few rabbit bushes, Cyler took a left down a path. "You'll like this. We went to the canyon last time, so now I'm going to show you my second favorite place."

Laken waited for him to explain further, but the silence stretched on. "Are you going to tell me what we're going to see?"

"It's a surprise."

Laken twisted her lips. "How long till I get to see the surprise?"

"Soon. Impatient much? Just enjoy the ride."

"That sounds familiar."

"Because you tend to be impatient in a lot of things," Cyler shot back. Laken's face flamed. "The ride is my favorite part."

"Keep talking like that, and we won't make it to your surprise," Cyler replied, his voice tight. "Damn it, keep up with this, and I won't even be able to look at the horse without getting aroused, and that's just...all kinds of awkward."

Laughing, Laken leaned her head against his warm back, focusing on the heat of the sunshine on her skin, the smooth rhythm of the horse, and now, the soft sound of running water.

"A creek?" Laken asked.

"Yup. Just ahead."

Laken twisted to see around Cyler. Sure enough, there was a small creek running through a basalt ravine, but what stole her attention was the color surrounding the rock. Bright orange and blue flowers grew beside the water, shifting gently in the soft breeze. "That's beautiful. What are those?"

"It's orange globe mallow and lobelia."

Laken took in the startling color against the mostly brown landscape.

"They can live here longer because of the water. I used to come here and pick flowers for my mom. She'd put them on the table, and more than once, we'd have to kill some bug making a run for it during dinner, but she didn't complain." Cyler chuckled.

"That's the risk with wildflowers, I guess," Laken replied, imagining the scene.

"There's usually a patch of rye grass that stays a little greener than most, and that rock over there is a good table." He pulled up Margaret and halted her. Holding out his hand, he offered to help Laken slide down. After taking his warm grasp, she placed her foot in the stirrup and slid off.

Soon they were setting up the tabletop rock with the packed lunch. "I love it."

"I'm glad." Cyler grinned, his blue eyes crinkling as he handed over a bottle of water. "Margaret seems pretty satisfied as well."

The mare was tied to a basalt column, a slack rein allowed her to munch on the green rye grass, her bit clinking slightly with her chewing.

Laken reached over toward the basket to help, but Cyler pulled the basket away, almost protective. "I've got this. Just sit there and let me take care of you."

She sighed, pulling her arm back. It was nice to be thought of, to be taken care of. She hadn't really noticed its absence until Cyler had started to do the little things, like making sure she had a nap. Or making her breakfast, or any other meal. He was usually there, whenever possible, and his first thought was always for her. It humbled her, blessed her, made her fall deeper and deeper in love with him each day.

Cyler handed her a sandwich, breaking through her thoughts.

She accepted with a smile and took a big bite.

Lunch was over all too soon, and after finishing, Cyler grew pensive.

"What's up?" Laken asked, studying his features.

Cyler met her gaze, his blue eyes searching hers. A small smile turned his full lips upward as he leaned forward. "Marry me."

Laken blinked, replaying the short phrase over and over, making sure that she'd heard it correctly. "Marry you?" she asked, just to make sure.

"Yeah. Marry me, Laken. Life is full of choices, full of opportunities, full of beauty. I never fully understood that. I don't want to live like I have been. Loving you is the biggest risk I've ever taken, and while I tease you about not giving you a choice, the truth of it is that I never had a choice either. It was you, right away. I fought a losing battle with my heart, but it was really a losing battle against the man I was afraid to be. And you... you helped me find myself again. I don't want to live life in a way that when I'm old like Jack, I look back and see everything I've lost. I want to look back and see everything I've gained. And I can't imagine looking back on my life and not seeing you living it with me."

Warm tears made silent trails down her face as she let Cyler's words pour over her soul, permeate it with love.

"So, to make it a little more official..." Cyler reached into the basket and pulled out a blue box.

Laken gave a watery laugh. "No wonder you didn't want me helping."

"I told you it was a surprise." Cyler grinned, opening the box and holding out a rose-gold ring. Emerald-cut diamonds made a trinity of beauty as they twinkled in their velvet case.

"Laken, marry me?" He knelt on one knee. His expression one of fierce hope, and it stole her breath as it seared its power on her heart.

"Yes," she breathed the word, tears streaming down her cheeks while she reached out and pulled him into a tight hug.

"You know how to keep a man waiting," Cyler taunted, pulling back to kiss her full on the mouth, branding her with his flavor, with his apparent joy.

His mouth was hot against hers, demanding and powerful as held her tightly in his arms. Slowly he softened the kiss then pulled away entirely.

"Come back." Lake leaned forward, trying to meet his lips.

"In a moment. There's something we need to finish." He lifted the ring from the box and held it out. Sliding the ring on her left hand, it winked in the sunlight, a perfect fit.

Curious, Laken glanced to him, about to ask how he knew her size.

"I measured your hand when you were sleeping," Cyler confessed.

"Devious."

"Nah, I prefer planning ahead," he corrected, pulling her in tight again then kissing her nose.

"We can go with that," Laken agreed.

"I love you," Cyler whispered against her lips before placing a lingering kiss there.

"I love you more," Laken returned softly before meeting his lips for a repeat performance.

"Doubtful, but I'm okay with you trying."

Laken giggled, reaching up then tracing his jaw with her fingers, a question forming in her mind. "Does Jack know? Is that why he kicked us out?" Laken asked, her eyes widening with realization.

Cyler nodded, lifting her hand to display the ring. "This ring was actually my mother's. I spoke with Jack about it, and he…well, he kinda surprised me. Again. I swear it's his new hobby, keeping me on my toes—or stepping on them. Take your pick." Cyler chuckled.

"What did he say?" Laken asked, studying Cyler's blue eyes.

"He said that we could redeem it for him." He shook his head, a slight smile tipping his lips. "I had mentioned having some reservations about giving you my mom's ring when it didn't exactly symbolize a strong marriage. I want more for you, for us. Jack simply reminded me that it's not the ring. It's who wears it." Cyler lifted her hand and kissed it softly.

"Jack's getting wise in his old age."

"It's about damn time," Cyler returned, laughing quietly.

"I love this ring. I'm thankful that it was your mother's. It's a beautiful thing to carry history."

"But not repeat it," Cyler added, a wry grin to his lips.

"True story. But I'm not worried." Laken reached up and cupped his chin in her hand, making sure she had his full attention before continuing. "I'm not afraid of trusting you with my heart, Cyler. I know it's in good hands. It might not always be easy. In fact, I'm pretty sure once or twice I'll want to punch you in the throat"—she giggled—"but that won't change the fact that...till death do us part." She sealed her words with a soft kiss.

"Till death do us part," Cyler repeated the promise against her lips.

Laken lost herself to the moment, to the kiss, memorizing each sensation, each scent, sound, and taste. And slowly, as Cyler pulled back, meeting her gaze, she closed her eyes, so thankful, so grateful, so at peace.

"We should probably get back. Jack's going to be chomping at the bit to know if you rejected me or not," Cyler badgered, reaching down and smacking her ass playfully.

"He's not wondering that. He knows," Laken corrected as they cleaned up their picnic site.

"Sure, sure." Cyler winked.

And soon they were on their way back to the ranch, Margaret plodding along. Laken enjoyed the scenery even more as she wound back up the hill.

Cyler tied Margaret up near the barn and helped Laken off. She took the basket to the kitchen as Cyler brushed down the mare. Then she made her way down the hall to Jack's room. After softly knocking on the door, she waited a moment before opening it up.

"So?" Jack was shifting himself so that he sat upright, his blue eyes twinkling with anticipation.

"It was a nice picnic," Laken replied, holding her hand behind her back. Jack narrowed his eyes. "And?"

"And Margaret is doing much better." Laken nodded, using her right hand to check the IV fluids.

After a quick study of the monitors she turned to Jack. His face was pinched, his gaze suspicious.

"What? Are you not feeling well? Are you in pain?" Laken taunted, thankful that she could at least pester Jack a bit.

"Huh." Jack folded his hands on his lap, his expression guarded. "Nope. Fit as a fiddle. A broken one, but a fiddle none the less. Can you hand me that book over there?" He pointed to a shelf to the side of the bed.

Laken turned to reach it.

"I knew it!" Jack shouted, startling her so that she dropped the book she'd just grabbed.

"Jack! You scared the life out of me. What in the world are you talking about?" Laken turned, glaring as she bent to pick up the book.

"Your hand. I see it. I see it with my own eyes, girl. You're a rotten liar." He clapped, chuckling happily.

Laken bit her lip, trying to force a stern stare. "You're sneaky."

"Like a silver fox," he shot back. "You're a mean one, Laken. I'd expect something like that from my son, but not you. I'm disappointed." He nodded self-righteously.

"What did she do now?" Cyler asked as he walked into the room.

"Your fiancée here tried to pull the wool over my eyes. I think she's ashamed of you, son." Jack coughed, but it didn't hide his grin.

"You should have seen your face though," Laken teased Jack. "You were so sure, and then your glower was impressive."

"Well, I knew he was going to ask, and I was ninety-nine-percent sure you'd say yes, but—aw hell, who can know the female mind? I've given up, so, there you have it."

"Nice to know you have so much faith in me," Laken replied, taking his blood pressure.

"Or me," Cyler added.

"Well, it all worked out. Can I see the ring up close?" Jack asked, and Laken held out her hand. Jack's fingers were cold as he gently grasped her hand and tilted it to get a better look.

"Yup. It's a beauty. Cost me a pretty penny too." Jack released his grip.

Cyler glanced heavenward. "Thanks, Dad." He turned to Laken. "For the record, I did have it reworked. Damn, I sound cheap." Cyler swore.

Laken laughed, her body shaking with the joy. "No, you sound like you wanted to give me something that money can't buy. Hope…redemption…life." Laken gave a warm gaze to Cyler, who met it with one of his own.

"She's a smart one," Jack agreed.

"Finally, you admit it," Laken teased, but her attention was stolen by the reading of the blood-pressure monitor. "Okay, I don't like this. Jack, how do you feel?" she asked, taking his pulse.

"No worse than usual, but I will say my heart is pounding a bit hard. But honestly, honey, I think it's just because I'm kinda worked up. I wanted this for you guys. I'm just happy."

Laken nodded but cut a look to Cyler. That might be the reason, but it didn't ring true to her training. "I'm going to see if we can regulate it a bit. It's a little low."

Then Jack's phone rang, and Cyler grabbed it, glancing to the screen, and left the room. Laken heard him answer just before hearing the door shut behind him.

"Probably Bo. I called him to double-check stuff with Breelee sniffing about. He's just calling back to confirm my affairs. He's a good man, for a lawyer, that is." Jack grinned.

Laken answered with a smile but took his blood pressure again.

As the cuff released, the numbers read just as low.

"Jack, you're going to have to lie back and rest. I'm going to give you some meds that will help your blood pressure, and you'll probably want to go back to sleep. First, let's lift your feet a bit."

Jack sighed and reluctantly sat back against the pillows, closing his eyes.

"I'll be right back with a cup of water." Laken darted down the hall and soon returned from the kitchen with a cool glass of water. She held out the two little pills to Jack and helped him sit up to take them. After draining his glass, he leaned back again, closing his eyes once more.

"Stop hovering. If you want me to relax, you gotta git, okay?" Jack commented, opening one eye.

Laken grinned, patting him on the hand before she left the room.

"Thanks." Jack's voice followed her.

But something wasn't sitting right. Something was wrong, and she couldn't quite put her finger on it. It gnawed at her as she walked to the kitchen. Reviewing his vitals, she mentally went through each scenario, each diagnosis. But nothing made sense. It was true that sometimes the body didn't have a rhyme or reason for doing things, but that wasn't exactly an answer. It just brought a different question.

Laken glanced at the clock. She'd give him fifteen minutes to fall asleep, then she'd check on him again. It was a good thing she'd had a nap that morning. She had a feeling it would be a long day, and a longer night.

For all of them.

Chapter 21

"So, we're good?" Cyler asked, holding his breath as he waited for the lawyer's answer.

"Yeah. She tried to push her weight around. Luckily, she's a bitty thing. Didn't do much for her cause," Bo answered.

Cyler sighed in relief. "What exactly was she trying to pull?" he asked, glancing to the door, and then taking a seat on the cement step.

"The usual. Emotional distress, emotional entanglement, prior engagement. None of it would hold water in court. But she had to try. They always do, you know. Just make sure you tell Jack that we're watertight. He was pretty upset, regardless of how I tried to tell him I'd done my job well."

Cyler chuckled. "Micromanaging. He's great at it."

"Tell me about it," Bo admitted.

"I'll let him know. Thanks for confirming. I'll be keeping my eye out over here. I don't think she'll give up easily—"

"They never do," Bo interrupted, sighing.

"I'll keep you in the loop," Cyler affirmed then ended the call.

Wiping a hand down his face, he tried to anticipate any moves Breelee would attempt. It was damn hard for him to wrap his head around crazy, but he tried regardless. His phone rang again, and he glanced to the Caller ID. It wasn't a number he recognized, but it was local, so he answered. "CC Homes."

"Hello, is this Mr. Cyler Myer?" a professional-sounding woman asked.

"Yes."

"Hello, Mr. Myer. I'm Elaine Morrison from HCEW, the company that your father established as his primary care during this transition time." She sounded kind, but there was an edge to her tone that had him narrowing his eyes, listening harder.

"Yes, I'm aware. You've been exceptional," he complimented, thinking of Laken's care.

"That's quite a relief to hear, Mr. Myer. We received a complaint about Nurse Garlington's care of your father, and while we've never received anything but commendations for her, we need to explore and investigate each complaint. Do you have any concerns about your father's care under Nurse Garlington?" the woman asked.

Cyler clenched his jaw, his mind already sure where the accusation had come from, but he took a deep breath to answer the woman. "Nurse Garlington is quite possibly the most exemplary example of palliative care I've ever heard of. Granted, my experience is limited, but to say I'm impressed is a gross understatement. If you wish to confirm, I'll be happy to ask my father. However, he might be slightly peeved you even were checking. He's grown pretty attached to her." Cyler softened his tone so that the woman would know he wasn't offended, simply amused.

The woman chuckled. "That's the response we're used to having concerning Laken—Nurse Garlington. I'm thankful you're pleased with the care you've received from her as our company's representative."

"I do have one question," Cyler said.

"Of course."

"Seeing as the only family present is myself, and I sure didn't file a complaint, it's quite concerning to me that someone felt the need to interrupt our affairs at this difficult time by filing a grievance." Cyler waited for his suspicions to be confirmed.

"We took the complaint from an anonymous person. They simply expressed—"

"Was it a woman? You see, there's someone that we're currently watching because she is a potential threat to our family." He paused, knowing he'd stretched it slightly, but Breelee truly was unpredictable at best. If she was up to something, he wanted to know.

"If you give me her name, I'll put that in the file. Unfortunately, I can't confirm anything since I didn't take the call," the woman said. "But we are sincerely sorry that someone would try to disrupt your family in this difficult time. I can assure you that we'll make a note that, unless we receive a complaint from your immediate family or a medical professional, we will disregard it."

Cyler nodded. "I appreciate it."

"Do you have any other questions?" the woman asked, wrapping up the conversation.

"Nope. Thanks." Cyler ended the call and huffed a sigh. Well, he was all but certain it was Breelee. *Damn woman.*

"You doing alright?" Laken asked shortly after the screen door squeaked, signaling its opening.

"Yup. Bo says everything in Jack's will is watertight. Breelee did try but didn't get anywhere, thank the good Lord." He shook his head. "Then I'm pretty sure she called your company to file a complain—"

"What?" Laken gasped, her face turning pale.

"Don't worry, sweetheart. I set the record straight and told them just how grateful we are for you, and how you've done nothing but given the most exceptional care to Jack. They believed it, because it's the truth." Cyler shrugged, patting the cement step beside him.

Laken sat, her shoulders tight with tension. "Why would she do that?"

"Jealousy, anger, desperation, take your pick. You can't quantify crazy." Cyler tugged on a loose strand of hair from Laken's messy ponytail.

"Thanks for setting the record straight. But I-I do have some guilt about… this." Laken pointed between the two of them.

"You're my fiancée." Cyler picked up her left hand and kissed it. "Family takes care of family. I learned that from you."

"Family. I can get used to that idea." She smiled softly, glancing down to her lap. "Cyler, Jack's blood pressure is concerning. I don't know exactly what to make of it, but he's resting now. What I'm trying to say is, if there's anything else you need to say to him, don't procrastinate. When someone has cancer, people always assume that they die from it, but really, the cancer makes your body so weak that sometimes it's not what kills you at all. And my gut is that we're on borrowed time." She met his gaze with a compassionate one of her own.

Cyler closed his eyes, taking a deep breath, then opened them, regarding her. "Thanks. I've said what needs to be said, but I'll plan on irritating him once he wakes up from his nap. It will be good for him," he added lightly.

"Good. Give him a taste of his own medicine." Laken stood up and dusted off the back of her jeans. "I happen to have some amazing news, and so I'm going to call Kessed and email Sterling. He's going to probably interrogate you from across the world, but at least he can't shoot you from that far. You'll have time to grow on him before he gets a chance to take aim," Laken teased.

"Good to know." Cyler arched a brow, chucking. "Give him my number so he can call. I'll do my best to get on his good side before he has a chance to maim me."

"Good thinking," Laken teased, walking into the house.

Cyler laughed when he heard Laken's squeal of delight from inside the house as she laughed. He assumed she was speaking with Kessed. It was a great moment, to hear just how thrilled she was to marry him, to take his name, make a new family. While he knew she loved him, was thrilled, it was like a cherry on top of the sundae to hear her express it when in a private moment with her best friend.

Gravel crunched, and Cyler walked around the house to see up the driveway. Who he saw made his blood chill then burn hot. *The nerve.*

His back flexed as he clenched his fists, heading toward the driveway, meaning to cut Breelee off before she even made it to the circular part.

As she saw him, she slowed down her BMW till it came to a full stop just feet in front of him.

Cyler crossed his arms and waited.

Breelee threw the car into park and stepped out. "Well, fancy seeing you here again. I thought you'd be gone by now," she remarked, narrowing her gaze.

"I live here—unlike you—which means this is trespassing." He pulled out his phone and started dialing the police.

"Wait. Damn, you're so uptight." She sighed impatiently. "Can't we just talk?" She tilted her head.

"No."

The police dispatch answered.

"Hello, I'm Cyler Myer. I have a woman trespassing on my property who's threatening my ill father." He arched a brow, watching as her color rose. After giving the dispatch his address, he ended the call and glared at her.

"You didn't have to do that." Breelee clenched her jaw.

"You didn't have to call in and complain about Laken's care," he shot back, watching carefully for confirmation.

"You didn't have to be such a pain in the ass and kick me out. Maybe I just want to say goodbye. Ever think of that?" She threw her hands in the air.

"Goodbye." He nodded once.

"To Jack, you idiot."

"He doesn't want to talk with you. At this point, what you want is to one, get your way, or two, alleviate some guilt by making a poor old man remember a part of his life he'd rather forget. Either way, you're being a selfish bitch, and we've asked you to leave. You keep coming back. You attack my fiancée and her job, and you wonder why I've called the police?"

"Fiancée?" Breelee narrowed her gaze.

"Yes. So, unless you want to wear those handcuffs as a fashion statement, I suggest you get off my property." Cyler took a step toward her. "Now."

"You know, I knew one day you'd find her. That certain woman who made you be...whatever this is." She waved her hand. "But for the record, I'm sorry that it wasn't me."

Cyler searched her gaze for some sort of duplicity but found none.

"History doesn't always repeat itself," he answered, remembering his earlier conversation with Laken.

"No, it doesn't."

The sound of sirens drifted from far off and Breelee looked back toward the road.

"Fine. You win. Say goodbye to Jack for me." She opened her car door.

"You're welcome to attend the funeral if you keep your distance." He spoke before he'd thought it through, but he remembered the way Jack had been banned from his mother's funeral, and no one should have to say goodbye from a distance. Even Breelee.

She paused, regarding him. "Thank you. But I'll be out of town by then." She gave a slight nod, slid into her car, and closed the door. Soon she was kicking up dust as she drove away.

Cyler felt relief wash over him like a rainstorm in the desert, his body soaking it up. He didn't trust her, but he didn't suspect she'd do anything else either. So, he turned and walked back to the house, grinning as he heard Laken's giggle once he'd opened the door.

"I know! It was amazing, Kessed. Wait. It's Sterling! I need to go! I'll call you back."

Cyler leaned against the doorjamb, watching as she fumbled with her phone and then answered.

"Sterling?" She grinned widely, squeezing the phone as if giving it the hug she wished she could give her brother. "That was fast! Did you see my email?" She bit her lip, listening, and as she turned, she caught sight of Cyler. Smiling, she walked over and took his hand.

"Yeah, it's true. But I'm kinda offended you think I'd joke about something like this," she teased then listened. "Actually, he's right here." She glanced to Cyler, her eyes narrowing slightly. "Fine, but be nice. He's going to be your brother, after all." With a shrug, she handed the phone over.

Cyler took it and gave her a wink. "Hello, Sterling."

"Okay, so I don't have time to play nice, so just answer the damn questions alright?" Sterling's tone didn't leave any room for argument, and Cyler suspected he was used to having his orders obeyed without question.

"What do you need to know?

"Do you love her?"

"Yes. More than I could tell you over the phone. It wouldn't do it justice."

"Good answer. If you're blowing smoke up my ass, if she's knocked up, or if you leave her for any reason whatsoever other than your sorry ass is killed, I'll cut you. We clear?"

"Clear." Cyler swallowed, half amused, half honestly concerned.

"And I say cut, because shooting you would be too easy of a death. I saw what happened to my mom before my dad took his head out of his ass and won her back. I won't see my sister do the same thing. You hurt her, and they will not find the body. Get it?" Sterling finished, the line crackling with silence.

Cyler shook his head, a small grin tickling his lips. "Sterling, if I do any of those things, I give you my full permission to end my sorry life."

Laken's eyes widened, and she reached for the phone.

Cyler pulled back, listening for Sterling's response.

"I'll hold you to that."

"I'm sure you will."

"Since we're clear, welcome to the family. May God have mercy on your soul."

Cyler barked a laugh. "Yeah, well, I'm happy to be here. And I look forward to meeting you someday."

"You better hope you grow on me a bit more before we shake hands," Sterling taunted, his tone amused.

"I'll do my best," Cyler replied, shaking his head. "Your little sister is in a panic. Can you her tell that everything's alright?" Cyler asked.

"Yeah, she's a nervous one. Probably chew my ass off for threatening you, but—"

"You're a good brother. I'll remind her when she complains."

"You're growing on me already." Sterling chuckled, and Cyler handed over the phone.

"What part of *be nice* do you not understand, Sterling?" Laken asked, arching a brow.

Cyler gave them a bit of privacy as he walked down the hall toward Jack's room. After a soft knock, he opened the door. Jack was sound asleep, his breathing shallow. He shifted in his sleep then slowly blinked awake.

"Hey," Jack said softly.

"Lazy ass," Cyler teased as he sat on the bed, giving a quick grin to Jack.

Jack rolled his eyes. "Never been lazy a day in my life. That's why Bo has to fight Breelee off with a stick."

"About that. I spoke with Bo and Breelee. There's nothing to worry about."

Jack narrowed his eyes. "You sure about that?"

Cyler nodded. "Yeah."

"Good." Jack sighed, closing his eyes.

"Going back to sleep on me?" Cyler baited, but he silently took in the pallor of Jack's skin and the way his breathing continued to be shallow.

"So tired." Jack opened his eyes. "And my chest—it's—think my heart's tired too, son."

"Is there anything you need? Should I get Laken?" Cyler stood and reached for the door.

"No." Jack breathed. "She'll just give me some more morphine, and I'm tired enough as it is. The pain...it isn't so bad...." Jack finished, his words trailing off.

Cyler nodded once then slipped out the door and went to look for Laken.

She met him in the hallway, her smile fading to concern as she took in his expression.

"Jack," she stated simply.

"He doesn't look good. He had a lot more energy this morning and—" Cyler rubbed the back of his neck. "Does it usually happen this quick? I mean, I know he's dying, but I guess I thought...the process would be slower."

Laken closed the distance between them, reaching out then lacing her fingers through his. "Everyone is different. Sometimes it happens slowly, inch by inch. Sometimes they are perfectly normal one day and gone the next. Some experience a rally of sorts, while others simply fade."

Cyler nodded. "So, what now?"

"I'm going to check his blood pressure again. There's been a marked decline in his oxygen levels, which is why I gave him the nose tube. If it's still declining..." She lifted a shoulder slowly, her face etched in pain.

"I see." Cyler shifted on his feet, glancing to Jack's door.

"I'll be right back." Laken slid her fingers from his and brushed by. She opened the door softly.

Cyler followed and leaned against the doorjamb, watching.

Laken studied the heart monitor, comparing it with her iPad notes. Her brow furrowed as she held a stethoscope to his heart, but she soon removed it from her ears and wrapped it around her neck. Jack moaned in his sleep, and Laken adjusted the morphine drip. Placing a hand on Jack's, she nodded once then turned to meet Cyler's gaze.

She tilted her head toward the hall, and Cyler stepped outside then waited for her.

Sighing, she confirmed his suspicions. "His body is starting to shut down. It can be days or hours, but based on the rate of decline from this morning, I'd say we have hours. The pain will increase, and I'll be managing it with the morphine drip, but that will also make him sleep longer."

Cyler glanced to the Jack's room. "So, he'll just"—he took a breath—
"fade in his sleep?"

"Possibly. Sometimes they wake. We can pray it's a very peaceful
passing," Laken replied softly.

"Is it...not peaceful...at times?" Cyler asked, not wanting to know the
answer, yet needing to be prepared.

"The pain can make them agitated, but I'm going to do my best to see
that it doesn't come to that," Laken answered honestly.

Cyler took a deep breath. "I need to make a call so they know I won't
be in tomorrow."

"I'll be here." Laken briefly placed a warm hand on his forearm then
went back into Jack's room.

Cyler grabbed his phone from his pocket and ducked out the door. After
a quick call, he explained the situation and cleared his week. Then he sat
on the cement steps, rubbing his hands through his hair.

Life.

Within twenty-four hours, he'd become engaged to the woman he loved
more than life, and probably would say the final goodbye to his dad. It didn't
even sting anymore to call him Dad. What a turnaround. It was shocking,
yet he'd never been so thankful for a change of heart—for both of them.
Cyler struggled, comparing the joy of his future with Laken and contrasting
it with the deep pain that came from saying goodbye to his only parent left.
The man might be a stubborn ass, but he was still his father.

With a reluctant sigh, he stood and walked back into the house.

Laken was sitting in a chair by Jack's bed, updating her notes. He nodded
to her, and she stood up.

"I'm going to give you a little privacy, Cyler. Jack might not respond,
but there's a good chance he'll hear you if you want to talk with him." She
squeezed his arm then left, closing the door behind her.

Cyler gently sat on the bed beside Jack, sighing. What did he say to
someone leaving this life? How did he even start a conversation? He
worked his jaw against the onslaught of emotion, against the feeling of
helplessness that washed over him. "Hey, old man," he whispered, forcing
a smile Jack couldn't see.

Jack didn't respond, but Cyler continued anyway.

"I'm glad I came back. Even if I didn't have the best of intentions at the
start," he confessed. "And I don't even hold it against you that you took a
swing at me." He sighed a laugh. "And just so you know, I will be having
that bonfire later this week with that coffee table. It's long overdue. And I
know you'd agree." Cyler glanced down to his hands. "I remember when

you broke your toe on that stupid thing. Of course, you were pissed as hell at me for taking Margaret out, but the coffee table won that fight when you kicked it. Honestly, I thought you'd get rid of it then."

"Mom—" Jack whispered, and Cyler's gaze shot over to meet Jack's.

"Mom?" Cyler questioned.

"—liked it," Jack finished, closing his eyes once more.

"Ah, that makes more sense."

Cyler glanced back to Jack, weighing his words. "So, this is kinda it... isn't it?" He clenched his jaw, keeping himself together.

Jack took a breath then opened his eyes. "Yeah. Reckon so."

Cyler nodded, glancing away. "Figured."

"Have a bonfire," Jack replied then gave a tight cough, contorting his face in pain.

"Dad?"

Jack lifted a hand dismissively. "Bonfire."

"Promise," Cyler assured him.

Jack nodded. "Son?"

Cyler leaned toward Jack, waiting. "Yes?"

"Thank you."

"For? I don't think being a pain in the ass deserves much gratitude." Cyler replied, trying to keep his tone light.

"No. For giving me a chance. It was all I wanted. All I prayed for. I—" Jack took another breath slowly. "I'm...at peace."

Cyler nodded again, needing to respond to Jack, but at a loss for his own words.

"Love her," Jack whispered so softly Cyler almost missed it.

"With all my heart," Cyler replied solemnly.

Jack swallowed. "Good." He drifted back to sleep, each breath making a slight crackle.

Cyler reached over and placed his hand over Jack's, startled by the cold temperature of his dad's skin.

If his body was shutting down, it made sense, but it was entirely different to feel it, rather than just know about it. Life was slowly sifting away, leaving a chill in its wake. Cyler closed his eyes, breathing deep, waiting.

Because that's all they had left.

Chapter 22

Laken leaned against the kitchen wall. It had been a half hour since she'd left Jack and Cyler alone to have some privacy. She needed to monitor him again, but she didn't want to disturb their private moments either. It was always a struggle. Being present to give care, yet giving families privacy when they needed it was a delicate balance. Often the two were in constant war with each other, so she tried to be as invisible as possible. Reluctantly, she walked down the hall and knocked softly on Jack's door before opening it.

Cyler's blue eyes met hers, pain furrowing his brow as he sat on the bed beside Jack.

The crackling noise in the air gave Laken a sign that Jack's lungs were compromised. A quick glance to the heart monitor confirmed that his pulse was abnormally high. If his blood pressure was still low...

Laken walked around the bed, carefully pulling out the blood pressure cuff and setting it around Jack's arm. After a few moments, it filled then gave her the reading she was expecting.

Low.

Laken leaned forward, studying the veins in Jack's neck, noticing how they stood out more defined than usual. Then his heartbeat took off a quick pace, causing Jack to arch his back with a groan.

"Laken?" Cyler glanced to her, his eyes wide with alarm.

"His heart has fluid around it, building the pressure so that it can't beat correctly." Tears fell down her face, watching as Jack relaxed and his heartbeat slowed.

"What's happening now?" Cyler asked, his gaze fixed on the monitor.

Laken swallowed. "It's time." She took in a deep breath through her nose, watching as the heart monitor slowly decreased its cadence, and she started to count each beat, knowing that it was a countdown to the last one.

We started life at zero, each heartbeat adding to another.

And we ended life with a countdown.

Cyler shifted, and she turned her gaze to him.

Jack's breathing stilled, the absence of the crackling noise far louder than a cannon in the small room.

Laken closed her eyes. She counted the monitor beats. *Fifteen, sixteen, seventeen, eighteen...twenty-one, twenty—*

The monitor flatlined.

A sob broke through her body as she looked to Jack. His face had relaxed, his hands opened slightly as if he was letting go. Peaceful, his expression was utterly peaceful, and Laken thanked heaven that he'd left this world in such a way, that the pain hadn't been too much, that he hadn't fought for each breath, but that he'd given it up softly, letting go rather than being torn away from this life.

With tears streaming down her face, she lifted an old ticking clock from the shelf and stopped the progress of the hands. With a click, the ticking stopped, stilling the time, forever displaying the minute that Jack's heart went just as silent.

After setting it back on the shelf, she turned off the silent monitor. The stillness in the room was thick.

"Goodbye," Cyler whispered softly, resting a hand over Jack's open palm.

Placing her hand in Jack's other one, Laken closed her eyes. "Rest in peace, Jack." She whispered a prayer then blinked through her tears as she moved over to Cyler.

Laken swallowed the lump in her throat, breathing deeply through her nose as she wrapped her arms around him, inhaling the familiar and comforting scent of his button-down shirt.

"It's not fair," he whispered brokenly, his chest taking a shaky breath.

Laken turned her face to burrow deeper in his chest before pulling away slightly. "Well, they always say life isn't fair. But you know what? The most beautiful things in life aren't fair either." Laken turned her gaze upward. "I mean, think about it. Life isn't fair, but that is exactly what makes it so astoundingly powerful. Even love isn't fair. The best love comes from a person giving, loving unconditionally, often loving when it wasn't earned or deserved. And death—" She sucked in a broken breath, closing her eyes as the tears continued to spill warm paths down her cheeks. "Death is the least fair. But I've never seen anything less powerful draw a family together, mend broken fences, and heal wounds that were impossible to repair. The beautiful part about death is that most times, it leaves life in its wake."

"Damn it all, why do you have to make everything sound so much better than it feels?" Cyler murmured, his tone half-frustrated, half-grateful.

"It's my job." Laken gave a slow shrug. "It's not because I don't feel it deeply. It's just perspective. Each goodbye that breaks my heart is only me searching desperately for the hope that can be possible afterward. That's how I survive, Cyler. Hope is my survival. And when I say goodbye to someone I've loved, someone I've come to care for as deeply as Jack, I realize that there's still blessing, there's still something amazing that is living and breathing—alive—because of him."

She took a breath and reached up to trace his jawline tenderly. "And right now, what I'm seeing is you."

Cyler smiled softly then kissed her on the nose before leaning his forehead against hers. "I see you too. And damn it all, he gets to take credit for that as well."

Laken pulled back, watching him.

Cyler sniffed, a wry grin teasing his full lips. "You know, it kinda pisses me off that he won. You know?"

"How so?" she asked, curious.

"I was so bent on revenge, on just hating his guts, and in the end, he did the impossible. I'm here mourning the man who redeemed himself so much in the past weeks, proving that it's never too late."

"It never is."

"As long as you have breath." Cyler nodded.

"And even sometimes long after, because a legacy? That never dies. And while the one Jack started wasn't perfect, he outdid himself in the long run." Laken glanced to where Jack's body rested.

"Yeah, yeah he did," Cyler agreed, his lips twisting in a sad smile. "I'm going to miss him."

"Me too." Laken closed her eyes against the fresh onslaught of tears.

She laid her head against Cyler's shirt once more, listening to the strong beat of his heart, savoring its strength, its power.

"Thank you," Cyler whispered into her hair.

"For?" she asked.

"For sharing your hope." He rested his chin on her head. "Because I didn't have the faith to believe that it could end like this, that there'd be a time I'd actually miss the son of a bitch." He chuckled. "But you did. And you pushed us both, and now I can look back on these last weeks with Jack and...be at rest."

"I didn't do much. You both just needed time."

"Time," Cyler murmured. "It's precious, isn't it?"

Laken sighed. "More and more each day."

"Laken?" Cyler leaned back, regarding her with his startlingly blue gaze.

"Yes?" Laken breathed.

"I'm thankful my time—however long it may be—gets to be spent with you." Cyler bent down and kissed her softly.

Laken pulled away from his lips ever so slightly. "Me too."

Me too.

Epilogue

Cyler watched as the man who had always been larger than life, seemed so small in the steel-gray casket. It had been a hard week, with lots of tears, but it was also a week full of hope, of promise. While they had planned Jack's funeral, they also had a wedding on the horizon. With each reminder of death, they had a reminder of life.

Laken squeezed his hand as the pastor read a passage from Ecclesiastes.

There is a time for everything,
and a season for every activity under the heavens:
a time to be born and a time to die,
a time to plant and a time to uproot,
a time to kill and a time to heal,
a time to tear down and a time to build,
a time to weep and a time to laugh,
a time to mourn and a time to dance,
a time to scatter stones and a time to gather them,
a time to embrace and a time to refrain from embracing,
a time to search and a time to give up,
a time to keep and a time to throw away,
a time to tear and a time to mend,
a time to be silent and a time to speak,
a time to love and a time to hate,
a time for war and a time for peace.
What do workers gain from their toil?
I have seen the burden God has laid on the human race.
He has made everything beautiful in its time.

Cyler smiled softly. *How appropriate.*

A beautiful red sun was setting over the horizon, a signal that a life had set as well while they waited in Ellensburg Cemetery. Jack's casket was slowly lowered into the ground as the pastor signaled for Cyler to approach the front. He reached down and grabbed a handful of dirt then sprinkled it over the top, closing his eyes as he prayed a final goodbye to the man who had proven that there was always hope.

Laken's hand wound through his as he opened his eyes, and she sprinkled dirt over Jack's casket as well. Cyler turned to regard the others that had joined in the graveside service.

Jack had indicated in his will that he didn't want a full-on funeral, just a quiet one in the cemetery. *"Let the sunshine bury me,"* he'd told Bo.

Cyler stood to the side with Laken as people walked by, giving their last respects to Jack and to him.

And as the sun hid behind Manastash Ridge, Cyler thanked the pastor and took Laken's hand.

It was time to go home.

It was time to start over.

It was time to build a new legacy.

A legacy built on hope, rather than revenge.

About the Author

Photo: Joyful Hearts Photography

Kristin Vayden is the author of twenty books and anthologies. She is an acquisitions editor for a boutique publishing house, and helps mentor new authors. Her passion for writing started young, but only after her sister encouraged her to write did she fully realize the joy and exhilaration of writing a book. Her books have been featured in many places, including the Hallmark Channel's Home and Family show. You can find Kristin at her website, www.kristinvayden.com, at www.facebook.com/kristinvaydenauthor or on Twitter: @KristinVayden.

Printed in the United States
by Baker & Taylor Publisher Services